THE FAMILY HOME

L. H. STACEY

Boldwood

First published in Great Britain in 2024 by Boldwood Books Ltd.

Copyright © L. H. Stacey, 2024

Cover Design by Head Design Ltd.

Cover Images: Shutterstock and iStock

The moral right of L. H. Stacey to be identified as the author of this work has been asserted in accordance with the Copyright, Designs and Patents Act 1988.

All rights reserved. No part of this book may be reproduced in any form or by any electronic or mechanical means, including information storage and retrieval systems, without written permission from the author, except for the use of brief quotations in a book review. This book is a work of fiction and, except in the case of historical fact, any resemblance to actual persons, living or dead, is purely coincidental.

Every effort has been made to obtain the necessary permissions with reference to copyright material, both illustrative and quoted. We apologise for any omissions in this respect and will be pleased to make the appropriate acknowledgements in any future edition.

A CIP catalogue record for this book is available from the British Library.

Paperback ISBN 978-1-80162-608-8

Large Print ISBN 978-1-80162-609-5

Hardback ISBN 978-1-80162-607-1

Ebook ISBN 978-1-80162-610-1

Kindle ISBN 978-1-80162-611-8

Audio CD ISBN 978-1-80162-602-6

MP3 CD ISBN 978-1-80162-603-3

Digital audio download ISBN 978-1-80162-606-4

This book is printed on certified sustainable paper. Boldwood Books is dedicated to putting sustainability at the heart of our business. For more information please visit https://www.boldwoodbooks.com/about-us/sustainability/

Boldwood Books Ltd, 23 Bowerdean Street, London, SW6 3TN

www.boldwoodbooks.com

*When my wonderful husband Haydn retired, I went out and I bought him a puppy cavapoo, who we called Barney.
Having a dog in the house again is just the best... He's brought a lot of joy to a lot of people.
With that in mind, I'm going to dedicate this book to every dog and cat lover in the world.
Because like you, I can't imagine my life without having a Barney in it...!*

PROLOGUE
DECEMBER 2014

With the sound of her husband's screams, yells and misguided prayers spinning around her mind, Imogen Gilby frantically gripped at the kitchen floor. Her blood-covered fingernails slid uncontrollably across polished ceramic tiles until, after what felt like an eternity, she reached the open doorway and launched herself through it, into the cold night air.

With an overwhelming sense of fear and guilt, Imogen gave a terrified look over her shoulder. Right now, right at this moment, her husband, Gerald, could be taking his last breath. But she couldn't help him. Not any more. All she could do was save herself and, with a deep intake of breath, she found a surge of energy and anxiously, she pulled herself through the darkness and into a frozen and unforgiving terrain, where the ground was sharp and painful. It attacked her body in a way that felt like she was being stabbed by a thousand tiny shards of glass that were penetrating her skin and she wished for nothing more than to slow down, to stop moving and to scream for help, but couldn't.

Desperately, Imogen searched for a weapon and, with hands

that were already torn and painful, she pushed them under the bushes in the hope that a garden tool had been thrown there, abandoned amongst the undergrowth, where only the nettles, ivy and bindweed now thrived.

As her breathing accelerated, she took another hurried glance over her shoulder and, with a renewed determination to survive, she dragged her body along the ground and as close to the garden wall as she could get. Staying in the shadows was the only way she knew how to survive and, even though her beautiful clothes, hair and body were now covered in both dirt and blood, she felt grateful for the darkness that enveloped her and gave her protection.

With her eyes closed for just a beat, she listened. The sounds that had been coming from inside the house had now stopped. The air was uncannily still and, with her breaths coming in short and sporadic gasps, Imogen listened for any indication that she was not alone, that her attacker had followed, and she prayed for the sound of sirens, for someone to arrive and help her.

Instead, the only thing she could hear were the tiny and occasional scurrying feet of the nocturnal animals that lived in the garden and for a moment, with her breath held tight, she lifted her face out of the dirt, and looked for the mice and the rats and quickly, she realised that, like everything and everyone else, even they had deserted her.

Blinking back tears, Imogen stifled a sob. Her whole body shuffled, inch by inch, caterpillar style along the edge of the wall, only stopping long enough to press a hand to her side where she felt the sticky warmth of blood seeping through her jumper. It coated her fingers, and caused the pain to surge through her in waves, making her grit her teeth and wish she could scream. But to scream would attract attention and, with her head tipped painfully to one side, she fixed her eyes on the wishing well that stood at the bottom of the garden. Behind it stood the church, right next to a long row of terraced houses. Each of the houses were shrouded in darkness, and Imogen desperately looked for the faintest flicker of light, anything to show her that just one person, in just one of those houses, could be peering through a window and that maybe, just maybe, they might see her and get some help.

She swallowed and wrapped her arms tightly around her body and, even though she could barely put up with the pain, she gave herself a hug. It was all she could think to do in an attempt to stop the relentless shaking that was overtaking her body, and from somewhere deep inside her she let out a long, sorrowful, animalistic scream that pierced the night air. Even though, by doing so, she knew there was a chance she'd give herself away.

The air was still, the temperature plummeting and, with her temper suddenly flaring up inside, Imogen let go of her body and began to roll her fingers in and out of tight, contorted fists. She knew that, if she was found, she'd have to prepare for a battle. One she knew she could never win. It was a thought that caused her to panic, and she clutched at the cold, frozen mud and, with all the effort she had left in her body, she propelled herself forward. She knew how close to death she most probably was. The thought of curling up and giving in crossed her mind, as a stream of hot, scalding tears clouded her vision.

Biting down on her lip, she stared up at the sky where dark looming clouds were circling above her. For just a few minutes, she lay down in the dirt, in the darkness and waited for the end to take her, but something deep inside her fought back and she refocused on the church and the graveyard beside it. Her only hope was to get to the sanctuary of the church, to the safety it might just provide, and once more she tried to push herself upright and pressed her back firmly against the wall as icy puffs of air expelled themselves from her mouth and she battled with the pain.

Short, sharp breaths were quickly followed by another long gut-wrenching sob. She could feel herself drifting in and out of the darkness. It was a feeling she tried to shake off, but her body no longer had a desire to live. Too much had happened, too many wrongs she could no longer put right. A life that had been lived in the shadow of others.

She'd never thought about dying before, but right now she was sure that dying would be a blessing. It would give her the perfect escape. A way of running from a world that had been nothing more than a lie and, even though by dying she would finally rid herself of the guilt she'd carried for so many years, she couldn't help but feel a sense of panic whirling around her. It was like a giant python curling around her thoughts and she began to think of all the people she'd let down. Their faces flashed before her with accusing eyes that tortured her soul and she thought about the lies she'd told, and the secrets she'd kept. But, as she did, her breathing faltered, and she could feel the imaginary snake constricting her throat and her lungs with a pressure that stole her breath and threatened to choke her.

In a last desperate attempt to save her own life, Imogen frantically threw her arm out in front of her and, as though her prayers had been answered, her fingers suddenly caught against something sharp, jagged and heavy. It was the weapon she'd hoped she might find and, with a frenzied grappling, she wrapped her bloodied fingers around it and dragged it towards her.

'Thank you...' Imogen mouthed the words and realised that she now had a way of protecting herself and a reason to live. For a moment, she took pleasure in the tiny drops of rain that had begun to land on her face, her lips and eyelids. It was a reminder of something real and good and she inched forward in a final attempt to reach the safety of the church. But the pleasure was short lived. From behind her, she heard the footsteps. They were heading straight towards her and, with the tool gripped tightly in her hand, she dragged her body behind the wishing well where a painful, twisted, half-smile crossed her face. She looked at the well that held so many of her secrets and realised that the time had come for her to make one final desperate wish.

1

PRESENT DAY – DECEMBER 2023 – HATTIE

With the early afternoon sun resting on the surgery window, Hattie Gilby closed her eyes and, for what felt like the first time in days, enjoyed the small amount of warmth that landed on her face, which for the middle of December was both rare and deceptive.

It was the first time in a week that the sun had broken through the dark, ominous rain clouds which, along with an arctic breeze, had made the temperatures drop. Her whole body had frozen each and every time a cold blast of winter air had blown in through the surgery doors that sprung open automatically every time a patient walked near them.

With her head resting against her hand, and her body slouching in her chair, Hattie stared at the computer, and groaned as another file dropped into her inbox and, even though it was almost time for her to leave for the day, the referral letter would need to be sent.

'Just my luck,' she growled under her breath, 'there's been nothing to do for the last hour and now...' She sighed with annoyance but knew that it was just a typical day at the surgery.

In the space of an hour, her work could easily go from frantic to mind-numbingly boring. Everything that happened depended on what patients walked in through the door. What their ailments were and, ultimately, what kind of aftercare they needed.

'Sorry, but I've gone and done it all wrong...' An elderly gentleman's voice broke into her thoughts and Hattie looked up as he approached the desk and removed his cap. 'I didn't know what I was doing and... I think I pressed the wrong button.' He leaned against the counter, and ran a frail hand anxiously across the liver spots that covered his scalp. 'Stupid machine. It wanted my date of birth and I hit the wrong number and now it doesn't know who I am.' He paused, and with the cap being twisted around anxiously in his hands, began to pace across the tiled floor between the desk and the screen. 'Not sure I know who I am myself, most days,' he muttered, 'only I have to see the nurse at half past two and...' He looked up at the clock. 'And it's about that time now, so... You couldn't be a love and give me a hand, could you?' He looked hopefully from Hattie to her colleague, Emma, who sat beside her, dressed in a pair of royal blue medical scrubs. To anyone who walked past, it was clear to see that Emma wasn't a receptionist, that it wasn't her job to answer the phone or to help on the desk. But, sitting at reception and hiding from the practice manager was her 'go to place' between patients and Hattie couldn't remember a single day in the past two years that Emma hadn't sat there chatting endlessly about her love life or the sex she was or wasn't getting. And even though it was down to Hattie to answer the telephone and to see to all the patients who couldn't operate the check-in machine, it seemed that, much to the detriment of her own work, it was also down to her to listen to everything Emma had to tell her.

Turning her chair towards Emma, she glanced hopefully in a

fruitless attempt to get her to help, but Emma had suddenly become engrossed in the computer screen that sat on the desk before her and, with an exaggerated flounce, she simply tossed her long, blonde hair over her slim, hunched-up shoulders and twisted her chair in the opposite direction.

Hattie glanced up and into the eyes of the elderly man, who was now leaning over her counter and giving her an anxious but hopeful gaze.

'It's Mr Marsh, isn't it?' Hattie asked politely as she made her way to him. 'Now then, let me see what you've gone and done and then we can put it right for you, can't we?' She clicked on the screen, pressed it to reset and stood poised, ready to help him with the detail. 'Go on then, your date of birth?' She leaned to one side and shoulder bumped him gently. 'You can tell me; I promise, I'm not going to tell anyone.'

Appreciative that Hattie was willing to help, Mr Marsh held a hand up to cup his mouth and surreptitiously whispered his details. 'First of May, nineteen forty-three,' he revealed, 'I'm eighty years young you know and, if I reach a hundred, do you know what I'm going to do?' He raised his eyebrow and nodded. 'I'm going to shout it from the rooftops, I am. That's provided I'm fit enough to climb a ladder.' He pointed upwards, and gave a mischievous smile that made Hattie forget her annoyance and she smiled right back.

'Oh, Mr Marsh, something tells me you'll be more than capable,' she replied with a laugh and pointed to the waiting room. 'Now if you want to take a seat in there, I'll let the nurse know you're here. I think her last patient went in just a couple of minutes ago, so she shouldn't be long.'

Sighing, Hattie returned to her seat and gave Emma a disparaging look. 'If you're going to sit there and stop me from working, the least you can do is help. I've got another referral letter to do before I can finish, so... the next one over forty is yours,' she whispered, keeping her eyes on the screen, and began to tap heavily on the keyboard in front of her. 'I swear this place has a distinct lack of decent looking twenty-somethings. Either that, or it's only the people over forty who ever get sick.'

'Hey, hands off. The young ones are mine. You know that,' Emma threw back. 'Besides, what would you want with a twenty-something male? You've got Charlie, haven't you?' Hattie's reaction to Charlie's name must have showed on her face because Emma leaned in as close as she could and looked at her intently. 'Hey, what happened, I thought the two of you were tight?' She held her hands up in the air, with her little fingers hooked tightly together.

'Yeah, I thought we were too.' Hattie continued to stare at her screen but felt the tears well up in her eyes. Talking about herself was something she rarely did. To speak about herself would bring up all sorts of memories she'd rather not talk about and, with her eyes pressed carefully together, she considered all the ways she could get out of being questioned about Charlie.

'You can't stop there,' Emma said. 'I tell you all about my love life, and the lack of it... so it's only fair that you tell me what happened. Did you meet someone else?'

'Why on earth would you even think that?' Hattie snapped. 'If you must know—' She paused and sighed – she wasn't sure how to tell the story. For the past couple of years, Charlie had been her world and now, well, now he wasn't. But Hattie could hardly tell Emma the truth. She could hardly say that Charlie had left because of something she'd done so many years before. Nor could she say that, even though he'd known all about her family, who they were and what had happened to them, he'd never really known about the life they used to lead. 'We had an argument, that's all. Charlie moved out.' Satisfied with her version of events, Hattie opened the file that had dropped into her inbox and leaned across to pick up her headphones.

'Oh no you don't.' Emma's hand dropped on top of hers. 'No one just has an argument and then, you know, that's it... there's always more to the story.' She opened her eyes wide, raised her eyebrows and stared. 'I mean, are you okay? What about the bills? If he moved out, are you living on your own, can you manage or did you move the next one in?' She rolled her eyes upwards. 'They don't exactly pay us a fortune here, so no one would blame you if that's what you did and, of course, you have to be able to afford the necessities, like wine on a Friday.'

Hattie knew that her lifestyle and Emma's were completely different, however she couldn't help but smile at her simplistic naivety of life, where all that mattered was getting home on a Friday and having a party until she woke up and realised that it was Monday.

'Emma, there's nothing more to say. We argued, and Charlie moved out.' She swallowed away the sob that threatened to expose itself and thought about Charlie and how, as if by magic, he was now in Switzerland, with the lads who had all miraculously managed to take a holiday from work, all at the same time, exactly one day after he'd left the flat. Which had all seemed just a little too coincidental for Hattie's liking.

Sitting back in her chair, Hattie closed her eyes. It was a story she didn't want to tell. Nor did she want everyone in the building to know her business.

'Oh my God... Did he leave you for someone else? Another woman maybe. Or... Jesus, Hattie, don't tell me he moved in with a man?'

Ignoring Emma's questions, Hattie flicked through the paperwork that covered her desk. She really didn't want to talk.

What she really wanted was to finish the letter and leave for home.

'Hattie?'

'Emma, forget it. There's nothing more to say. Charlie was a dick. He moved out. It's over. That's it.' She turned, glanced up at the clock and willed the seconds to turn into minutes.

'But aren't you scared, living all by yourself? You know, after what happened to your parents?'

It was a comment that made Hattie stop and stare. She had no idea that her work colleagues knew about her past. But clearly word had been passed around and, whether she liked it or not, she'd probably been the topic of everyone's conversation since she'd begun working here.

'You know about that?' It was all she managed to say as she watched the way Emma lifted her handbag out of the drawer, took out a small mirror and admired herself in it. A gold lipstick was carefully chosen from a small pouch and, with the precision of a surgeon, she applied the soft, pink shimmer to her lips.

'Of course we know. You don't think you can keep secrets like that one, do you?' Emma puckered her lips and rubbed them together. 'Now, if you need someone to come and stay with you,' she said, 'all you have to do is call me. I could come over for a few days. Maybe for the weekend. We could have a girly night,' she gasped, 'with pizza and everything and you... you could finally tell me all about it.'

Feeling her whole body deflate at the thought, Hattie looked up from her computer and stared at the door. She could feel her cheeks burning with embarrassment and, with her mind spinning, she thought of all the times Emma had tried chatting to her, questioning her, digging for information about her life. Hattie thought of all the ways she'd avoided answering her questions or those of anyone else who worked at the surgery and, if she was completely honest with herself, she'd made it her mission to avoid making any of them friends, because friends ended up chatting and exchanging life stories. They would begin with conversations about what they were cooking for tea and would quickly turn the chatter into a comparison of the happiest and worst days of their lives and the last thing Hattie wanted to talk about was her life and the night that had changed everything. She'd always kept the details to herself about the night she'd found her father's stabbed, slaughtered body in the kitchen of their family home. Or the way her mother had been brutally attacked and had almost died. Both stories were conversation stoppers and, even though people often wanted to hear the gory details, they just didn't know what to say, or how to react.

'To be honest, Emma, and don't take this the wrong way, but I like being alone. The peace and quiet is something I look forward to, especially after sitting here all day being interrogated.' Her words were full of resentment, and she said them in a voice that even to Hattie was a little louder than she'd have liked. 'My plans for tonight include nothing more than a boiling-hot bubble bath and a proper romance book where all in the world is good, because then I don't have to answer any questions.' She knew that she sounded like a petulant child but she didn't care and, through narrowed, angry eyes, she glanced down at the drawer, dragged it open and lifted her bag out and onto her knee. It was all she could do to avoid Emma's fierce-looking frown and for something to do she began to rummage in her bag and surreptitiously glanced down at her mobile phone to see a whole list of missed calls and messages displayed on the screen – a sight that brought a sense of panic to her mind. Calls from Adam, her brother, and from her older cousin, Louisa, wouldn't normally be shocking, not in themselves. But an accumulation of more than a dozen missed calls, along with numbers she didn't recognise, could only mean that there was something wrong. Jumping up, she began to pace back and forth and mentally she began preparing herself for what was to come. The thoughts and scenarios flashed through her mind. She could see her brother, Luke, her mother and, once again, she could see her father's body, lying there in a pool of bright red blood. They were all thoughts she didn't want, images she didn't want to relive and, with her phone still held tightly in her hand, Hattie grabbed her coat and raced for the exit.

2

PRESENT DAY – DECEMBER 2023 – HATTIE

'Okay, Louisa, take a breath.' Walking at speed as she spoke, Hattie tried to dodge the rain as well as the people who were walking towards her and listened intently to what her older cousin was saying. 'Tell me exactly what happened.'

'I went to see your mum,' Louisa said, 'I always go on a Friday. Grant works most days, but Fridays are the busiest apparently for cremating people, and the kids go to football. Visiting your mum gives me a couple of hours without them and I enjoy those few hours where they're not screaming at me for whatever it is they want or need next.' She sighed and paused dramatically as the sound of the children could be heard arguing in the background. 'Like now, when one wants fish fingers for tea, the other wants sausages and yes, you guessed it, Kitty doesn't like either. So, she's mooching around the kitchen looking for what else she could have instead.'

'So, Grant still works at the crem?' Hattie shuddered at the thought of burning those you loved and could still clearly remember the words her father had once used: 'You only burn rubbish, and people are not rubbish which is why we bury them respectfully.'

'Yeah, he's still there. It's a job, Hattie, there's not many of them around these days and it suits him. He always gets the weekend off, which is great for us as a family.' Louisa said defensively. 'You don't like Grant, do you?'

'Louisa, sorry, I diverted and yes, of course I like Grant, but you called me, about mum.' Hattie moved to stand under a shop awning, pretending to look through the window at the freshly baked bread. 'And by the look of my phone, you called repeatedly. Was it important?'

'She isn't well.' Louisa finally said. 'They readmitted her to the hospital, earlier in the week.'

Closing her eyes for a beat, Hattie waited for Louisa to continue. The phone went silent for so long that Hattie held it away from her ear and stared at the handset. She'd got used to the idea that her mother was ill and that, since the attack, she'd been constantly in and out of hospital and that her prognosis had never really improved. Intensive care had been followed by critical care. Then, there had been the months of rehabilitation, followed by the years of physiotherapy. Every course of treatment had been followed by different operations, none of which had improved her health and Hattie had lost count of the multiple hospital wards she'd visited.

'Louisa... it's bad this time, isn't it?' Hattie asked with a sob that was followed by a deep, inward breath. The silence at the other end of the phone line had become too much. It was more than obvious that her cousin didn't want to tell her the news and Hattie turned away from the shop window to turn her eyes up to the sky. The winter sun had disappeared, and the rain had taken its place again. For the first time since she'd begun to walk to work rather than driving, she regretted the decision.

'Louisa, please tell me what's happened?' Pressing the phone tightly to her ear, Hattie tried to swallow. Her throat had gone dry, and her legs felt as though they were about to fail her.

'I can't lie, Hattie, she isn't good. She's had some tests and the results came back this morning.' A sob left Louisa's throat and Hattie could imagine her sat in the corner of the cottage that had once been her parents'. Her brood of three children mooching around her ankles and a cat or two curled up on her knee. Louisa was only three years older than Hattie, although she'd always seemed much older having to grow up quickly at the age of sixteen when both of her parents had died in a car crash. And, although Hattie's parents had tried to look after her, Louisa had quickly decided to go it alone and look after herself, which hadn't always turned out for the best.

'What test results?' Hattie demanded. 'No one told me she was having any?' Pressing the phone to her ear, she wished she'd waited to make the call. At least if she'd been at home, she could have sat in silence instead of being surrounded by pedestrians and a shopkeeper who kept marching to his door with his hands on his hips, sighing and marching back in.

Glancing around for somewhere better to stand, Hattie ran her gaze along the other shops and the two village pubs. Even though she'd lived here for the past four years, she'd rarely used the local amenities, preferring to do her shopping out of town where no one knew her.

'Hattie... We've all been trying to phone you... and there's no easy way of telling you this. She's got cancer. As though she hasn't been through enough. Now she's got bloody cancer and it's just not fair, is it?'

Hattie leaned against the wall as the air left her body and it felt as though she could no longer breathe. 'Where is she?' she finally managed to ask. 'Did... did you say she was back in the hospital?'

'She's in Friarage in their cancer treatment ward, but there's nothing they can do. They've said that we have two options – move her into a hospice, or she could go home,' Louisa said, 'But whichever you choose, it needs to happen quite soon and, personally, I'd go for the hospice. At least there they have professionals, people who are there the whole time and, you know, she wouldn't be alone.' Hattie could hear the difficulty Louisa had in saying the words. Her voice had become little more than a whisper, her words slow.

'A hospice?' Hattie asked. 'Isn't that where people go to die?' As she uttered the words, she realised the stupidity of the statement and the enormity of the situation hit her. A hospice meant that her mother had weeks, possibly only days, left to live and without hesitation she began to regret all the times she'd missed a visit. The excuses she'd made and all the things she still had to say but had no idea how to say them.

'Hattie...' There was a pause between words. 'I know you haven't been back to the house, not since, you know... but it is time. I really think it's time you came home. There's things to do, and there will be a lot to organise.' Her voice was full of concern. She knew how much Hattie hated the thought of stepping back into that house, of how many memories would hit her the moment she did.

'I... I don't think I can...' Hattie whispered as she heard a commotion in the background and could sense that Louisa had placed her hand over the handset. 'Will you three stop it or I swear to God, I'll turn the bloody Wi-Fi off and no one will get to play the game,' she shouted out loud.

Amid the sound of three young children groaning and moaning, Hattie's mind went back to the way she'd grown up with her two younger brothers. The fighting and commotion had been a normality of everyday life, as had the constant lectures, which would result in all of them being sent to their rooms for what felt like hours on end. At the time, she'd have never considered the idea that one day she wouldn't be at home, or that she'd ever move away. But now, nine years later, she knew that she'd have to go home and really didn't know how that would make her feel.

'Hattie, you have to come home sometime,' Louisa said as though reading her mind. 'I mean, if you really don't want to go back to the house, you could stay here, but I don't think you'd like it. You know how small my cottage is. The kids are always running riot, it's bedlam during all the hours they're awake and most days I feel unbelievably sorry for the neighbours.'

'I can't, Lou. I have to stay here, I have...' She was going to say she had Charlie, but she suddenly realised that she didn't have him any more. She was all alone. And now she knew that everyone at the surgery had been discussing her business, she didn't feel as though she'd ever be happy about going back there either. 'Do you know what, Lou, I don't have Charlie...' she admitted. 'And maybe I should come back.' Feeling suddenly emotional, she thought about the way she'd unintentionally distanced herself from her brothers. The phone calls between them that had become fewer and fewer and, selfishly, Hattie thought about how she'd feel if she drove all that way and they didn't want to see her. But then, if they didn't want her to be there, why had Adam tried to call her?

'Hattie, there's something else you should know. You know how your mum hasn't spoken, not coherently, to anyone for the past nine years?' she asked. 'Well, lately... she has. And she's been asking for you. It feels as though she's got something to say, Hattie, something that matters.'

3

PRESENT DAY – DECEMBER 2023 – HATTIE

With her heart pounding heavily in her chest, Hattie stepped out of her car in Ugathwaite to stand in front of the vicarage, the house she used to call home.

Standing on the pavement, she hovered beneath a single, hazy streetlight that flickered with slow, intermittent flashes. It gave the road an eerie feeling as white clouds of fog rolled in from the fields and, unconsciously, she gripped her keys tight between her fingers, formed a fist and allowed the keys to poke out aggressively between them.

Staring intently, she could see that the house was shrouded in darkness. It was a clear indication that neither of her brothers were home and, while still holding the keys in one hand, she pulled her phone from her pocket with the other and flicked at the screen as her phone began to vibrate.

'Adam, where are you?' Closing her eyes for a moment, Hattie pushed away the internal anguish she'd felt about coming back. It was something she'd always known would happen, especially after leaving in the way she had, and, even though she'd tried, she hadn't been able to convince either of her brothers to go with her.

'I'm at the hospital, Mum isn't doing too good. Her breathing is quite laboured and, to be honest, Sis, I don't want to leave her...' As Adam whispered the words, he opened and closed a door and Hattie heard the door click to a close behind him.

It was a moment that made Hattie take a deep inward breath, bite down on her lip and begin to quiver with an emotion she had been continually supressing for the past nine years. 'Give me a min. I'll come to you. Which ward am I aiming for...?'

'No, please, don't do that. That's why I called.' Pausing, Adam took a breath and Hattie could hear the sound of his footsteps clicking along the hard tiled floors of the hospital corridor. 'I'm looking outside right now and the fog, Hattie, it's pea soup round here. Even I wouldn't drive in it and, to be honest, I think you'd be better off sitting it out and waiting 'til morning.'

'But...' Taking a breath, Hattie leaned against the drystone wall and looked up to stare at the house more closely. The ivy that had grown up the walls had already taken over the bricks and some of the windows. It looked as though it had been continuously growing upward and now it appeared to be on a mission to swallow the gutters and the downpipes whole. 'But... I'd rather be there,' she added unequivocally. She looked between the house and the car, took a slow breath in and could feel the rhythm of her heart accelerate. Being here alone, waiting for Luke, hadn't been a part of the plan and immediately she rolled the keys in her hand and took a step back towards where she'd parked. It was a conscious decision to park the car on the side of the road, rather than pulling into the driveway, but now she wondered why she'd done it. Had she intended making a fast exit, making sure she wasn't trapped in the drive behind other vehicles, or was it that getting out of the car and opening the gates would have been far too decisive?

'Seriously, Luke won't be long and yes, before you ask, he's still as grumpy as hell, but you two need to talk. You need to sort things out, once and for all.'

'Adam. I could be with you in less than twenty minutes, I'm sure the weather isn't so bad that I wouldn't get there. I mean...' She turned, stared at the fields where the fog rolled slowly towards her. 'I just came over the valley, it can't be that bad already, can it?'

'Hattie, just wait for the weather to alter. You know what it's like up here, it can change in minutes and there's enough for you to face here tomorrow, without lining yourself up for it tonight. Besides, Mum's asked that we all come together, she wants us all to be here at the same time and she's saying that she's got something to tell us and... it sounds important, Hattie.' The sound of a car passing by and slowing down made Hattie look nervously around her and, with her eyes fixed on the tail-lights, she held her breath until the car disappeared around the corner.

'Adam, don't you think it's odd that she didn't speak to us for years and now she can?' It was a question that fell from her lips as she thought back over the years, to the hours she'd sat beside her mother's bed, chatting away, talking about everything and nothing. She'd always been under the impression that her mother couldn't speak, when, in reality, it had been that she simply hadn't wanted to. 'I find it all a bit strange, don't you? I mean... why would she do that?'

'She isn't chatting, Hattie. Her words are not fluent, not like they were, and she struggles to put full sentences together.' He paused, reflectively. 'Maybe she was embarrassed and didn't want us to see her like that.'

Leaning against her car, Hattie could feel the moisture from its surface seeping into her jeans and, with a sigh, she took a step forward to stand in front of the wall. The last thing she wanted was to be here. Stood outside this house. Alone. Without Adam. He was the older of her two younger brothers, the more grounded and dependable, who'd at least made some effort to keep in touch with her and, right now, the thought of him not coming back was overwhelming. She felt a stifled sob leave her throat.

'Hey. Come on, don't get upset. She must have had her reasons and right now none of us know what those reasons are. I just hope that tomorrow gives us some answers and that it isn't the truth I always feared.' As he spoke, his voice broke too, and Hattie's heart plummeted at the thought that Adam was at the hospital, coping with their mother alone.

'And what is it you think she'll tell us?' Her mind flew back to a day when she'd found him searching their mother's office with fury in his eyes. It had been a day when he'd become obsessed with a note that had been written, a passing comment their mother had made. 'I know what you thought back then, what you suspected, but just because Louisa was adopted, it doesn't mean that we were,' she added. 'And it wasn't a secret – her parents actually told her about it, as soon as she hit sixteen. I can still remember how shocked our mum had been, and I'm sure that if there had been something to say, they'd have said it back then. Don't you think?'

A loud bang made Hattie spin on the spot and, with eyes that were wide and filled with angst, she searched the square that stood at the other side of the road. It was a large area where trucks used to park that, since she'd left, had been turned into a communal space for the community to enjoy. The concrete had been replaced with grass and park benches and the borders had been filled with trees and bushes, that even though it was winter still created at least a hundred different places for someone to hide, especially now that the fog had begun to roll in and was quickly surrounding each of the trees as it went.

'...to stay here, there's a chair beside Mum's bed, the nurses gave me a blanket last night, so I'll get myself comfy and at least then someone is with Mum.' It was more than obvious that Hattie had missed something that Adam had said and in her annoyance, she stared at the handset.

'Okay, okay, I'll stay here...' It was all she could say and, after confirming the time that they'd all meet the following morning, Hattie ended the call.

Contemplatively, Hattie ran her fingers along the drystone wall until she reached a small wooden gate that was old and worn and, like the rest of the house, in desperate need of some tender loving care. The gate was covered in loose shards of paint, which she flicked away with cold, shaking fingertips. Something she'd have never been allowed to do while her father had been alive. Back then, there would have been no shards to pull. The gate would have been painted annually right before spring, in a bright red colour to match the front door.

Taking a step back, Hattie wavered before walking forward and quickly realised that she'd always thought about coming back but hadn't and there had been days when she'd thought that she'd never come back at all. Yet here she was and, with her chest constricting, she gave the gate a determined push and felt the resistance beneath her fingers as it gave out a loud, ominous grating sound that filled the air, leaving Hattie in no doubt that the gate was broken and trapped against the tarmac. Standing to one side of the path, she peeped between the conifers to look at the house next door. By standing in one place, she could move her head from side to side and take in one small part of the garden at a time and, hesitantly, she looked along the path, to where a low wall divided the front of the garden from the back. It had been a wall she remembered their father building, a wall that was supposed to be much higher but a miscounting of bricks had meant that it was low enough for them all to jump over. In front of it stood a Christmas tree she'd rescued from the side of the road as a tiny twelve-inch sapling. It had been a bitterly cold day, but, even so, she remembered she'd walked around for what had felt like an age, deciding where she should plant it, picking a place in the back garden close to the wishing well. But, when her father had forbade it, she'd been made to plant it at the front of the house, next to the wall, instead.

It was a memory that caught her by surprise and quickly she tried to conjure up one or two of her happier days. She needed reminders of the good times, the days when she'd had fun and had felt loved in the days before her world had fallen apart.

Glancing from one part of the garden to the other, she finally rested her gaze on the shed. It was the place where she'd shared her first kiss. And the old wooden swing chair that had long since fallen from its chains was where she'd sat, holding hands with her first love, who had felt oh so important at the time. There was the patch of land where she'd always stood her bike, and the long, low, concrete ledge that she'd often played on as a child. Unable to resist, Hattie pointed her toes, stretched out her arms and, like a funambulist balancing on a long and dangerous tightrope, walked along its edge. In her childish imagination, the rope had always wobbled precariously, but today and because of all the extra growth in the bushes, her wobble was real, and she struggled to stay upright, until, eventually, she jumped off at the end and clapped her hands in delight like a child, awarding themselves for their own amazing performance.

Hearing a noise, she once again peeped through the conifers

to see the shape of a car pulling up on the drive next door. It was a house that had used to belong to old Mrs Hicken, a peculiar woman who over the years had had one or two run-ins with Hattie's parents. She'd always had something to say, something to complain about and Hattie wondered if there was a chance she still lived there. But the newly painted frontage, and the sight of a younger woman standing in the upstairs window rocking a baby back and forth in a slow, but obviously well-practised, rhythm, told Hattie that it was highly unlikely.

Giving the young woman an envious smile, Hattie realised that everything about the village, including the old neighbours, would have changed. But, then, who could blame them. No one in their right minds would intentionally live in a house next door to theirs. Not by design and certainly not by choice, and it amazed her that anyone had chosen to live there now.

Leaning back against one of the trees, Hattie went over her options. In an ideal world, Luke would have already arrived home. He'd be kind, welcoming and would completely ignore the fact that she hadn't been back to the house for the past nine years. Nothing would be said. But life wasn't that simple. With her fingers still holding on to the keys in her pocket, she wondered whether she should just let herself in. But the thought of meeting with her brother was already causing her stomach to do somersaults without him arriving home to find her snooping around in the house that he still lived in.

Suddenly, she felt the weight of the world press down on her shoulders. It was the pressure that she'd felt before and the guilt and doubt that had filled her mind. She'd felt exactly the same the last time she'd been here and, without warning, her knees went weak. Her mind spun with a million apologies she knew she'd have to make and then, without warning, the taste of acid hit the back of her throat. Her stomach retched and every inch of her body began to shake with a trepidation she'd hoped would never come back.

'It's different now. Everything's different. It wasn't your fault.' She said the words, over and over, like a mantra. She swallowed nervously, wiped her mouth on the back of her hand. Then, like the blade of a knife cutting through her thoughts, she heard the church bells toll. It was a sound she should have expected, but one she hadn't wanted to hear. Not after the last time, when she'd been staring into her father's dying eyes, with no choice but to kneel in the blood that surrounded his body, and she'd listened to the toll of the bells as his pulse diminished. It was a night she wanted nothing more than to forget and, with her eyes pressed tightly together, she pushed her fingers firmly into her ears and prayed for the tolling to stop.

Fixing her eyes firmly on the front door, Hattie deducted that, like the gate, it hadn't been painted for a number of years. Each of the brass door numbers were now only held on by a single screw, which left each of the numbers to hang untidily upside down and she couldn't help but wonder what her father would say and how angry he'd be. For all the world to see, he'd been the kindest, gentlest man. But the reality had been that he'd ruled the house with his Bible and, like the flickering of images at the beginning of a film, small nuggets of memory filled her mind as one image after the other flashed right before her.

After speaking to Louisa, she'd been sure that coming back to the house was the right thing to do and, knowing that she owed it to her mother to be here, she'd packed a bag, phoned the surgery and let them know she wasn't going back. It had been a call she'd dreaded but, once it was over, she'd been filled with an immense sense of relief and, even though the rent on her flat still needed to be paid, she knew that looking for another job would be right at the top of her list, just as soon as she'd been to visit her mother.

With her fingers trembling with the cold, Hattie reached for the door and lay her hand against it. 'And then I'm going to look for the truth,' she said in a low, but definite, voice. 'Now that I'm back and, even if it kills me, I will get justice for what happened to my family.'

4

PRESENT DAY – DECEMBER 2023 – SOPHIE

After hearing the gate scrape open next door, Sophie Alexander crept through her dimly lit house and into her son, Noah's, bedroom, and while using the curtains as a barrier to hide behind she peered out through the window, to look over the front of the house and onto the garden below.

Shielding Noah with her hand, she smiled at the way he held on to her like a baby limpet, all arms, legs and a mouth that was currently welded to a spot on her shoulder where he desperately tried to suckle her skin.

'Come on. Stop that,' she whispered, 'you've just had your supper, greedy guts and you can't be hungry, can you?' she sang the words in her soft Irish accent and rocked him rhythmically from side to side as she glanced out of the window and stood on her tiptoes as she spotted a young woman who appeared to be creeping around in the garden next door.

Tipping her head to one side, she watched the woman's movements suspiciously and tried to remember how long it had been since she'd noticed anyone on the garden path other than Luke, Adam or the team of carers that had turned up, morning, noon and night to look after Imogen. There had often been a constant stream of them, along with a series of parcel deliveries and fast-food guys that had turned up on a regular basis. But no one else had been there for months, which was why she was now taking an unhealthy interest in the woman who was venturing around in next door's neglected garden, watching the fog roll towards her, like a length of voile being dragged across the fields, turning everything white as it went.

Pulling the curtain to one side, Sophie smiled as the woman held her arms out to each side and began to walk slowly along a long narrow ledge that bordered the garden, before jumping off and clapping like a child. Her shoulder-length auburn hair bounced around her shoulders and, just for a moment, a heart-warming smile crossed her face. But then, as though a switch had been flicked, she gave an anxious look over her shoulder and stared uneasily into the distance as though she were fully expecting someone to appear out of the fog that surrounded her.

'So... who are you, then?' Sophie whispered over the top of Noah's head. 'A friend, a girlfriend? What do you reckon, Noah?' Rocking her son from side to side, Sophie patted Noah's back, and prayed that he'd go back to sleep. With a yawn, she thought of the last conversation she'd had with Luke. Just that morning they'd chatted as he'd left for work, which had been a vast improvement on when they'd first met and he'd rushed past her with no wish to communicate at all. At least now he'd pass the time of day, yet she couldn't help but feel a little slighted that he hadn't mentioned the impending visitor. Although that probably meant that Luke wasn't aware she'd be coming at all and that maybe she was a friend or a girlfriend of Adam's?

Moving to the chair beside the window, Sophie perched on its edge and continued to rock Noah back and forth. It was a good place to watch the world going past, and with Noah laying against her, busily sucking on his fist, or rooting for milk, it was a good place for her to relax and to take a few moments.

'Shhhhh. There you go, Noah. Now then, why don't you take your nap like a good boy, before your daddy turns up.' She paused and thought of Finn. 'He'll be calling in to see you soon, so he will,' she said, softly. 'In fact, why don't we both take a bit of a rest. Just for a few minutes?' She allowed herself to lean back in the chair, where she closed her eyes and listened to the constant drone of traffic that went past outside. It was a noise she liked, a reminder that right outside her front door the world was still turning and that, even though she hadn't seen a soul for the whole day, they were still out there... still walking and driving right past.

Her pyjamas were covered in baby food and, without a doubt, she needed a shower. She didn't really have time to sleep and more than anything she had to get dressed before Finn arrived and before he realised that, for the second time that week, she hadn't got dressed at all.

'There doesn't seem much point, most days, Noah, does there? Nothing ever happens and no one, other than your daddy, ever comes to visit.'

It was true. Her friendship group was all back in Ireland. Her life here a total contrast to the life she'd had before, where people had dropped in and out of each other's houses on a daily basis, coffee would have been made, and gossip shared. Here, she'd fully expected that she and Finn would have been together. For them to bring Noah into the world and for the three of them to be a family. It was the dream she'd hoped for after meeting Finn at a medical convention in Durham. He'd courted her relentlessly until he'd finally convinced her to move here from Dublin. Which was something she initially hadn't thought about doing, but one too many visits to England had seen her pregnant with Noah and, even though her pregnancy had been a complete surprise to them both, they'd both been happy and eventually she'd agreed to the move.

But their cosy existence hadn't lasted long. Finn had insisted that they live in the village where he'd grown up as a boy and, for some bizarre reason, Sophie had found herself agreeing. And now she wished she hadn't. Ugathwaite was far too quiet. She missed the hustle and bustle of Dublin and, even though Finn had sold her the dream and told her how amazing it would be to live in the country, she'd quickly come to dislike it.

'Please, Finn,' she'd pleaded, 'I don't like it here. I don't like living next door to that house.' She remembered standing in the room they were decorating as a nursery and pointing through the window. 'Do you know what they call that house, the one next door? I heard them. The women in the clinic. They all call it the "murder house", so they do. The things that happened in that house, they're terrifying. A man was slaughtered, right there, in his own kitchen! Do you know that?' She'd stopped and pulled a face. 'And that poor mother, she was beaten so badly, she went and lost her mind and, now, she's in and out of hospital like a God-damned yo-yo. One minute she's home and there are a dozen carers a day and then, whoosh, she's shipped back off like a bag of rubbish and spends weeks in hospital with only the odd visit from her family.' She'd paused, held a hand to her swollen stomach where an unborn Noah nestled safely inside.

'Sophie, it's just a house,' Finn had responded. 'And what happened there, it's over. It's history. It was years ago. Imogen Gilby is just a frail, old woman and I can assure you, there's no impending danger, not any more and not to us.'

'How do you know, Finn? Maybe there is. She might be waiting for the killer to return, for them to finish what they started. In fact, I'm amazed that she ever dares to come home at all.' As she'd said the words, she'd caught the way Finn's eyes had glazed over. The sag of his shoulders and the deep sigh that had fallen out of his mouth. 'Seriously Finn, the stories of the murder reached the news in Ireland and, if I'd known that we were going to live in the house right beside it, I wouldn't have come,' Sophie had insisted. 'It's creepy, possibly dangerous and... and what about our baby?' She'd once again placed a hand protectively over her pregnant belly and peered suspiciously out of the window, giving the house next door a long and unsettled look. 'What if it happens again? What if history does repeat itself and...' She'd fallen against Finn, wrapped her arms around his waist and lifted her face to stare directly into his eyes. 'And what if me, you and our baby end up caught in the middle of it all?'

'Come on, Soph, don't be daft.' Finn had lifted his hand to her face, cupped her chin and placed a soft, tender kiss firmly on her lips. 'Lightning doesn't strike twice, not like that, and besides, I grew up in this village. I love it here and yes, I have some good and some bad memories, but mostly good. I have friends here, Sophie. Good friends and my family, my gran is here too.'

'Finn. You never go out with your "so-called" bloody friends so don't give me that and, up to now, not one of them has ever been to visit you in this house,' she'd said almost smugly, until she'd realised how sad that sounded. 'And what about me? What about my friends? My family? The people I know are all in Ireland. Have you ever thought about that, about what sacrifices I had to make to be with you?'

'Soph, please, give it a rest,' he'd said abruptly. 'Try it, just for a year, for me and if you hate it half as much as you think you will, I promise, I'll take you back to Ireland on the very next flight. Deal?' He'd paused, smiled. 'So long as my gran can come and live with us.' He'd laughed and ducked playfully, as she'd swung out with a mischievous punch.

'Not on your life, Finn Alexander. I'm not living with your gran. Not ever. Do you hear me?' she'd answered jovially, but, deep inside, she'd meant every word. 'But, saying that, you spend so much time at her house, we might as bloody well.'

He'd paused, looked at her thoughtfully and reached out for her hand. 'Seriously, Sophie. The whole idea of us coming here was to get away from the city and surely to God, we've all got to be safer here than we would be in Dublin, or in London, or in any other stupid city that England has to offer, don't you think?' He'd pulled her back into the safety of his arms, held her tightly against him. 'And, to put it bluntly, Soph, look at what we've got here. My gran gave us this house. Do you realise how big a gift that is? If you were still in Dublin, you'd still be in that one-bed basement flat with its black mould travelling up the walls.' He'd pulled a face, pressed a kiss against her forehead and smiled lovingly. 'I know it was all you could afford but you wouldn't want to go back to that, or to subject our son to living like that, would you?'

Sighing, Sophie had known that Finn was right, and that the conversation had been over just because Finn had said so. Naively she'd agreed to the year-long trial, to the waiting and to the hoping that, somehow, she'd be happy. Yet here she was, nine months later and, after one disagreement too many, Finn was living back at his gran's.

'Sophie, it isn't forever,' Finn had said with a sorrowful look over his shoulder on the day he'd moved out. 'But I can't live with the bickering, I can't do anything right and you, well, you won't let me prescribe something for the postpartum rage...' He'd turned back towards the door. 'Sorry for being blunt, but I won't have Noah growing up with people arguing around him, not on a daily basis, it really wouldn't be fair.'

Now, when she thought back to the days after she'd first moved here from Ireland, Finn had barely ever been at home. He'd almost always been at work and, when he had come home, the arguments had begun within moments of him walking through the door. Sometimes it had felt as though he'd purposely annoyed her, as though by creating an atmosphere he'd have a reason to leave and yes, maybe sometimes she had expected a little too much, but her moods had bounced around, leaving her with no energy to try and make the relationship work, not when Finn had seemed hell-bent on letting it all go.

'You should have just gone back to Dublin...' she told herself for the millionth time. 'You should have gone back to Ireland where you had friends, and people around you to help raise your son.' Which would have been simple, apart from the fact that she loved Finn. Somehow, she had to find the energy to fight and to make the effort, especially now that Noah was born, but she was only willing to do that if Finn fought too. 'I'll make things right, so I will,' she said, convinced that, given the chance, she could resurrect the relationship and get it back to the way it had been when they'd first met and fell in love.

'Come on, Noah, let's get you to sleep.' In a voice that was almost a whisper, Sophie thought back to the moment when Noah was born. It had been a time when her life had spun on an axis. In a split second, she'd fallen in love, hook, line and sinker. It was a feeling that hadn't changed, even when she sat for hours at a time, like she had tonight, tapping him gently on his back, praying for sleep.

'Your mummy,' she said to Noah. 'She's going to find a way for you to have a mummy and a daddy, both who love you, and both who live under the very same roof.'

With Sophie's thoughts firmly on Noah, she closed her eyes, rested her head back against the chair and allowed herself to drift into a world where thoughts of a woman, walking around the garden outside, were pushed to one side and the only thoughts that mattered were those of her, of Finn and of Noah and the life they could live in the future.

5

PRESENT DAY – DECEMBER 2023 – SOPHIE

'Is he asleep?'

Jumping at the sound of Finn's voice, Sophie's eyes shot open with a start and immediately she felt herself bristle. She'd had every intention of taking a shower and making herself presentable before Finn arrived and, irritably, she looked down at the pair of bright pink Disney pyjamas, covered in spittle, along with the odd splash of sweet potato and banana that Noah had eaten for lunch, along with a muddy paw mark that Jasper had managed to land on the top of her leg. All of that, along with no make-up and her unbrushed hair tied up in a messy topknot, made her curse at the thought of how awful she looked.

'Finn, you frightened me half to death! You could have knocked on the door,' she grumbled hurriedly. 'You don't live here any more, or did you forget? And I know your gran owns the house, but you can't just walk into it, you do know that, don't you?' Spinning around in her seat, and through tired, painful eyes, she tried to focus. The bright light of the hallway made his silhouette appear tall and ominous and her mind flew to the Bible studies she'd read as a child and, for a split second, all she could think about was the angel Gabriel standing before her with a face like lightning and eyes like flaming torches. It was a thought she quickly blinked away and did all she could to find Finn's handsome face hidden amongst the shadows.

'Yeah, sorry,' he whispered while loosening his tie, 'I... Well, you know what I'm like, I just don't think and I'm that used to just walking in. It didn't occur to me that I shouldn't do that any more.'

'Well, you scared me half to death.' She took in a deep breath, stretched one arm above her head and searched the room until her gaze landed on the clock. 'What time is it, are you early or late?' Pushing herself upright, Sophie squinted as Finn moved into the room, giving her the chance to catch sight of his cold, ruggedly handsome face. There was a shadow of stubble that covered his chin and, as usual, he was dressed in a dark blue suit with a delicate stripe, along with his polished shoes and a perfectly matched tie.

Tonight, unusually, he'd eased his tie away from his neck and it hung untidily over the top of his pale pink, cotton shirt. It was a small indication that told Sophie how stressful his day had been, and immediately she felt sorry for snapping at him. With a quick look at Noah, she could see that he too was unimpressed by his father's sudden appearance and had fallen back into a deep, restful sleep. Noah sleeping was always a sight that made her heart swell. He had long, blonde eyelashes, the perfect rosebud lips and a thumb that kept going up and down to his mouth, where for a few seconds at a time he'd scramble to suck it.

'Do you want me to take him?' Finn asked with an apologetic smile. 'And, no, I'm not early, something came up and I'm running a bit late. Again.' He sighed regretfully. 'I had a heavy day at the surgery, in fact I had one of the worst days ever.'

'Really?'

'Yep, we had a patient who went and died on us in the waiting room. One minute she was sat there, happily chatting about the weather to old Mrs Pemberton. The next, she was gone. Dead. Just like that.' He moved back to the bedroom door and flicked on the light. 'Of course, we had to clear the room, postpone appointments and call for a private ambulance, which all takes time...'

'Oh Finn, that's awful.' Suddenly, now the light illuminated the room, Sophie glanced down at her clothing and once again wished she'd changed.

'Soph, did you get dressed today?' Moving across the room until he was stood by her side, she saw the way that Finn looked her up and down and then at Noah, whose eyes had flicked open. A smile had crossed his face and, suddenly, he lurched himself forward and Finn lifted him up and into his arms. 'I've told you before, I could prescribe you something and, in my professional opinion, I think you need to consider it,' he said as he looked at her face with the same look of concern he'd given her almost every day since Noah had been born. 'And I'm saying that as a doctor, not as a husband.'

'That's right, Finn, why don't you throw tablets down my throat because that'll make everything all right, won't it?' Sophie could feel her temper rise and angrily kept her gaze fixed firmly on the window. Finn's answer to everything was to prescribe something to take. A pill for this, a tablet for that or a therapy session with someone she'd never heard of. Feeling annoyed, she thought about all the occasions during the day when she'd considered getting dressed, and then there were all the things that had always stopped her. There had always been a job to do. Noah had needed feeding or changing and Jasper, who was still only a puppy, had often demanded her attention. There had been beds to make and laundry to take care of. After which, there had been little time or enthusiasm left to do anything just for herself.

'I'm not sick, I've just had a bad day. Noah didn't settle, he...' She felt the tears spring to her eyes. She couldn't bear the look of disappointment that showed on Finn's face and, deep down, she felt a sense of disappointment too. 'So, to answer your question, I don't want your bloody tablets, what I'd like is a bit of help. Rather than standing there throwing out the criticism, maybe you could come over in the morning, give me the chance to have a shower while you give your son his breakfast and, maybe then, you could end up wearing it all over your clothes rather than me.' Pushing a hand through her hair, she felt her bottom lip quiver. Life had not turned out how she'd hoped and, with her hand resting on the curtain, she kept on looking outside. The curtains, covered in brightly coloured lions, tigers and other zoo animals, were a design that had often made her smile, but tonight all she could see was the way they were squashed against the radiator by Noah's crib. How close the changing table stood beside it. How many nappies were piled up on top along with baby grows and every cream that a newborn might need. And then, on the other side of the room, stood at least thirty cardboard boxes. All the unpacking she still hadn't got around to. 'I just don't seem to get the time to do anything and...' She looked down at Noah, who was now sleeping like a baby in his daddy's arms. 'And I was going to say that your son never bloody sleeps. But, ironically...' She tutted, sat down in the chair, dragged her hands through her hair and gave Finn a tight, questioning smile. 'You have no damned idea how hard it is for me, Finn. Being here on my own, and I know that, even if you lived here, you'd still go out to work, but the responsibility of being all by myself, all of the time... Well, it gets a bit much.' She turned back to the window. 'And then there's Jasper. I had him out in the back garden earlier, but he keeps digging and I still didn't get the chance to take him out for a proper long walk.' Looking up at Finn for some kind of reaction, she picked up one corner of her dressing gown and began to twist it angrily around her finger. 'Everyone wants a part of me and, quite honestly, I'm not sure that there's anything left of me to give.'

'Fine. It's fine. I hear you. I'll go down and I'll take Jasper out for you.'

'For me? Don't say *for me*, Finn. He's your dog too.'

'Sophie, come on, don't be like this.' Tipping his head to one side, Finn dropped a gentle kiss on Noah's forehead. 'I've brought pizza.' He motioned towards the door, and looked as though he were about to walk through it. 'I thought we might eat together, at least. Shall I go and stick it in the oven while you go take a shower?'

Nodding, Sophie felt the tears that had threatened finally fall, but she turned to the window, so that Finn didn't see. 'Yeah, sure...' She pulled the curtain to one side and stared through the thickening fog at the garden next door. 'Who do you think she is?'

'Who?'

'There was a woman. She was stood on the path. In Luke's front garden.'

'How should I know?' he replied. 'What did she look like?'

Pondering the thought, Sophie continued to peer out of the window. 'Well, she was my age, but I think she looked taller, although I couldn't really tell from up here. And, she had longish auburn hair that swished about a bit at the bottom.' She nodded as though confirming her description. 'I'd say she was really quite pretty.' Looking down at the windowsill, Sophie tried to remember the detail. But, other than the shoulder-length hair, she couldn't remember much more and for a while her mind clouded over, and she began to wonder if she'd seen the woman at all or, like so many other things, whether or not she'd been a small part of her dream.

'Sophie. You do know that Luke's visitors are none of our business, don't you?' He took a step towards the window, furrowed his brow, and tried to look over her shoulder. 'Besides, I've never taken you for being a stalker.' He playfully pushed her out of the way as he looked outside with a thoughtful gaze.

'Do you know what, Finn? I'm going to take that shower...' Sophie said the words but didn't move. Instead, she began to take Noah's clothes from the radiator before adding them to a pile that stood on top of the changing mat. 'And while I'm in the shower, maybe you can look after your son, while trying to cook pizza. Oh, and while you're down there, don't forget to set the table, make up Noah's bottle, empty the dishwasher and walk the bloody dog. Because, once you've done all that, all at once, without messing up, you might start to realise that seeing a new face in the garden next door really could be the highlight of your day.'

Finn shook his head but took a step back. 'Fine. Alright. I'm going downstairs to throw the pizza in the oven, whizz Jasper around the garden and look for whoever it is you've seen hiding in the trees. Once I find them, I'll interrogate them and then I'll come back and tell you all about it.' He smiled sardonically. Pressed his lips lovingly onto Noah's cheek and lay him down in his crib. 'I won't be too long, baby boy.'

Sophie looked down at her son who now slept peacefully. But the irony that Finn had put Noah in his crib while he went to do his chores hadn't been lost on her completely. Nor had the way he'd shot down the stairs like a bullet, to take out a dog who he'd barely ever walked and all because she'd mentioned a woman with long auburn hair, hiding in the garden next door.

A final glance saw the woman briefly step out from her hiding place and look up at where Sophie watched her from the window. Catching each other's eye, both women could see a lifetime of mistrust in the other's face and, for just a few short moments, they stared directly into one another's souls.

Oddly, as Sophie stared, she was no longer worried about whether or not the woman was here to see Luke. Or whether she was a long-lost friend of Adam's. What she did worry about was Finn. She knew he'd had a life here before they'd met. A time when some of his memories had been so good, he'd jumped at the chance to live here again. The problem was, she knew that there had been some bad memories too. Things he'd never spoken about, not to her, and all Sophie could imagine was that, at some point in his life, Finn had stepped out of a big black hole, one that he had no wish to step back into or revisit.

'I could be very wrong, Finn... but I think you know exactly who that woman is. The only thing I don't know is whether she was a part of your good life, or a part of your bad one.'

6

NINE YEARS BEFORE – HATTIE

Sitting up with a frightened jolt, Hattie stifled a yawn as she listened to the loud, persistent noise that came from someone banging violently against the front door.

Shuffling up against her pillows, she glanced across her bedroom and squinted as she noticed the small burst of light that shone beneath her door. It came from the hallway and gave her just enough light to glance around the room and with her mind spinning from the alcohol she'd drank just an hour or two earlier, along with a terrifying end to her evening that she hadn't been expecting, Hattie reached for her phone and flicked at the screen. 'Who the hell?' she grumbled. The screen had gone black; the battery had died, and without a single flicker to give her any hope of using it she threw it back at the bedside cabinet and watched as it dropped off the edge and landed beside a bright red linen dress that lay discarded in a heap on the floor. It was a dress she'd only just taken off. One she wished she'd never worn. But also a dress that would have given her father palpitations, if he'd ever seen her in it. Which was probably the best reason she could think of to never wear it again.

Holding her breath, she waited and listened to the banging. She hoped that her father would answer the door and that, when he did, the visitor would come and go, without causing too much trouble, like she'd known to happen so many times in the past. Being the vicarage meant that they'd often have the lowest of the low turning up night and day, looking for handouts. Both men and women who'd often become angry and violent, especially on the days when they'd expected the church to give and, even though their father had always given what he could, they hadn't always received all they'd hoped for. But, then, she feared that the visitor was there to see her and that her night was about to get much worse than it had been.

Pulling the duvet up and under her chin, Hattie considered hiding beneath it. She wanted nothing more than to take refuge until her hangover had subsided and, knowing that her mobile had died, she searched the other end of the room for a clock. 'Two thirty-six,' she muttered under her breath. She'd been home for less than an hour and, even though it felt as though she'd slept for much longer, it was still the middle of the night and Hattie resented the intrusion.

Of course, the chances were that the visitor was there to see her father – he was often needed in the middle of the night and some of the parishioners had a genuine reason for knocking. They would often look to their faith at times when a relative was nearing their end and they'd ask her father to sit by their bedside, hold on to their hand and give them the last rights. Newborn babies were christened when their parents were terrified that they wouldn't survive until the morning, the homeless needed food to eat or somewhere to live and, all in all, her father felt like the property of the village. The one person they all went to, whenever something out of the ordinary happened or when a spokesperson was needed.

But, tonight, the knocking was different. It was angrier, louder and more persistent than normal, making Hattie throw her head back against the pillow, and blow out angrily and fearfully through puffed-up cheeks as the constant banging bounced off the walls and continued to echo around the house.

With her father's footsteps padding down the stairs, Hattie held her breath and listened to his normal grumblings, and his overzealous shouts of assurance. 'Okay, okay, I'm coming.' But the visitor either hadn't heard or had chosen to ignore him and continued banging the door. 'Now then, I've said I'm here. Give me a minute.'

For a moment, Hattie's mind flew back to the idea that the person was there to see her and, while holding her breath and listening intently, she went over the whole night in her mind. It had been a date she shouldn't have gone on and a situation she hadn't wanted to be in, where threats had been made and, now, with the hammering on the front door, she prayed that she hadn't brought any trouble to her parents' front door.

'Hattie, what's going on?' Still holding her breath, Hattie watched as the door was slowly pushed open with the long, slow tell-tale creak that came from a hinge her father had always refused to oil: 'I like to know when you're out of your bed in the night, young lady and I quite like the fact that the door gives you away.' Hattie knew it was just another way her father had of controlling her. A way of knowing where she was and what she was doing. But his over-controlling ways had made her even more determined to live her own life. She was nineteen years old and grimaced at the thought of what he'd do if he ever found out how often she sneaked down the old servant's staircase and left the house without anyone knowing. At first she'd simply gone out with friends and spent time in the pubs and nightclubs in Northallerton. But tonight had been different, tonight she'd been talked into helping Louisa. There had been the offer of easy money where she could earn two hundred and fifty pounds in just one night, and all she had to do was go on a date, wear a nice dress and hold on to the arm of a man who'd been old enough to be her father. What she hadn't realised was how high the expectations had been and how quickly the situation had escalated, leaving her to feel vulnerable and with her dignity just a little bit wounded. And now, with her fingers tracing the place on her neck where she was sure she'd been bruised, she was more than fearful of the threats that had been made and the repercussions that could easily follow.

With the door swinging open and the room now half-lit by the light from the hallway, she could see the shape of her younger brother, Luke. He was just thirteen years old and a couple of years younger than Adam, although taller and leaner. She found herself amused by the way he'd walked into the room on his tiptoes, with both of his arms held out in front, looking like Shaggy from an old episode of *Scooby Doo*.

'You're a bit old for this, aren't you?' She patted the duvet affectionately and watched as her younger brother shuffled across the room and sat on the edge of the bed. 'Both you and Adam got away with creeping into my room as toddlers. But you're a young man now. I'm not sure Dad would approve...' Giving the door a dubious look, Hattie put her arms around her brother and pulled him into a hug. 'We'd probably get sent to hell in a handcart, just because you're in here,' she whispered with a smile. 'You know how strict Dad is about these kinds of things and you can be sure there'd be something in that bloody Bible that'd tell him it's wrong.' She thought about how her father's mind would explode while writing all the sermons he'd expect them to sit through.

'Hattie... why would he send us to hell?' Luke questioned

with a frown. It was more than obvious he'd just woken up and, while taking advantage of the rare hug he was giving, Hattie thought back to the quiet, young boy he'd always been. An introvert in a household full of the gregarious. Quite the opposite to his older, rugby playing brother Adam, who wasn't happy unless he'd caught everyone's attention. 'The banging woke me up,' he sighed and, like a child much younger than his years, he lay down beside her. 'They do sound angry, don't they?' Lifting his head up from the pillow, Luke twisted anxiously as he tried to listen to the sound of her father's grumblings.

'Okay, okay. As I've said. Give me a minute.' Father's words were followed by a grunt and a final turn of the key as the door was opened and a woman's loud, Liverpudlian voice filled the hallway. The loudness made Hattie gasp as she listened to the voice that seemed to bounce off every wall, until it echoed forcefully around the confines of her bedroom.

'Where the hell is she?' The words were venomous and more than threatening. 'I swear to God, if you've harmed a hair on her head, I'll go down for murder.' The noise bellowed around the house, as one internal door after the other was opened, and then slammed shut again with force.

'Okay, Mrs... er... I'm not sure who you're talking about right now, but, if I can help you, I will. The... the office, it's this way.' Even at this hour, and with the woman screaming at the top of her voice, her father was trying to be polite. He was good at caring for others, even though Hattie resented the amount of time he spent at the church.

'Imogen. Imogen... Could you come down for a moment? I... I think this lady might be here to see you.' Her father shouted the words in a voice that was just loud enough to be heard, but was still calm, and to the outside world sounded almost hypnotic.

Sitting upright, with her eyes fixed on Luke's, Hattie pressed a finger to her lips as she heard her parents' bedroom door open and close. The sound was quickly followed by the sound of soft footsteps. A sign that her mother was heading towards the bathroom, where, as normal, she'd make herself presentable before going downstairs.

'She was here last night...' the woman's harsh voice continued. 'I've been told she was in the family way and came to see your missus... and, since then, she hasn't been back to the house. Nobody's seen her. It's like she's disappeared. Right into thin air.' Another door was opened and slammed, making it more than obvious to Hattie that the woman was marching around, pushing her way in and out of rooms and looking inside. Hattie kept one eye on her own door and wondered if the woman would be brazen enough to venture upstairs.

Tiptoeing across the room, Hattie positioned herself behind her bedroom door, where she peered through the crack. She watched as the bathroom door opened and, with the elegance of a movie star, her mother stepped onto the landing and began to move slowly and deliberately down the staircase, turning the light off as she went.

The sudden darkness gave Hattie the perfect opportunity to slip out through the door and, with the collar of her pyjamas pulled up to hide the bruising, she wedged herself behind an old mahogany tallboy that stood at the top of the stairs. From her hiding place, she had a clear view of the vast hallway where she watched as her father, Gerald, made a failed attempt to usher a scantily dressed woman into her mother's office. But her short skirt, low-cut top and breasts that were trying to escape were obviously making him nervous and, with an exasperated glare, he turned his attention in the direction of his wife and looked hopeful that she'd take control and that he'd be immediately relieved of his duties.

'Berni, isn't it? We've met before. It's good to see you again.' Imogen Gilby calmly nodded her head in acknowledgement. 'Here, wipe your tears.' She handed the woman a tissue and gave her a look of concern as Berni wiped her eyes to leave long black streaks of mascara painted down each of her cheeks. 'Please. Why don't you come into my office. We can talk in here.' It was a voice that Hattie had heard her mother use at least a thousand times before. A tone that was firm yet gentle, caring and empathetic all at once. 'It's more private and... you have to understand, my family are asleep.'

'I really don't give a toss about your so-called family.' Berni screeched. 'You don't think anyone around here is taken in by your la-de-da ways and your false sense of importance, do you? We all know who you are. I remember what you did and, quite honestly, people like you just make me sick. You're no better than we are, and I have no idea what gave you the right to—'

'That's enough,' Imogen snapped as she walked across to her desk. There she picked up a pen and tapped it anxiously against a desk pad and wrote something down. Hattie slid down the stairs with Luke close behind her until they reached the half-landing and, with the curtain hiding them from view, they peeped around its edge until they could see right into their mother's office.

'I just want to know where my daughter is. She didn't come back to the house, and I've spent the whole night looking for her.' The woman pulled at her top, to reveal a little more of her breasts. 'Word has it that she came to see you.' She stretched out her arm, an elongated finger pointing directly towards where Hattie's mother stood. 'What I don't understand, is why?'

With a glance towards Luke, Hattie furrowed her brow and

pulled the curtain further around them. It was a place she often hid to watch the comings and goings of her mother's clients. There was always one or two each night. Some were well to-do businesswomen, and others were like the woman who currently stood in the office doorway at the bottom of the stairs. She was scantily dressed and looking for answers. Although, even now, because her mother rarely spoke about it, Hattie still wasn't sure what a psychotherapist did, or what services they offered apart from talking to people about their problems.

'Berni... you know I can't tell you why she came to see me. I have a duty to my clients...' Imogen shook her head and looked from Berni to her husband with a furrowed brow. 'Whether she's your daughter or not, I really can't say who has been here. Or why they came. I'm so sorry.'

'Well, I know for sure that she didn't need one of your counselling sessions. But, if she didn't come for that, why else would she come here? It's not like she had the money to pay you. Not when she's already a month behind on her rent.' She nodded and, once again, pulled a new tissue from the box and wiped at her eyes. 'The boss man, he isn't happy. He wants paying and Alice, she needs to get herself home and back out on the streets.' She glanced over her shoulder and lifted one side of her lip in a sneer. 'You might think it's okay to tell people like us how to live their lives. To flash your money. But you're no better than we are.' She turned back to the office, looked Imogen up and down. 'Your life, it isn't so damned perfect, is it? It never was, was it?'

With her heart beating like a bass drum, Hattie caught her breath. Berni had taken another swipe at her mother's lifestyle, which made Hattie bristle with annoyance. It was more than obvious that the woman had something to say, and Hattie made a mental note to find out who she was and why she was being so nasty. In the meantime, she turned her attention to her father, who'd now stopped pacing and stood with a hand on the front door handle. Suddenly he jerked it open to stand on the threshold and suck at the cool night air. Looking left, then right, he appeared to check out the houses that stood to each side of theirs and Hattie felt sure that he was just a little worried that somehow the commotion might disturb their neighbours, even though the houses were some distance away.

'Berni?' Turning with a newfound confidence, Gerald tentatively held out a hand towards her as she walked back into the hallway. 'Berni, I'm going to put the kettle on and make us some tea.' He gave her a genuine smile, then closed the front door and moved towards the kitchen, where he hovered in the doorway. 'It always helps, no matter what the situation. Don't you think?'

Suddenly the woman fell silent and took a swipe at the tears that had once again begun to roll down her cheeks. 'If she wasn't coming to see you, who was she seeing? One of your boys? Is one of them the father to her baby? If they are, they are going to pay for it!'

It was a sentence that made Hattie catch her breath and, anxiously, she gave Luke a questioning look. But, when his face gave nothing away, she stood up, and as quietly as she could she nudged him back up the stairs and in the direction of his bedroom before Berni said any more. 'Quick. Go on, get yourself back to bed,' she said.

'Gerald, don't worry about the tea.' Her mother's voice drifted up the stairs in a soft tone. Even at a time of crisis she had a way of remaining both calm and steady. 'Berni. My boys are far too young for Alice, and I didn't deny that she was here. What I said was that I couldn't tell you *why* she was here.' She smiled thoughtfully. 'I'm sure that Alice can't have gone far. So, I'll tell you what I'm going to do. I'll put my coat on and we'll go out and look for her, together. How does that sound?'

The Family Home 53

Moving as quickly as she could, Hattie crept back inside her bedroom, to stand by the window where she hid behind the curtain to look outside. She felt her gaze automatically focus on the cars and the trucks that were parked across the square. It was a place where Hattie had often seen Alice go. As did the other prostitutes that came to the village. The square was a place where the truckers often parked for the night. An easy picking for a prostitute who was looking for extra work and Hattie had no doubt that this is where Alice might have gone. Especially after she'd watched so many head that way before for a quick chat in the car park that had ended up with one of the women dropping to her knees, or climbing up and into the cab, for a quick thirty-minute session. Either way, both the prostitute and the trucker got exactly what they wanted, and, because she'd often seen the prostitutes walking away laughing, Hattie had never seen the harm in what they were doing. Not until tonight when a kiss had turned into a rough exchange and, after a few terrifying minutes, Hattie had jumped out of the car and, with the only dignity she had left, she'd confidently walked in the opposite direction to her own home, while all the time looking back and waiting for her aggressor to drive out of the village. Only then had she headed for home, where she'd gone in through the back door and climbed back up the old wooden staircase that led to the safety of her bedroom.

And, until tonight, nothing had fazed her. She'd never been shocked by anything she'd seen, especially when life happened right out there, in the square, in open view of anyone who might want to watch. However, right now, she was watching her mother walk down the road, arm in arm with a prostitute as though they were long-lost friends and, carefully, Hattie watched the exchange. It was more than obvious by what had been said and what she was witnessing now that both Berni and her mother knew each other well. It was an odd combination of women, of personalities and backgrounds. Unless, of course, their backgrounds had crossed in the past and in a way that Hattie could only imagine, in a way she fully intended to explore.

7

PRESENT DAY – DECEMBER 2023 – HATTIE

Alone and in the dark, Hattie inched along the driveway. It was the closest she'd been to the house in nine years and she could vividly imagine walking through the house to the spot where her father had been brutally murdered. It was enough to make the nausea return, the feeling of impending doom settling on her shoulders, and silently she cursed Luke for being so late.

'Come on,' she cursed anxiously under her breath, 'where the hell are you?' She bit down on her lip and held her breath as she heard the sound of a pair of heavy boots walking past at speed. The thickening fog was impeding her view, and she began to wonder if the approaching feet belonged to friend or foe. It was enough to force her into taking another step backwards, where she caught her back against a tree and a sharp, jarring pain shot through her.

Waiting until the stranger had walked past, Hattie lifted her phone to her face, checked the time on it and continued to curse. Her brother was really late and, with her eyes trained on the small part of the road she could see, she watched for Luke's arrival but could clearly recall the conversation she'd had with

Adam and his non-committal way of telling her that Luke was still as grumpy as hell. Deep inside she knew that the loving brother she'd previously known had been replaced by one that barely cared at all and, with a heavy heart, she mentally prepared herself for what he might say when he finally arrived.

'Seven thirty-four...' she whispered under her breath as her fingers tapped at the screen of her phone. With a sudden determination that she wouldn't wait a moment longer, she walked back to the gate, only to jump backwards as Luke's handsome face suddenly emerged from the fog. She felt a burst of pride as she spotted his face. Then, wholeheartedly, she felt a million regrets. He was the baby brother she'd once hugged in her bed. But, now, at just twenty-two years old, he was practically a stranger, and she couldn't help but feel an overwhelming sense of disappointment for the years they'd lost, as he marched straight past, without a single glance in her direction.

'Luke?'

'What the hell do you want, Hattie?' Luke asked as he jammed the key in the lock and kicked out at the bottom corner of the door. He smirked with satisfaction as it bounced heavily against the inside wall, making the whole house vibrate with his anger.

As the light went on inside, Hattie's foot hovered on the threshold. She was overwhelmed with trepidation and almost afraid to put her foot down on the inside because, once she'd stepped inside, once she'd returned, it would be like the breaking of a curse and she had the sudden urge to run – to go back up the garden path, out of the old, broken gate and back to her car where she was sure she'd feel safe. Everything about this house felt evil and dangerous. Although, during all the years she'd lived there, she'd run in and out of the door without hesitation. It had been her family home. The place where she'd lived and, even though her father had been strict and her mother all consumed with her work, she hadn't ever felt unsafe. Not until those few days that had preceded her father's murder. A night when she'd vowed that she'd never come back, not until the killer was caught. Now, stepping over the threshold, she felt as though she was reneging on a deal. One she'd only made with herself and, as she inched over the threshold and into the hallway, she felt every particle of air leave her body, making her grab at the newel post just to stop herself from falling.

Standing there, with her fingernails digging into the woodwork, Hattie scanned the hallway. It still had the same deep red wallpaper, the faded ivory-coloured panelling with a dado rail that went across the top, and a pair of long, dark grey curtains that were now covered with small irregular-shaped holes.

'Luke?' she said again as her brother continued to ignore her.

'What?'

'You could at least say hello, couldn't you?' she questioned, as the feeling of hurt surged through her. 'It isn't easy coming back here, and...' With her eyes fixed on his, she wished for him to soften, for him to welcome her home, just as she'd hoped, but instead Luke rolled his jaw until it became set rigid with annoyance. He looked her up and down and gave her a cold, distant smile.

'Hello, Hattie,' he grumbled with an air of hostility that emanated from every inch of his tall, muscular body. Short, dark strands of hair poked out from beneath a navy-blue beanie. His cheeks were red from the cold and his deep, charcoal eyes were as cold as ice as they stared straight through her. 'I'm sorry you're finding it hard being back here, but some of us didn't have a choice. Now, are you staying long? Because, do you know what? Hard as it is living here, we seem to have been managing just fine without you.'

It was a reaction that hit her in the stomach like a fist. She looked over his shoulder towards the open front door, where she saw the fog was growing even thicker, like an impenetrable blanket.

'Look. I shouldn't have come,' she said. 'Only, Adam phoned, and so did Louisa, and they said that Mum was sick and that I should come sooner rather than later. That she wanted to see us all.'

Luke crossed his arms defensively. 'No, Hattie, you shouldn't have come. Adam might have phoned you, because, for some reason only known to himself, he thought you had a right to know what was happening...' He shook his head. 'But I don't. It's not like you've ever really been bothered before, is it? So, if you want to leave, don't let me stop you.'

'Luke!' Reeling with anger, Hattie could feel herself purposely taking short, sharp breaths. She wanted to retaliate, to tell him of all the times she'd gone to the hospital, the hours she'd sat by her mother's bedside and the constant clock watching, that ensured that she'd always left before they arrived. But didn't. She knew she could have done more. Could have been here more and, even though she hated being at the brunt of Luke's anger, she knew how much she probably deserved it.

'Look, Hattie. You're here and you obviously want to talk.' Aggressively, he punched out at the door that had once been their mother's office. 'So, let's talk. Let's go into the office and you can say whatever it is you want to say, then you can go back to wherever it is you've been hiding and I... Well, I can get on with my life. Living here, in this good, old family home, that everyone talks about, and nobody wants to live in. Including me.'

Hattie turned and pointed down the long, narrow corridor that stretched from the front of the house to the back. It was the passage that led to the lounge, and to the kitchen where she'd found her father's body. It was a place she really didn't want to go and a room that had tortured her dreams, but, to beat the feeling she had inside her, she knew that she had to walk into that room and see that the body was gone, that the blood had been cleaned and that the nightmare of her past could finally be put behind her. Besides, the lounge and the kitchen had been the rooms where they'd always congregated as a family and that was where she wanted to go, and not into her mother's office.

'Can't we go to the lounge?' She had a sudden urge to run along the corridor, push open the doors and look behind them to see that nothing had changed and that behind each of those doors it was still the way her mother had left it.

'No, I'd rather go in here,' he snapped.

'Luke, don't be like this...' She didn't know what else to say, or how to calm his obvious animosity. 'I just spoke to Adam?' She watched the way Luke marched through the office and straight to the window, where he stood looking out. To his right stood their mother's desk. Behind it, a long row of tall walnut bookcases. Each bookcase was stacked high with old, dusty books, box files and encyclopaedias that had been pushed into every space. In front of the window stood the same chocolate-brown leather settee. It was a place she'd sat so many times as a teenager and, even though it was cracked and faded, she still had the urge to sit and be ensconced in the familiarity it would give her. Carefully, she reached out and ran a hand delicately across one of its arms. 'He's staying at the hospital—' she pointed out of the window '—because of the weather. He said I should stay here tonight and that we should all go to see her in the morning.' As she said the words, she rolled her eyes upward, knowing that right above this room was the bedroom she'd slept in for the first nineteen years of her life and that, right now, she was less than ten feet from where her old bed had stood. 'Mum's old settee,' she whispered fondly. 'It's where her clients used to sit. Do you remember them? There was always one or two here, every night of the week, and...' She hoped that, by chatting about the past, she might lighten the mood. 'She always loved this room and it... Well, it feels kind of odd, coming in here, you know, without her being here.' For a moment, Hattie could still see the way her mother used to sit behind her desk, the tailored dresses she used to wear. The sunglasses that were almost always perched on top of soft auburn hair that fell gently around her shoulders, and her smile that was always warm, welcoming and full of empathy. 'My ladies come here to talk to me, Hattie,' her mother had once explained. 'Some of these women, they sell their souls to the devil. But, deep down, they're not bad people. They need our help; you know that don't you? And your father and I, well... we try to help them the best way we can.' Hattie remembered the way she'd tapped her cheque book with the nib of a pen. A clear indication that money had been given. 'And this room,' her mother had continued. 'It has to look professional and, above all else—' she'd nodded proudly '—it has to feel safe.'

It had been a statement that Hattie had often thought back to. She'd seen the irony in the fact that her mother had created a safe space for others, but that this was the place where she'd been left broken and so close to death, that she'd ended up crawling through the dirt in the hope she'd find someone to help her.

'What happened to us, Luke?' Hattie finally asked, 'What happened to our family?' Her gaze scanned the room. Her body absorbed the atmosphere that was more than painful and, with her lips pressed tightly together, Hattie tried to think of all the things she'd wanted to say. All the conversations she'd imagined she'd have with her brothers. But, being here, back in this house, was all-consuming and, suddenly, her mind had gone completely blank, and she had no idea what she should do or say. Once again, with her eyes on the door, she considered leaving.

'What happened?' he growled. 'Are you talking about the fact that our father was slaughtered on the kitchen floor, or that our mother was brutally attacked in a way that ruined her life and ours?' He took a step backwards, raised his eyebrows. 'Do you know what people say around here, Hattie? They think our father attacked her and that she dealt him the final blow. That they attacked each other.' He rolled his jaw in anger. 'But with no proof the whispers just carry on and Adam and I, we've had to deal with all of this alone, because you fucked off and you didn't come back.'

Taking slow, deliberate breaths, Hattie stared back down the hallway. She had an urge to tell Luke the reasons behind why she'd left. She had so many regrets and felt so much remorse about everything that had happened. If she hadn't taken that job, she wouldn't have ended up at the sharp end of her father's wrath and, ultimately, the argument it had led to. Right there in the kitchen, where his body was found. If they hadn't argued, if she hadn't stormed back to her room, her father might have been anywhere else in the house and the whole catalogue of events that had followed might have been avoided. She opened and closed her mouth, tried to say the words, but couldn't. In the end, she just shook her head regretfully and knew, without a doubt, that Luke had every right to be angry. She didn't and couldn't blame him for hating her. To him, she'd simply packed a bag and, even though at the time she'd tried to convince them to go with her, she had left. And now she was back, and she was going to give him another reason to hate her even more.

8

PRESENT DAY – DECEMBER 2023 – HATTIE

Moving to sit down, with her eyes fixed firmly on her brother, Hattie concentrated on the man Luke had become. He had a rugged, handsome face. His shoulders were broad and muscular and he filled his denim jacket to the point of bursting. While she'd been away, he'd turned into a fine young man and she ached for him to give her a smile that she remembered as both affectionate and captivating.

As though he were sensing her discomfort, Luke furrowed his brow, removed his hat and pushed his hands through his short, trimmed beard and then angrily up to ruffle his hair. He was no longer the gangly teenager she'd left behind. Nor was he the toddler who'd constantly climbed into her bed and cuddled up beside her. 'I don't like the dark,' he'd often whispered. 'Or the noises. They scare me.'

'However you paint it, Hattie, you left us. And now you're back and what I want to know is, why?' He took a step forward, threw out a hand and slammed it against the seat beside her.

Catching her breath, Hattie pressed her back firmly into the settee and paid close attention to the way Luke's fingers curled into tight, threatening fists. She didn't like the way his skin had turned white with tension. It was an act that made her heart pound heavily in her chest and, with her eyes fixed firmly on his, she felt a determination not to show him how much he scared her.

'You need to back off, Luke. Right now,' she finally growled, before taking a long, deep breath. 'I might have fucked off, as you put it. But finding Dad like that, with half of his damned head caved in, surrounded in blood, really didn't make me feel like staying. Do you know how much I dread walking into that kitchen? How scared I was of coming back to this house?' She paused, swallowed. 'So why don't you give me a break. I'm not the goddamned enemy.'

'Aren't you?' he asked. 'But you were clearly Daddy's favourite.' He stood up, lifted his hands up in the air, his palms upwards. 'The one he loved the most.'

His words were bitter and twisted and hung heavily in the air between them. Hattie glared at him. 'What the hell are you talking about, Luke?' She swallowed, as his face moved to just inches away from hers. 'Our Dad loved no one but God.'

'You really don't know, do you?' he asked. 'Or you do, and that's why you're back. You heard that Mum is about to die too and now... you're here to claim the house, and the bloody inheritance they both planned to leave you.' He shook his head slowly from side to side. 'What I need to know is why the hell they want to leave it all to you and not to the three of us?' he asked. 'And, if you do sell this place, where the hell am I supposed to live?'

'Luke, for God's sake.' She felt her breathing accelerate, and sank her fingers into the leather arm of the settee. Her mind spun with a million questions, that no one could answer. She'd once seen a copy of her parents' will and, for years, she'd been more than aware that it had only named her. But she didn't know why.

'You knew, didn't you?'

'Yes, but...' She felt the room move around her. 'I found it, the will.' She shook her head in annoyance. 'I didn't even think it was current or that it would mean anything and I certainly thought that, by now, Mum would have changed things.' Anxiously, she looked down at the carpet and continued to dig her fingers into the seat of the settee. 'I thought she'd have written a new one...' She furrowed her brow.

'Yet... here you are, ready to scramble around and claim every last crumb,' Luke grumbled.

'I didn't ask to inherit the damned house and, if you think I'm happy about it, then you damn well need to think again.' The house was the last thing she'd have ever wanted and, once again, she felt as though the weight of the world had suddenly landed on her chest and was slowly and deliberately stealing her breath. She slowly inched further along the settee, wanting to put a distance between her and Luke and she felt a sense of relief when he stood up straight, but then spun around and threw his hand outwards, hitting the wall in obvious anger with his fist.

'Luke...' Exasperated, Hattie closed her eyes and swallowed hard. She'd always known that coming back here was going to be hard. But she didn't want to own this house, or to live here for longer than she had to. What she did have to do, though, was make peace with her brothers.

Shaking his head, Luke pulled a Bible down from the shelf and threw it aggressively towards her. 'Do you know what, Hattie? They say the Lord works in mysterious ways. Well, do you know what?' He spat the words and pointed to the Bible.

'You're welcome to it. 'Cause everything in this house is nothing more than pure fucking evil and, if it were up to me, I'd burn it. I'd burn the whole damn lot, down to the ground.'

Hurt by Luke's anger, Hattie swiped the Bible off her lap as though it had burned her. She watched the way it bounced across the floor and came to land next to a pile of box files. They were stacked beside the desk and, unusually, unlike the rest of the room, none of them appeared covered in dust.

Hattie wrapped her arms tightly around herself and watched the way Luke stared through the window towards the gate at the bottom of the garden that was still hidden by the fog. In his reflection in the glass, she could see the way his face had become distorted with emotion. The anger and frustration that clearly showed in his features and the effort he was obviously making to hold it together.

'Luke—' She stopped, thought about her words, and leaned forward to pick up an old, tarnished picture frame. For a moment, she simply stared through the dust at the picture of her family. It had been taken at a time when she'd thought they'd been happy. A day when both their mother and father had proudly stood behind an old wooden bench, their three children dutifully sat before them. All of them smiling for the picture.

'I wish I could give you all the answers. I wish I knew what happened in this house that night. But I don't and I don't for one minute believe the police theory that our mother stabbed our father. The damage to his head was horrendous, she couldn't have possibly done all of that, not if she'd been stabbed herself.' Her hand went out to sweep the room. 'I know he was difficult at times and hard to live with, but she loved him. She loved him far too much to kill him.'

Closing his eyes, Luke nodded in affirmation. 'But she left us, Hattie,' he whispered. 'She's been silent for so many years, not really communicating with any of us. On that night, we lost them both, but then we lost you too...' He took a deep breath, and with eyes full of unshed tears, he stared straight at her. 'The difference is... you could have and should have come back. But you didn't.'

'Luke.' She felt her bottom lip quiver. She didn't like arguing. Not with Luke and she ran a hand through her hair and gazed longingly around a room she'd once used to love and admire. 'I had to leave. I was terrified. Someone had been in our home. They'd killed our father and left our mother for dead and I... I felt vulnerable, threatened and I couldn't bear the thought that whoever did this was probably someone we knew.' With the picture frame still held in her hand, she tapped a long, pointed finger firmly against the glass.

'Why do you say that?'

'Look at the evidence, Luke. They were in the kitchen. Our parents, over the years, had a lot of people in and out of this house. But not in the kitchen. That was the room where no one but friends and family went. It was a private space and, if they were in there, then it must have been someone our parents knew.'

Turning, with eyes full of tears, Luke stared at her with his mouth wide open. 'Do you really think it was a friend of the family?'

'Yes...' She rolled her eyes to the ceiling. 'It could have been someone that went to the church, or someone that one of us knew.' She patted the settee and watched the way Luke flopped down to sit beside her. His shoulders had suddenly dropped and he gave out an audible sigh and lifted her hand to clasp it in his.

The anger had gone; the animosity had dissipated and, in its place, was the kind, gentle brother she'd once known and loved. For a while she just stared at their conjoined hands and wished that life had been different.

9

PRESENT DAY – DECEMBER 2023 – HATTIE

Blinking repeatedly, and with tiredness still burning her eyes, Hattie turned over in her bed for what felt like the hundredth time that night. It was the same bed she'd slept in as a teenager, the bed her parents had bought her for her fourteenth birthday and nothing had changed, apart from the duvet cover and the oversized pair of Charlie's pyjamas she'd ended up wearing as they had, somehow, ended up in her case. After a whole night of talking to Luke she'd just thrown them on and was now lying in a bed that was hard, cold and felt more than unwelcoming. It had lumps and bumps in places that she clearly didn't remember, and she found herself tossing and turning until eventually she lay, with just the light from a small table lamp lighting the room.

Staring, she looked at the patterned wallpaper that she'd really liked almost a decade before and concluded that it really had seen better days. There were large areas in the corners of the room where the paper had lifted away from the wall. It was a sight that disturbed her and, in her frustration, she punched at the pillow, gave out a deep, sorrowful sigh and closed her eyes in despair.

The damp, putrid odour that had infiltrated the house was almost intolerable. It was more than obvious that the heating had barely ever been switched on and she held her hand up to cover her mouth and her nose while staring out of the window at the eerie, skeletal shape of a tree that grew right outside, its branches waving around in the breeze. As she looked past it and towards the horizon, she hoped for sunrise, for the first glimpse of the morning. Instead, she saw nothing but the grey murkiness that lurked beyond.

Impatient now, she began to rummage around on the bedside cabinet, searching for her phone that currently lay amongst an accumulation of dust and cobwebs. She'd noticed it all as she'd hesitantly made the bed up the night before and now, with a tentative swipe, she ran her finger across the cabinet's surface and did all she could not to cringe inwardly. 'It all needs cleaning,' she whispered. 'Every single inch.' It was more than obvious that no one had been in this room since the day she'd left. Even an old hairbrush she'd left behind still lay on the dresser, along with an old tissue box and a half-empty bottle of a perfume she'd never really liked.

Disconnecting the power to the phone, Hattie tapped at the screen where a new list of messages and missed calls appeared. With a swipe, she scrolled through them.

CHARLIE MOBY 20.03

Missed Call.

CHARLIE MOBY 20.04

Missed Call.

CHARLIE MOBY 20.09

Hattie. Pick up. I need to speak to you. Where the hell are you?

CHARLIE MOBY 20.10

Hattie, the flat's a mess. I can't find any of your things. Have you gone away or what... let me know where you are.

CHARLIE MOBY 20.15

Missed Call.

CHARLIE MOBY 20.24

Missed Call.

CHARLIE MOBY 20.59

Hattie. Did you get my message? Phone me. I'm worried.

CHARLIE MOBY 21.13

Missed Call.

CHARLIE MOBY 21.17

Missed Call.

CHARLIE MOBY 21.21

Missed Call.

CHARLIE MOBY 21.26

Missed Call.

CHARLIE MOBY 22.15

Missed Call.

CHARLIE MOBY 22.16

Missed Call.

CHARLIE MOBY 22.18

Call me.

CHARLIE MOBY 22.27

Missed Call.

CHARLIE MOBY 22.32

Missed Call.

CHARLIE MOBY 22.45

Missed Call.

CHARLIE MOBY 22.59

Hattie. FFS, pick up. Pick up now.

Hattie could imagine Charlie sat with his phone in his hand, repeatedly stabbing the screen. He'd never liked being ignored, nor had he ever been the most patient person and the fact that she hadn't answered wouldn't have gone down too well, hence the repeated calls, although she didn't know how he'd have the audacity to complain. Not after disappearing to Switzerland and posting all the images on social media in a way that had felt as though he'd been twisting the proverbial knife. With a flick of her finger, she found herself once again looking through Charlie's timeline, and felt her annoyance as his tanned, charismatic face looked back at her from the screen. He was rugged, with mousy blonde, rough-cut hair. A style that, although it looked as though he'd literally just jumped out of bed, had actually taken him hours to style and she'd lost count of the times she'd watched him stand in front of a mirror with a large tube of hair gel that he spread across his fingers and manipulated each hair until they all pointed in a direction he approved of.

Blowing out through puffed-up cheeks, Hattie flicked the screen to show another image of Charlie stood on the slopes. He wore a bright blue ski jacket that Hattie had never previously seen, along with a matching beanie that covered his hair and, even though his eyes were covered by the wraparound sunglasses, she could still imagine the pale blue eyes, blonde eyelashes and thick brows that defined his handsome face.

Scrolling quickly, she saw pictures of Charlie on the slopes,

Charlie with his friends, stood in a row drinking coffee in a cafe or sat in a hot tub drinking a beer. Then, as though one beer wasn't enough, there was another of him sat in the bar, with dimmed lights and cocktails. Sighing, Hattie held the phone away from her face, tipped it on one side and pursed her lips in disapproval. She'd always been able to tell when Charlie was giving a genuine smile and, maybe it was just wishful thinking, but she was sure that the smile he had plastered across his face had just been for effect.

'Amazing that you arranged all of this at such short notice, wasn't it, Charlie?' She growled the words and remembered how hurt she'd felt when she'd heard about the trip, exactly one day after Charlie had moved out as though he were rubbing salt in her wounds. And then to discover that all of his friends had managed to book the same flight and go to the same hotel, at a single day's notice. She nodded slowly at the phone. 'If you think for one minute that I believe that none of this was planned, Charlie Baker, you must take me for a fool.'

Taking in a deep breath, she pushed herself up against the pillows. Even though the last thing she really needed was a showdown, she hit the call button and waited for Charlie to answer.

She'd wanted to keep things platonic between them, knowing that at some point she'd have to go back to the flat and finish packing the last of her things. 'Charlie, look, last night, it was a difficult one. I'm sorry I didn't respond but I didn't even realise you'd called until this morning and...' She was going to try and explain about her mum, that she'd switched her phone onto silent, but didn't get chance, as Charlie's soft, Irish accent rose up in volume to drown out her voice without any effort.

'Oh. So, you're still alive, are you?' he yelled, 'Well, I suppose I ought to be grateful for that.'

'Charlie, I—'

'Save your breath, Hattie. You packed your bags, and you did it without giving us a second thought. I mean, I can't believe you did that. You couldn't just wait for me to get home and talk about things, could you?' He threw the words at her without taking breath. 'I got home to that woman from the flat upstairs telling me you'd left. That you ran in from work and packed a bag and had thrown it in the car like a jet-propelled missile.'

'Charlie... I...'

'For all I knew, you'd ended up in a ditch... or, or something even worse.'

'Wait a goddamned minute,' she replied. 'Don't you have a go at me, Charlie Baker. 'Cause I don't think you thought twice about buggering off to Switzerland with your mates, did you?' Furiously, she threw the words at him and tried to work out how Charlie always made sure that he turned into being the victim.

'Don't be smart, Hattie. It doesn't suit you,' he replied. 'I came home full of hope that we could sort things out.' He paused, and Hattie could hear a dramatic, long intake breath at the other end of the phone. 'But leaving like that... And then... to top it off, you didn't even answer your phone. You couldn't even speak to me and give me an explanation, could you?' Again, there was a break in his words, a pause before he began speaking in a much lower, softer tone. 'I was worried about you and, when I couldn't get hold of you, I was almost planning your funeral.'

Throwing her head back against the pillows, Hattie sighed with despair and pulled a face at the phone.

'Charlie, stop turning this around on me. I wasn't the one who buggered off to Zermatt.' She pressed her lips tightly together, gritting her teeth, and held back the tears. She couldn't believe that somehow Charlie had once again managed to make her feel guilty, that, without actually waiting to find out why she'd really left, he'd made himself the victim. It was one of his traits that infuriated her the most. She hadn't wanted the call to turn into an argument but, as she closed her eyes, she thought about the night when Charlie had left. 'You called me a hooker!' she yelled. 'You found out that I'd been on one job as an escort and, in your mind, I'd been selling it on every street corner. Didn't you?' She could feel the trembling within her begin, her shoulders became tense, and her chest heaved in and out with anger. 'That was your final blow as you walked out the door. Do you know how that made me feel, to hear that from the man I'd loved?'

'Loved? Right. That's how it is, is it?' He growled the words. 'I can't remember the exact words I used, but I didn't call you a hooker.'

Biting down on her lip, she could still see the way he'd looked at her through narrowed eyes and, because a flash of guilt had crossed her face, he hadn't given her the chance to explain, or to justify what she'd done. 'I was an escort, Charlie, not a prostitute and yes, I had sex before I met you, but I never slept with the one client that paid me.' Sitting forward, Hattie could feel her voice wobble. She wasn't proud of what she'd done but she'd been a rebellious nineteen-year-old, one who'd been easily led by her cousin. 'Do you know how many successful businessmen there are that don't have a wife or a girlfriend? How many of them are invited to dinner parties, where a plus one is expected?' she questioned. 'I went on a single job, where I wore the right clothes and smiled across a dinner table at all the right people, and I ate lobster. For the first time in my life, I ate lobster.'

'The holiday was crap, by the way,' he suddenly added without making any reference to what she'd just said. 'All I could think about was coming home, sorting things out. But you'd gone. I was worried and I haven't slept, Hattie. I love you so much,' he grovelled. 'I've been awake for most of the night, so how about you put me out of my misery and get yourself home.'

Closing her eyes, Hattie moved to the window and forced it open. Like everything else, the lack of use over the years had left the window stiff and it made a loud, grating noise as she elbowed it open. 'Do you know why I left, Charlie?' She pulled air into her lungs and waited. As usual, the silence was deafening, and she could imagine Charlie sat at the other end of the phone trying to work out how he could once again turn the conversation around and make it all about him.

'It hurt me, Hattie. Knowing that people were talking about you... that one of my friends knew something about you that I didn't.'

'Charlie, stop,' she demanded. 'I didn't leave because of that. My mum is dying, she's on end-of-life care and I came home because my brothers need me. And, yes, I'm sure you did love me, once, but it's over between us. I'm not coming back.' She paused, thought about what she had to say next. 'I need to be at home,' she said.

Closing her mind to the barrage of words she knew would follow, Hattie pulled the phone away from her ear. The last thing she needed was Charlie switching on the charm and turning the conversation back to his advantage. She pushed her head through the open window and rested her elbows firmly on the ledge and, once again, dragged in a deep breath of air that was bitterly cold. She closed her mind to all Charlie was saying, took in the view with her gaze directed on the road. She realised that there were barely any vehicles going up or down the road. It was still too early for the children to be up and playing in the park and the sounds and commotion that normally came from the village had fallen practically silent – just as it had on the night when her life had changed. A night when she'd been unable to stop the chain of events that followed, just like she knew that she wouldn't be able to change the events that were about to come.

10

PRESENT DAY – DECEMBER 2023 – SOPHIE

'Jasper, come on boy, hurry up.'

With a layer of frost covering the garden path, Sophie stamped her pale pink Wellingtons against the tarmac. She pulled her hands further up and inside the arms of her dressing gown and, with the temperature plummeting, began to wish she'd pulled a thick pair of socks onto her feet, rather than the thin cotton ones she was currently wearing.

Holding tightly to the lead, she watched and waited for Jasper to go to the toilet, and felt her frustration grow as the puppy did all he could apart from the task she wanted him to do. He sniffed at every blade of grass before twisting, turning and running around each of the bushes at speed. It was a game that left the lead tangled to the point that she had no alternative but to trudge across the grass to help him escape and, with a sidewards glance at the house, she began to envy the fact that, if all had gone to plan, Finn was inside and right now he'd be sat with Noah, eating breakfast.

Once again, he'd arrived early and walked in without knocking. Then, just as though he'd still lived there, he'd begun to work his way around the kitchen, wiping the sides, filling the dishwasher and effortlessly making Noah his favourite cheesy toast fingers. All of which left her feeling lost, incapable and a failure at almost everything she'd ever done since moving to England, including being a mother.

'I guess I should feel grateful that he turned up at all,' she grumbled while secretly admitting that Finn taking over with Noah had helped her a little. She couldn't help but wish that he'd been the one to take Jasper out into the garden, especially seeing as he'd been dressed in a thick wool coat and would have been much warmer than she was.

With the lead now free of the bushes, Sophie gave Jasper a tug and walked back towards the gate. 'Come on, hurry up. We can't stand outside all day.' She wriggled the lead and sighed as she looked across the square and to the fields beyond that were white with frost. In the distance, a white, cloudless sky bordered the horizon, and a picturesque farm with a field full of cows completed the picture. She had to admit, Finn had been right: the view from this house could definitely be classed as breathtaking. Especially on a day like today, but it wasn't Ireland and, right now, she wanted to go home.

'Come on, Jasper, get on with it,' Sophie urged, then laughed. 'Get a puppy, they said, it'll be fun they said. He and Noah, they can grow up together, they said.' She smiled as Jasper plonked his bottom down on the ground and joined her in looking thoughtfully upwards. 'What they didn't tell me was that I'd be out of bed on a freezing cold morning, with my feet turning blue.' Running a hand affectionately across the top of his head, Sophie couldn't help but smile at the huge, owl-like dark eyes and the apricot ears that twitched in the cold but then jumped backwards as a loud, sudden noise came from the house next door. The sound of a latch moving was followed by a window groaning as it opened, and a woman's voice could be heard.

'I didn't leave because of that,' the woman said. 'My mum is dying, she's having end-of-life care and I came home because my brothers need me. And yes, I'm sure you did love me, once, but it's over between us. I'm not coming back.' Standing on her tiptoes behind the tallest of the conifers, Sophie used its branches for camouflage and, while catching her breath, listened intently and couldn't help but try and put the jigsaw together. 'Okay, so you must be the sister...' she deduced. 'Now then, what was it they called you?' She tried to remember a brief conversation she'd once overheard and then she allowed her mind to flick back to the night before and the look on Finn's face when she'd mentioned the woman that stood in the garden. She suddenly couldn't help but feel suspicious. 'You're obviously a part of Finn's life he doesn't want to talk about,' she whispered, 'so, for your sake, I hope you're not staying.' Sophie sang the words under her breath and continued to look up to the window where the woman, wearing a pair of oversized pyjamas, was half leaning out. 'I wouldn't mind if you were pretty or if you knew how to dress, but you obviously don't,' she said bitterly and then looked down at her own pyjamas that were shrouded by a dressing gown. She wondered if, the night before, Finn had known that the sister was here, and if he did how he felt about her being back...

'Soph...'

Turning at speed, Sophie spun around to see Finn's partially naked frame standing in the doorway with his shirt and tie held out in his hands, and a pink streak of yogurt staining the cotton.

'I did warn you that your son is good at shot put, didn't I?' She stifled a laugh and did all she could to bite down on her lip without looking back up or drawing any attention to the woman in the window.

'He sure is. Good job I always carry a clean one.' Laughing, Finn went to step over the doorstep. 'Something I learned after a patient once bled all over me.'

'I'll get it for you,' Sophie quickly added as she passed him Jasper's lead and held a hand up towards him, making him take a step backwards. 'Now, go on, press that little button on your key ring and open up the car.' She nervously looked up and over her shoulder to see the woman smile and lift her hand in a wave. It was a friendly gesture, one that Sophie should have responded to, but with her mind working in overdrive she had to make sure that, the moment the woman saw Finn, she'd be under no illusions that he wasn't available. So, in a performance worthy of an Oscar, Sophie stepped towards her husband, gave him a confident smile and, with her arm reaching upwards, she hooked it behind his neck and pressed her lips firmly against his.

'Hey, what's that for?' He furrowed his brow in surprise, but smiled as he took a step back into the house. 'I thought...'

'Never mind what you thought, you might have moved out for a while, Finn Alexander, but you are still my husband,' she said in a firm but determined whisper. 'And don't you forget it.'

Once again, she looked up and over her shoulder. She knew that Finn was still just out of sight, that the woman hadn't seen the look of shock on his face, or the confusion that followed, and felt pleased that her performance had worked in her favour and that the woman in the upstairs bedroom window would have clearly got the message.

11

PRESENT DAY – DECEMBER 2023 – HATTIE

Her hands trembling with emotion, Hattie practically threw the phone at the bed. In the matter of a week, her whole life had changed and now she had to find the strength to go to visit her mother. It was a journey she didn't want to make, but one she'd always known would come. Every week since her mother had been attacked, there had been one hospital appointment or another. Each visit had left them all with their emotions bouncing off the walls, and each time they'd been called into the hospital they'd all expected the worst. But, this time, the worst was actually about to happen. There wouldn't be many more calls, visits or chances, and Hattie could feel her heart compressing in her chest at the thought that one day soon she'd have to say her final goodbye and, even though she'd gone over the words a million times in her mind, she still didn't know what or how to say it.

Jumping in the shower, she stood with her face under the water. It was hot, therapeutic, and mentally she prepared herself for all the questions she needed to ask. Hattie just hoped that, once she asked them, her mother would speak, rather than stare silently into space, just as she had for the last nine years.

'If you always could speak to us, why didn't you?' she asked, but kept coming back to the only question that mattered. 'If you knew who attacked you, if you saw their face, why didn't you tell us? Why didn't you tell the police, rather than let them think for all those years that you might have been the one responsible for inflicting the final blow?' It was a thought that spun around her mind, one that wouldn't go away and, after standing in the steam for a good few minutes longer than necessary, Hattie was disturbed by a loud and continuous bleep that filled the air and the sound of the fire alarm brought her back to reality.

Throwing her eyes wide open, it suddenly occurred to her that the room had filled with steam and, after dragging open the shower door, she grabbed at a towel, threw it around her body and stepped onto the landing where, with the use of a smaller hand towel, she began to waft at the alarm that had been stupidly positioned right outside the bathroom door. Just then the front door flew open and, for a few moments, she stood, open mouthed, staring down the stairs. Right there, in her hallway, looking as though he was about to fly up the stairs like Superman, was Griffin Alexander, her friend, lover and ultimately the one who'd got away.

'Hattie?'

'Griff... what the hell are you doing here?'

'Are you okay?' Running towards her, his hands went up to her shoulders, his fingers tipping her chin towards him as though checking every part of her face for damage. 'I was just getting in my car. I heard the fire alarm and...' He searched her eyes intently with his. 'I didn't know you were home?' He paused, took in a breath, then nodded. 'Okay, I'd heard that someone was home, that a woman with auburn hair was patrolling the garden and...' Staring into her eyes for just a moment too long, he leaned in, kissed her lightly on the cheek. 'I hoped it was you.'

Taking a step back, Hattie held a hand to her chest and took in the man he'd become. He was tall, still ruggedly good-looking, while wearing a smart suit, with a shirt and tie, and she felt a sudden surge of pride rush through her. 'You, the suit,' she said breathlessly, 'I take it you qualified, that it's Doctor Alexander now?' She bit down on her lip suggestively, as a wide, disarming smile crossed his face and he nodded, almost apologetically. 'Okay, well, Doctor Alexander, I don't mean to sound rude,' she laughed, 'but what the hell are you—' she held up a finger and waved it up and down, in a comical wand like manner '—doing here?'

'I live next door, well, not officially,' he tried to explain. 'But I did. And my wife, she still lives there and... Oh God, this is complicated.' He laughed, brushed an imaginary fleck of dust from his suit and looked down at the floor. 'I come home pretty much every morning and every night, to see Noah, my son.'

Keeping a tight hold of the towel, Hattie felt her mouth go dry. Her throat felt restricted and, suddenly, she could barely swallow. 'Griffin, wow. That does sound complicated.' Only then did she notice the woman she'd seen earlier. She was stood behind him, holding a baby tightly in her arms. 'And this must be Noah?' Hattie said as she tipped her head to one side and furrowed her brow in question.

'Griffin, you say?' The woman looked up at Hattie from the bottom of the stairs, with a thoughtful, questioning look. The baby, who she jiggled up and down in her arms, suddenly rested his head against her shoulder as though quietly confused and waiting for answers. 'Well, well, well, I'm not sure I've heard anyone call you Griffin since we were married in church.'

12

PRESENT DAY – DECEMBER 2023 – SOPHIE

As Finn did a slow reverse until he reached the bottom of the stairs, Sophie took a watchful step forward and, with a deep intake of breath, pushed Noah firmly into his arms. She had every intention of staking her claim, and was in no doubt at all that she had something to prove to the woman who was currently stood at the top of the stairs, wrapped in a very small bath towel with her wet auburn hair hanging limply around her pale, naked shoulders. Especially when her face looked flushed and pink from the shower, and the coy, timid smiles and battering of eyelashes, all aimed directly at Finn, hadn't got past her.

'Sophie, this—' he bounced Noah up and down on his hip, while holding out the other arm and giving the woman a captivating smile '—this is Hattie, she's a friend. She's also Adam and Luke's older sister.' Turning Noah towards him, Finn kissed his son on the forehead. 'And this is Noah... go on Noah, say hello to Hattie.'

Standing back, Sophie did her best to smile through teeth that were clenched so tightly, her jaw began to hurt. 'I'm... well,

I'm pleased to meet you but, Finn, we're being rude,' Sophie said firmly. 'It's quite clear that Hattie is fine and that the house isn't on fire like you thought. So, why don't we go back home until your friend manages to get herself dressed and...' Sophie paused as she spoke. It should have been a comment that jolted Finn into action. To get him to leave both the house and the woman behind. But all Sophie could see were the looks that were being thrown in both directions. She could sense the electricity that filled the room and she wondered what kind of conversation Finn and Hattie would be having, if she hadn't ran into the house behind him.

'Oh, don't worry about me, I don't mind.' Hattie reached for another towel that had been draped across a radiator and pulled it tightly around her. 'There you go, all covered up. Besides, we haven't seen each other for years and I'm intrigued, what's with the change of name? It was always Griff, or Griffin, at school... I don't ever remember anyone calling you Finn.'

With her hand reaching out to touch Noah's fingers, Sophie rolled her jaw in annoyance. It was more than obvious that Hattie was looking her husband up and down, with admiring eyes, and Sophie took a protective step forward and rested a hand against his arm.

'Yeah, Griffin, Finn, the names somehow just morphed from one to the other at uni,' he laughed as he stepped away from Sophie's touch and leaned both himself and Noah against the balustrade. 'Look.' He glanced at Sophie before looking back up the stairs to Hattie. 'Why don't you come round sometime? I'm home most evenings. I always pop back to visit this little one and it'd be good to catch up.'

Standing back, Sophie crossed her arms defiantly. She didn't like the way Finn had made it clear that he only came home to visit his son and, with her eyes flashing between Finn and Hattie, she felt the anxiety of the situation growing inside her. Right now, she wanted to be anywhere else in the world, apart from here, and felt a slight feeling of victory when Hattie moved uncomfortably to hide herself behind the newel post while all the time nodding and giggling with Finn in a way that only happened when sexual chemistry was present. Sophie was in no doubt at all that there was a lot more to Hattie and Finn's relationship than them being just good, old friends.

In an attempt to quell the tension, Sophie ran her eyes around the house. She could see moth holes that were scattered across the bottom of the curtains and large patches of wool that had been eaten away in the corners of the carpet to leave areas where there was little to no carpet at all.

'It looks like I could be back for a while,' Hattie suddenly chirped up. 'Mum, she isn't well. She's been diagnosed with cancer. It's gone way past the stage where it's treatable and Adam called me and asked me to come home.' She took in a breath before lowering her eyes. 'She's in Friarage at the moment, but they're talking about moving her to a hospice. So... I don't think it will be... you know, long and, so, yes... while I'm here, it'd be great to catch up, that's if...' She tipped her head to one side and gave Sophie a quizzical look. 'That's if you don't mind me stealing him away for a few hours one night.'

'No, of course I don't mind. I'm only Finn's wife,' Sophie said through gritted teeth. It wasn't like her to feel jealous, or to speak out of turn, but the thought of Finn disappearing off for a nice cosy night out with the woman wrapped in a bath towel made her blood boil and spill over. She reached out, ran a hand protectively over her baby's head. 'But Noah's just nine months old and, as you can see, he's a proper daddy's boy already. So, if you're thinking of stealing him away, then I think Noah might have something to say about that. He does like to keep his daddy all to himself.'

An uncomfortable silence filled the air and Sophie began to step from foot to foot. She knew she'd made things awkward, and she wanted to leave, but she didn't want the happy reunion to carry on in her absence. Spontaneously, she held her hands out to Noah and clapped them to catch his attention, but felt the disappointment surge through her as he turned back to Finn and waved his arms in the air, vying for his daddy's attention.

'I should probably get dressed,' Hattie was saying, 'this towel clearly isn't big enough and—'

'No, it isn't really, is it?' Sophie added sarcastically as she breathed in deeply. She didn't want to show how anxious and intimidated this woman made her feel and she couldn't ignore the fact that, even dressed in a bath towel, Finn obviously liked the way Hattie looked and immediately, a million different questions began to spin around in her mind. The biggest one being, why hadn't Finn and Hattie ended up together, especially when she could see that all these years later there was still a clear connection.

'Well, I guess that's my cue,' Finn said as he flashed Sophie a look. 'We'd best leave you to it. Noah and I just had our breakfast, which we both ended up wearing, and...' He made a point of sniffing the air. 'And I'd say that we're now in need of a nappy change. Which is apparently something else I seem to be an expert at these days.' Pressing his nose tightly against his baby's cheek, Finn blew out a raspberry and beamed with delight as Noah repaid him with a delighted chuckle. 'We don't care if you're a smelly bot, do we?' Once again, another raspberry was blown before Finn turned his attention back to look up at where Hattie still stood. He took a breath in, a sure sign that he was nervous about asking a question. 'Look... that catch up. Let's make it sooner rather than later.' Smiling, he glanced at Sophie, but frowned as he saw the way she'd crossed her arms and stood with her foot tapping up and down like a petulant child.

'Oh my God, why didn't I think of this before?' Sophie suddenly said as brightly as she could. 'Why don't I cook us all a nice meal? Maybe a curry or a spag bol, and the two of you can sit across the table from each other, with your doe eyes, while I head for the kitchen with our son and wash the bloody pots?' Sophie could feel her temper accelerate. She didn't want to be a jealous wife who got angry every time her husband spoke to another woman. What she wanted was to be welcoming and friendly and the kind of wife that made Finn's friends feel at home. But, for some reason, Hattie was different, the tension or chemistry between her and Finn was tangible. It was a sight she didn't want to watch and an emotion she didn't want to feel. Not now. Not ever. And, with an exaggerated flounce, and while her dignity was still barely intact, Sophie spun on her heel and headed out of the open door. Where she felt surprisingly liberated, until the moment her foot caught on the tarmac and, with an agonising twist, she found herself flying forward until she came to land, close to the conifers.

13

NINE YEARS BEFORE – HATTIE

Sitting on the floor, with her back pressed against the settee, Hattie rested her book in her lap and flicked through the pages without reading a thing. Instead, she stared into a fire that had been lit for most of the day and, even though the flames licked at the back of the chimney, she couldn't help but shiver. Her body felt unbelievably cold, and she reached for a soft blanket that lay on the settee behind her and pulled it tightly around her.

Getting warm seemed to have evaded her since the early hours of that morning. Something hadn't been right about the way her mother had acted, or the way she'd walked down the street arm in arm with Berni on their quest to find Alice.

'Hattie.' Her father's voice echoed down the hallway as the front door slammed behind him and the sound of his boots stamping across the thin, worn carpet came down the hallway towards her. 'Good. You're safe, I just wanted to let you know there's been a development.'

Appearing in the doorway, Gerald Gilby looked pale. He held a hand to his chest like he did during a sermon and, concerningly, his eyes looked dull, their normal sparkle gone.

For a man who had never appeared to be fazed, even after witnessing the most horrendous sights, Hattie had never seen him look so daunted and, for a moment, she wondered if his legs were about to fail him.

'Dad, are you okay? What happened... Is it Alice?' Tossing the blanket to one side, Hattie sat forward and waited patiently as her father paced back and forth. 'Have they found her?' she asked hopefully, but the slow, disgruntled shake of his head told her otherwise. His hand reached out for the door-jamb, and his fingers gripped the frame until they turned white with pressure.

'They, they found... her bag... it was beside the river,' he stuttered. 'I've... We've phoned the police... and some of the men... they're going to set off along the riverbank to look for her, if she's fallen in, time is critical...' He paused. 'But in the middle of winter, the river is cold and vicious and...' He swallowed hard. 'I don't hold out much hope, Hattie.'

'She wouldn't survive, would she? She went missing hours ago.' Hattie's hand went up to her mouth as she spoke. 'And, if she fell into the water, she'd most probably be—' Stopping before completing the statement, she knew the outcome and, like her father had said, her chances were slim. Which meant that, whether they knew it or not, the men were now looking for a body. 'Did someone do this to her?'

'Hattie, I don't know. All I do know is that she's the same age as you. Still a young woman with her life ahead of her, and, by all accounts... she was heavily pregnant.'

'Is that why she left?' Hattie asked sharply. 'Was she...' Her hand went up to her mouth, her eyes wide and questioning. 'Was she afraid to tell her parents? I mean, surely if she were heavily pregnant, they'd already know. Wouldn't they?'

'I don't know.' Taking in a deep breath, he gave her a long, intent stare. 'All I know is that she has to be out there, she has to be somewhere.' He leaned forward to where she sat, reached out, and lay the palm of his hand lovingly against her cheek and held her gaze. 'If anyone ever hurt you, I'd...' Unusually, the words caught in his throat and Hattie tried to remember the last time she'd seen her father get emotional. It was something he never did and, even when conducting a funeral when all around him people were in floods of tears, he was always the one to remain stoic and calm.

'No one's going to hurt me.' She stood up, gave him a heartfelt smile and fondly pushed an arm around each side of his mildly rotund stomach, resting her head against his chest. 'Is there anything I can do to help with the search? Maybe I could go to the church, see if there's anything I could do to help there?'

'No!' he immediately shouted in a voice that made Hattie jump anxiously backwards. 'I want you to stay here, it's safer and...' He pointed to the fire and pushed his lips into a smile that didn't quite reach his eyes. 'It's warmer. I'd much rather you looked after the house... because Hattie—' he looked down at the floor, regained his composure '—if we find her. *When* we find her, it would hardly be something I'd want you to see. Once you've seen things like that, you can't unsee them... they stay with you for the rest of your life, especially if she's been in the river.' Lifting his hand from her shoulder, he looked down at his watch. 'Some of the local farmers are going to walk their own land. No one knows the topography like they do and, between us all, we should be able to cover quite a big area by morning.' He furrowed his brow, turned and looked into the mirror that hung on the wall. In it, he gave himself an awkward smile, checked his appearance and made a show of straightening his clerical collar. 'As soon as we have some light, we'll search the more difficult areas, but, for tonight, we'll have to take the torches and do what we can...'

'You think she's...' Hattie sat back down to lean against the settee, where her stomach began to churn. She wanted to ask if her father thought that Alice was dead, whether she'd been hurt while working, and, with a feeling of sickness rising up in her throat, Hattie thought about the situation she'd been in the night before and how easily that whole situation could have escalated.

'I think...' Sitting down on the settee beside her, her father rested a hand on her shoulder. 'I think that girls that live the way Alice did will always get themselves into bad situations. Unfortunately, I see it all the time, which is why I want you to stay here, where you're safe.'

Taking in deep breaths, Hattie tried to stay calm. She couldn't promise her father she'd stay in the house. Yet she knew that going against his wishes was wrong. The night before, bad things had almost happened. She'd found herself in a situation where she'd been out of control. Things had quickly escalated and a night that had been surrounded by glamour and wealth, had suddenly become one where she'd been both physically and verbally assaulted. It was a thought that sent a rush of fear coursing through her.

Rolling her eyes upwards, her mind went back to the day before and to the way Louisa had cajoled her into doing the 'nice, easy job'.

'Come on, Hattie, all you have to do is wear the dress,' Louisa had said, 'hold on to his arm. Be attentive. Smile at all the right people. It's easy and what's more, Bill Fraser is rich. He's charismatic. He has more money than bloody sense. The only thing he doesn't have is a date for tonight.'

Louisa had made it all sound so easy and being the younger cousin, Hattie had always looked up to her. She'd often chatted to her about things she'd have never told anyone else and above all else, she'd always wanted to please her. Which was why, when she asked her to help her, Hattie had always found it hard to say no.

'But what about Griff?' Hattie remembered asking. 'You know I like him and if he sees me out with another man, he'll think...'

Louisa had tipped her head thoughtfully and comically from side to side. 'Look. I've double booked. You'll be doing me a massive favour and hey...' Louisa had said with her tongue pushed firmly in her cheek. 'If you're waiting for Griffin to make a move, then this is the perfect way to make him jealous. One or two selfies of you all dressed up to the nines...' She had stood back and with a finger she waved it up and down in the air. 'He'll see you in a way he's never seen you before and trust me, he won't want to risk you going out with another man again.'

Sighing, Hattie had thought about Griff and the one night of intimacy they'd previously shared. It had been a night when she'd been walking home through the village. Griffin's car had slowed beside her. The window had dropped and, with an attractive smile that she'd have walked on water to see, he'd offered her a lift. The journey hadn't been long, just a few minutes at best, but the conversation had continued for the next two hours. Until eventually she'd gone to climb out of the car and, with an intensity she'd never previously known, he'd pulled her back towards her, grazed his lips with hers and, once he'd been sure that it was a kiss she was happy to share, he'd parted her lips and used his tongue to tease her until she'd moaned out loud with pleasure. It had been the night before Griffin had left for university and with only the briefest of promises that he'd meet up with her, the moment he got home, he'd been gone and still to this day Hattie waited for him to call.

'I don't think I had him a first time,' Hattie had admitted, sadly. 'He didn't call when he got back from uni and, even though Adam kept on at me to call him, kept saying that he wanted me to get in touch, I didn't.'

'Why not?' Striding around the room, Louisa had reached out to the Christmas tree, moved baubles from the top to the bottom. 'Because I know you like him.'

'It wasn't my place; he's the man, he should have called me.' Defiantly, Hattie had leaned in and moved the baubles back to their original positions. 'Don't, Mum will know if you moved them.'

'Then the two of you need a bit of being pushed together, don't you, and nothing will do that faster than if he sees you with another man.'

'But won't that put him off for good?' Hattie had sat back thoughtfully. Since that night, she'd hoped that Griffin Alexander would whisk her off her feet. She'd waited, hoped, and interrogated Adam at every opportunity. And, even though she'd tried to be in the right pub, or club, on the right day at the right time, the mood had always been wrong. It had been too loud, too quiet, or there had been too many people. She'd never once managed to get him to herself and, in the end, she'd flushed violently with colour every time he'd walked in, until a time when she could barely speak at all, and she had to admit her experiences with men had been limited. 'What if he found out I'd been an escort. What would I say to him, if he asked?'

'You don't need to say anything. Like everyone else would think, you're Bill Fraser's date for the night. Nothing more. Nothing less. Sometimes, Hattie, saying nothing at all can speak volumes. Just take a few pics, post them online and say what a wonderful night you had. Let jealousy do the rest.' Holding her hands up as though in prayer, Louisa had battered her eyelids frantically. 'So, what do you say? Pweeeeaaase, Hattie, would you do it for me?'

Naively, and with the sole thought of making Griffin jealous, Hattie had agreed to the date. She'd been carried away with the whole glamour of searching the best boutiques for a dress. They were the kind of shops she'd never been in before and it had felt exciting. For once, she'd actually felt like a grown up, especially when she'd pulled the bright red, lined dress over her head and allowed it to drop down and around her ankles. It was long, with a split that went straight up at the front and gave a tantalising peek of her leg as she walked. The Bardot-style top was seductive as it went across her shoulders and she just knew that, if her father ever saw her wearing it, it would give him a million palpitations.

Once dressed and with her make-up artfully applied by Louisa, Hattie had stared at her reflection in the mirror. The image that had looked back was unrecognisable and, with a confidence she didn't realise she possessed, she had made her way down the back staircase and out of the house, to where Louisa had sent a car to pick her up. It was going to take her straight to the client and without a doubt, she'd felt like a million dollars. Until it had been time for them to leave.

'I'll take you home,' Bill Fraser had said with what Hattie had thought to be a genuine smile. 'My car's out front, and this —' he'd held his glass up in the air, rattled the ice that still hovered in the clear bubbly fluid '—it's just tonic, no alcohol, so I'm good to drive.'

Feeling a little worse for the amount of alcohol she'd devoured, Hattie had naively accepted the lift and, after a night where a part of her had felt as though the date was real, she hadn't wanted it to end. She'd wanted the glamour and the romance to continue and had even felt her stomach fill with a fluttering of excitement when he'd pulled his car into the square. It was an area that was hidden by large, evergreen bushes and, in a well-practised manoeuvre, he'd reached forward and unclipped her seat belt, pulled her towards him and kissed her. It had been easy to melt into his arms, to allow herself to swoon as his mouth had roamed over hers, but then she had felt herself gasp as his hands began to move across her breasts in a rough and persistent way.

With her hands firmly against his chest, she had inched slowly backward in her seat, given him what she hoped would look like a thoughtful smile. 'Bill,' she'd whispered, 'I've had a wonderful evening but...'

'Don't even think about it...' Once again, his hand had caught her around the back of her neck and, almost violently, he'd dragged her towards him. 'You're not leaving. I haven't had my money's worth...' Suddenly, his mouth was pressing down against hers, his tongue parting her lips. It invaded her mouth, making her gag, and his hand was moving up the inside of her leg, at speed. It was a movement that made Hattie squirm sideways in her seat, as her hand grappled for the door handle. The more she writhed, the more insistent he became and, as his hand reached her underwear, she heard the material tear and, for a few painful moments, she felt his fingers push themselves deep inside her and, in her panic, she lifted her hand and swung out at him as hard as she could.

'Get off me,' she had screamed as once again she reached for the door, caught her fingers under the shiny silver catch and, with her mind swimming with the alcohol, launched herself forwards but felt Bill's hand forcefully drag her back in her chair.

'You bitch... What the hell did you slap me for?' he'd yelled.

'You should have expected what was coming. It's what always comes. You get paid and I...'

'Can you hear yourself?' Her voice was now nothing more than a terrified sob. 'You're full of expectation, of what you're owed, you don't think about what anyone else wants and you may have paid me for tonight, but you didn't pay for sex, and I do not have to give it.' Moving herself as far away from his grip as she could, Hattie once again had reached for the door handle. Her breathing was deep and sporadic, her eyes wide with fear. 'I'm going home now and you... you need to drive away before I phone the police and have you arrested for assault.'

In a single, rapid movement Bill Fraser had grabbed hold of Hattie by the neck and held her tightly until his eyes were staring straight into hers. 'You go anywhere near the police...' He slowly nodded. 'Anywhere near and you will be sorry.' For a moment, his fingers had tightened to a point that Hattie could feel the blood pounding in her head. It was getting louder and louder to the point where she felt herself move in and out of a darkness she didn't understand and then his mouth was once again on hers, but this time, it was firm and onerous. 'I can take everything from you in a heartbeat, do you understand that?' he'd whispered between the kisses. 'I have ways of making your life a living hell, so don't you forget it.' His voice had been loud, angry and threatening, and then, with a determined force, she'd felt the car door spring open behind her as he wrenched it open, and she was physically thrust out of the car and onto the tarmac.

'You bastard!' she'd yelled in an undignified way, as she'd scrambled to her feet. Her neck was sore, her arm was grazed, and every inch of her body felt invaded. He'd touched her in a way she'd never been touched before and she had the urge to run inside, jump into a shower and wash herself clean. But his threats had been real and, right then, she didn't dare walk straight to her own home, she didn't want him to know where she lived and, with her finger pointed towards the car in a wand-like fashion, she felt the anger of what had happened boil up inside her. 'You... you deserve all you get. I hope they throw away the key!' She'd thrown the scathing words at him in a final act of retaliation before walking as confidently as she could in the opposite direction.

'You alright there, love?' one of the truckers who'd parked up for the night had suddenly shouted across the square. 'Are you hurt? Did he hurt you?' Climbing down from his truck, the tall, stout-looking man had headed towards her but, with tears springing to her eyes, she held her hands out, palms forward as though in an act of surrender.

'I'm fine, please...' Embarrassed about the way she'd been thrown from the car like an unwanted animal, she'd turned and walked away. She'd just wanted to be alone, to put the whole event behind her, but already she could feel the pain that surrounded her. 'I'm just going to go home.' Turning, Hattie had walked slowly away and, only once she'd seen Bill's car drive away in the opposite direction, did she turn and walk back towards her home, where she went in through the back door, through the kitchen and up the old servant's staircase that led her back up to her room.

* * *

Rousing from her thoughts, Hattie heard the sound of the front door slamming behind. Her father had left the house and for a good few minutes, she simply stared at the Christmas tree that stood in one corner of the room. It was crammed full of ornaments. Fairy lights danced in a fast and sporadic sequence and, just for a minute, Hattie wished they would stop. It didn't seem right that the tree was so jolly or that it was even lit up at all while Alice was missing and the village was out there, looking for her. Then, like the sound of doom, the church bells tolled in the distance. It was a sound that made Hattie hold her breath and she wondered if they were being used as a sign and whether their constant clanging meant that Alice's body had been found.

With her heart racing, Hattie ran to the patio doors. They stood at the back of the room and overlooked the back garden and the fields beyond that were currently surrounded by a deep, disturbing darkness. The only light that could be seen was that of the torches that were far in the distance. It was a sure sign that the men were sweeping their lights back and forth across the furrowed land and that, even though the bells had tolled, the search for Alice continued.

It was only then that something caught her eye. A flash that was much closer and a movement that made Hattie squint so she could see more clearly. She saw Louisa storming towards her with a face like thunder, her distinctive long dark hair blowing around in the breeze. She wore a skirt that was far too short, along with a pair of high boots that went right up to her thighs and the shortest leather jacket that didn't look anywhere near warm enough to wear in the winter.

'What the hell happened?' Louisa demanded as she angrily burst in through the patio doors. 'I got you that job in good faith. He paid good money. And you...' She pointed aggressively. 'You tossed him off,' she shouted. 'Do you know who the hell he is? How rich he is? And how much work he's given me in the past?' She marched into the room and stood as close to the fire as she could get with one hand on a hip that was brazenly pushed out to one side.

'Lou, your face...' Hattie gasped in horror as the lamplight lit up Louisa's bruised and tear-stained face. She took a step forward, lifted a hand and, with shaking fingers, went to inspect the bright red bruising that went down one side of Louisa's face, but jumped backwards as Louisa violently knocked Hattie's hand away.

'Don't touch me,' Louisa snapped. 'Because, do you know what?' She glared with a look of pure hatred that Hattie had never previously seen. 'This,' Louisa continued as she lifted a finger and jabbed angrily at the area of her face that was fast turning blue. 'This is your fault.'

Moving slowly backwards, Hattie shook her head in defiance. 'He hit you?' she finally managed to say. 'He hit you, because of me?' She was confused and angry and suddenly she took a step back to question everything. 'Why would he do that?'

'Let's say he thought he was owed more for his money.' Walking to the mirror, Louisa studied her reflection before adding, 'And you slapped him. Why the hell did you do that?'

'He tried...' Hattie closed her eyes; she suddenly couldn't believe she'd naively climbed into his car. At one point, she'd actually believed she'd been on a date with a handsome, charismatic and rich entrepreneur, who seemed to really like her. It was a thought that now left her feeling unbelievably hurt and stupid. 'He tried it on, I asked him to stop and he wouldn't, so yes... I slapped him.' Closing her eyes, Hattie thought about the torn underwear, the fingers that had violently been pushed inside her and the pain that had followed. 'He...' she began, but couldn't continue. She had no idea where to begin or how to even explain how much it had hurt.

'Jesus Christ, Hattie, how old are you?' Dropping heavily to her knees, Louisa stared at the Christmas tree. Enviously, she ran a finger across the parcels beneath it, tipped one of the labels so that she could read what it said. 'You have no idea how lucky you are, do you?' She pointed with a wavering finger up to the tree. 'You have it all. Don't you? All of this, the whole build up to Christmas, your brothers, your parents... the people who love you.' Her voice broke as she spoke. 'I've never had that, Hattie. Of course, I've had your family around me, but it isn't the same as being brought up as an adopted only child. And because you've always had it all, you're unbelievably naïve.' She looked up, with a look of disdain. 'And it wasn't him that hit me, you fool. He wouldn't dirty his own hands.' She laughed sardonically. 'He sent the boys round. He wanted his money back and...' She swallowed hard, pulled her handbag off her shoulder and tipped an array of make-up onto the carpet. 'He fully expected me to give him it. He said you'd humiliated him in front of others, that you attacked him and that someone had to pay.' With a long, stifled sob, she lifted a small compact mirror off the floor and began to pat her face with the powder.

'I've still got the money, it's in my room. You can give it him and tell him to shove it where the damn sun don't shine... I'll...' Hattie jumped up, ran to the door, but stopped as an ear-splitting scream filled the room and Louisa began to throw items of make-up at where Hattie stood.

'I swear to God, Hattie, you are so fucking stupid.' She stood up aggressively with her nose just millimetres away from Hattie's. 'If it were that simple, don't you think I'd have called you? Don't you think I'd have literally given him a couple hundred quid myself? That's not what he wants. Don't you get it? You humiliated him, in front of others.' She pointed towards the square at the front of the house. 'And that costs money, Hattie... serious money. You don't think for a minute the two fifty I gave you will cut it, do you? Do you really believe that's all he paid?' Holding out a hand, Louisa tugged at Hattie's clothes. 'Where do you think the dress came from? Or the shoes and the diamante necklace? Do you think the boutique just gave them to us, like a gift? Because I've got news for you, Hattie, they didn't. Bill Fraser, he paid for them.'

Sinking down to her knees, Hattie stared at Louisa. Her black leather boots were covered in mud. She had a hole in her tights and the hem of her skirt was starting to drop. 'How much?' She wanted to ask her cousin how they could even ask for the money back but, by the look of Louisa's face, these weren't the kind of people that would be willing to negotiate and the threats he'd shouted kept coming back to her in waves.

With silence filling the room, Hattie's eye caught the ever-annoying flicker of the Christmas tree lights and went over the words that Louisa had just said to her: 'You have it all.' It was true – compared to Louisa, she did have it all. She lived in a house where her parents loved her, unlike Louisa who lived alone in a house she'd inherited right after her parents were killed in a car crash, when she'd been just sixteen years old. 'Louisa, how much did he pay you?'

Scrambling around on her hands and knees on the floor, Louisa began to collect the make-up she'd thrown. Some had rolled under the settee; other pieces had landed in plant pots and an eyeliner lay in the hearth and was melting with the heat.

'It doesn't matter.' She looked everywhere in the room apart from at Hattie. 'It's not your fault. I never should have got you involved.' She moved slowly across the room, gathering the items as she went and finally, she sat down on her bottom, crossed her legs and sorrowfully looked up into Hattie's eyes. 'It's my problem now, Hattie, and I'm going to have to put it right. Just like I always do.' She sighed with emotion. 'I'm going to earn the money back, tonight. But, for one last time, I do need you to help me...'

14

PRESENT DAY – DECEMBER 2023 – HATTIE

The hospital car park was nothing more than a swarm of cars and frustratingly Hattie drove up and down each of the rows numerous times before spotting a space. It was tiny and looked much too small for anything more than a Mini to park in, which, for her, was a problem. She wasn't good at parking and, with a sigh, she studied the space and, after she'd pondered the idea of pulling forward for just a few seconds too long, she watched with an exasperated gasp as another car slid into the place.

'Damn it,' she growled. 'If you'd get on with the job in hand and stop thinking about urgh...' She realised that her mind was fully consumed by Griffin, or Finn as he now seemed to be known. Seeing him that morning had been a shock and, even though she'd suspected he still lived in the village, he'd been the last person she'd expected to see bursting in through the front door and running into the house thinking it was on fire. It was, however, a nice thought that he'd seen himself as the one to run into the flames and save her. Which, of course, only could have been true if he'd known she was there and instead, he'd run in with a look of fear and trepidation on his face, which had changed the moment he'd seen her and she'd immediately noticed that recognisable sparkle and his bright blue eyes – and, for a few seconds, she'd wished she could turn back the clock and that her life had turned out differently.

'I guess I should be lucky that the door was unlocked,' she whispered with a smile, but then furrowed her brow. Was it lucky? For the first time in years, she'd been in the house, fast asleep and alone, and for some reason Luke hadn't thought to lock the front door behind them. But then, if he had, Finn wouldn't have got in and maybe that cute moment they'd shared wouldn't have happened.

'He's a daddy now,' she whispered to herself. 'He has a wife.' The thought created a void inside her she couldn't understand. A mixture of regrets over the hows, whys and what ifs and she stared down at the gear stick and wondered what had gone wrong. Everything had been going so right. She and Griff had finally found new ground. They'd become a couple just days before her parents had been attacked and then, for some reason he'd backed off at a hundred miles an hour. Leaving her to wonder if it had meant anything at all, or whether it had just been something that happened at a time when it shouldn't have? Reaching for the glove box, she pulled it open in the hope that there would have been a leftover stash of sweets. A bar of chocolate or something that would satisfy the craving she could suddenly feel.

'Would it or could it have all been different?' She wasn't sure. After her parents' attack, everything changed, and back then she'd had no time or mind power to think about anything, including Griffin. Every day, she'd felt as though she'd been walking through mud. Every one of her senses had been numb, and the only thing that had mattered had been her mother and, for a number of days and nights, she'd practically camped by her bedside and prayed. She'd spent hours asking God for help, for him to spare her mother's life. Until eventually her prayers had turned to anger. She'd become frustrated and argumentative with a God she couldn't even see, for allowing this to happen and, eventually, every day had felt as though it had blended into the other.

Hattie shook herself from her painful memories and, after a few more minutes, eventually found a space to park her car. Getting out, she scanned the hospital walls. She'd been stood in this same spot so many times before she felt as though she knew every brick, every door and all of the elongated windows that were so narrow and tall, they reminded her of arrow slits. The problem was, she could never decide whether or not the patients would want to defend their positions, or simply escape the illness that kept them inside.

'Hattie... hello... over here...' Louisa's voice suddenly cut through the noise of the traffic. 'Hattie, it's me. Give me a minute to park this thing and—' A hand suddenly appeared through a car window on the next row of cars and waved around frantically. 'Wait for me, we can go up together.'

'I didn't know you were coming?' Hattie shouted back, as she watched the brand-new SUV begin to zip up and down until Louisa swung the vehicle effortlessly into position, before jumping out and practically running across the car park.

'Oh my God, Hattie, come here. Give me a hug.' Without warning, Hattie felt herself being pulled into the arms of her cousin, who had lost her thin, willowy appearance. Her hair was still dark but was no longer the jet black that Louisa remembered and it was shorter now, a more manageable length that just kissed the top of her shoulders. 'I know we talk on the phone all the time, but it's been too long since I actually saw you,' she continued. 'Now then, let me look at you.'

'Was it my fault?' Hattie blurted out without thinking. 'He threatened me, that night. He said something about being able to take away everything I had, that he could make my life a living hell, and for the past nine years I've been too scared to ask you just in case all of this happened because of what I did.' She paused and then, with her eyes staring directly into Louisa's, whispered, 'What we did.' She stopped, took in a breath, and felt her eyes fill with tears. 'I've always wondered if it was him. If he did this?'

'Oh Hattie, is that what you think?' Once again, Hattie was pulled into her cousin's arms. 'Oh, my love. Have you been thinking this for all these years? That somehow it was all your fault and that, what? That they killed your father because you refused a man sex in the back of his car?'

Taking a hurried step back, Hattie felt her foot catch painfully against the kerb. She was almost unbalanced but she pulled her arm quickly away as she felt Louisa make a grab to save her. 'I'm fine... Louisa, please.' Taking her time. Hattie kept her attention on the floor and stared at it for what felt like a moment too long as she waited for the feeling of nausea to pass. She blew her breath slowly outward in an attempt to regain her composure. 'He hurt me. He assaulted me and then, then you asked me not to say anything to the police about him?' Hattie questioned. 'You said that if I were to talk about what I'd done, of what had happened, that I'd be the one to end up in prison. That they'd see me as an accomplice, and that somehow they'd find a way of blaming us both for what happened.'

Leaning against Hattie's car, Louisa crossed her arms defensively. 'Hattie, I was trying to save my own ass. Surely, you knew that. Didn't you?' she asked. 'I panicked, and I certainly didn't want them potentially linking me to what happened and going through my client list or my bank account. Some of the men in there were worse than that Fraser bloke, they really would have done a number on me if I'd given out their name to the cops and... I feel awful and I'm sorry, I shouldn't have done that to you. If we'd come clean, maybe they'd have caught whoever did it.' She bit down on her lower lip. 'Instead, your mum's been the one stuck in her own prison ever since, trapped in that body and mind of hers.' She glanced towards the hospital and, with her bottom lip quivering with emotion, she wiped a tear away from her eye. 'Hattie, I swear to God, if I thought for a minute it was one of the punters, I'd go to the police myself.' Again, she looked over her shoulder and paused thoughtfully. 'But, even so, it's a murder and an attack that's still not been solved and, every day since it happened, it's crossed my mind that someone is still out there. That someone did this and, even though I've done all I can to make her comfortable, to give her some semblance of life, it still doesn't alter the fact that she didn't get justice.' She waved a hand around in the air dismissively. 'Oh, and I'm not looking for any thanks. I've not done anything too fancy. But I do try to get her out and about a bit. We've been to the seaside. A couple of trips to Whitby each year and to Scarborough.' She paused and smiled thoughtfully. 'We even went to Helmsley for an afternoon tea, now that was a nice day and, even though she didn't eat very much, your mum, she seemed to enjoy it.'

Hattie nodded contemplatively. For all the years since her parents had been attacked, she'd been sure that Bill Fraser had sent someone to the house to teach her a lesson and, inadvertently, he'd met with her parents. Although now Louisa had put it so bluntly, why would a man go around killing people just because he hadn't got sex?

'Your mum will be so pleased you came.' Feeling her hand being squeezed affectionately, Hattie looked up to see the tears that had flooded Louisa's eyes. 'She doesn't talk much. Quite intermittently, but she has begun to say your name. So, I do know she wants to see you.' She smiled and, affectionately, patted Hattie on the top of each shoulder.

'But what does she say, Lou? And why now, why has she waited so long to speak to us?' It was a question that had gone around in her mind for years, yet especially since the day before when she'd found out that her mother's silence had been by choice.

It was a thought that had repeatedly played itself in her mind. Especially after she'd spent many an hour sitting beside her mother, chatting away in the hope that she'd answer. And now, she was about to say something that was important for them to hear. Something she hadn't felt was important enough for her to say at any point in the past nine years. Which just felt wrong.

'Darling girl, she doesn't speak like she did but the fact that she wants to see you all means that, whatever she has to say, it has to be something important. Something she wants you to know before... she dies.'

15

NINE YEARS BEFORE – HATTIE

'All you have to do is stand in there, and keep quiet,' Louisa said later that evening as she pointed to the old brick-built bus shelter. 'It'll be fine, honestly and, the sooner I can do some business, the sooner we can go.' Her teeth chattered with the cold and her body shivered relentlessly in clothes that looked so wet they were almost transparent.

'Lou, you can't be serious?' Hattie sniffed the air, the smell of urine hitting the back of her throat, and she felt the nausea turn in her stomach. 'It stinks. In fact... it wouldn't surprise me if every man in Northallerton has relieved himself in there, right on that very spot.' She held a hand over her mouth and breathed in slowly. 'I can't, seriously, Lou. I'll throw up. And where did your friend go? Isn't he waiting, to give us a lift home?'

'Hattie. Grow up. All I need is for you to watch my back.' She tried to smile but the unsaid doubt behind her eyes gave her away. 'I just have to get a bit more money and...' She paused, ran a hand through her long, wet hair. 'Well... it can't be that hard, can it? I've been having sex in here since I was fifteen... and getting paid for it, well, it's just not that different? All I'm asking you to do is stand here and say nothing.' She waved a finger at the road, and then smiled at a car that slowed down to look.

'Lou, you can't be that stupid,' Hattie yelled. 'I mean, I know you've done the escorting for a while, but this is different and, right now, it's cold, it's wet and there's absolutely no reason for you to do this. In fact, you can't do this. It isn't safe... and my God, I have no idea how the hell you once again talked me into this or what would happen if my dad found out. I promised him I'd stay home where I was safe.' Hattie paced back and forth. She did all she could to avoid stepping into the shelter, but the rain was persistent, and she didn't feel comfortable in the clothes that Lou had practically forced her to wear. They were causing her to get wide-eyed stares from the men who were driving past, with the odd comment being shouted through the car windows. One man, who was sat in the passenger seat lifted his phone, clicked to take a photograph and quickly Hattie lifted a hand to cover her face and could feel her cheeks burning with both the humiliation and the anger that every man who walked past thought she was a hooker too. It was a feeling that made her skin crawl with disgust and she desperately wanted to go home, where she belonged.

'Look at them, staring at me through their dirty, beady eyes. They think I'm on the game.' She pulled at the skirt as though she were only just realising how short it was and, with the cold winter air cutting into her skin, she leaned heavily and despondently against a wall. 'And if I'm only the bloody lookout, why the hell did I have to dress like this?'

Giving another car a wave of her hand, Louisa kept one eye on where Hattie stood. 'Do you know what, I have no idea, 'cause after the way you acted last night, I'm telling you now

The Family Home

you'd be the worst prostitute ever.' The comment was harsh, unnecessary and hurtful, causing Hattie to take a step inside the shelter, where she blew out slowly to calm her emotions. It had never been her intention to become or even look like a prostitute. She hadn't wanted to be an escort. Everything she ever did was to please someone else and with her arms held tightly around her body to keep herself warm, she tried to think of a way she could leave. A way she could go back to being at home, living a calm, sedate life that didn't involve standing by the side of the road, watching Louisa's back. But she couldn't. To do that, she'd be leaving Louisa all alone and even though, right at this minute, Hattie didn't feel as though she deserved her loyalty, she couldn't abandon her either.

'I have no idea why you're snapping at me. The only reason I went on the date was because you said that it'd make Griffin look twice. You said that all I had to do was post pictures of me with another man on my social media and like a miracle he was supposed to pay me more attention.' She stopped and glared in Louisa's direction while she walked to a car, leaned in through the window and the driver handed Louisa money, which was swiftly tucked into the small bag she had looped over her shoulder. For a moment, Hattie stood, watched with a furrowed brow, and waited for her cousin to walk back to her. 'And, might I add, these are pictures that I wasn't allowed to take. Pictures you'd have known I wasn't allowed to take and one of the first things Fraser threw at me when I first met him.' Hattie shouted. 'No photos, no video, no evidence.' She repeated the words verbatim as she remembered them. 'And what was that all about?' she asked as she pointed to the car that drove away.

'Don't stress. He owed me some money,' Louisa growled with a stern look over her shoulder. 'If you'd only played along and given Fraser what he wanted, neither of us would be here tonight, would we?' She stood back, thoughtfully. Then, she pushed her tongue firmly into her cheek. 'You've never done it, have you?'

Unexpectedly, Hattie felt hurt by Louisa's words. She'd always been proud of how careful she'd been with the opposite sex and didn't like the fact that somehow it was now being used against her. 'God, Louisa, you're childish and, what's more, it's none of your goddamned business whether or not I've had sex. It's got nothing to do with us being stood at the side of a road, looking like trash. There just has to be another way of earning the money, other than this...' Hattie questioned vehemently. 'And if Fraser's that upset, why don't I go to him, apologise for whatever it is I'm supposed to have done and then...'

'Then what?'

'Oh, I don't know. But you do realise what you're about to do, don't you?' Hattie could feel the panic rising up within her but noticed the distant gaze in Louisa's eyes. It was more than obvious that, whether Hattie liked it or not, Louisa wasn't going to listen. 'Do you know what, Lou. I'm not doing this.' Hattie turned away from the shelter. 'I'm going home.'

'No, you're not.'

'Oh, yes, I am...'

'Hattie. I'm begging you.' Anxiously, Louisa grabbed hold of Hattie's hand and dragged her back towards the shelter. Then, with hands that shook with both the cold and with fear, she pressed them down onto Hattie's shoulders and stared directly into her eyes. 'I'm begging. You can't leave me...' Looking at the road beyond, Louisa gave Hattie a pensive half-smile. 'I'll make you a deal. If any of the men look nasty. Or if they... oh, I don't know... if they do anything you don't like, just step out of the shelter and I swear, the minute they see you, they'll realise we're together and they'll stop. They'll leave like a shot. I promise.'

'And what if they don't, Lou?' Looking up and down the road, Hattie wanted nothing more than to leave. To go back home and sit in front of the fire, just as she'd promised. But she couldn't. She couldn't leave Lou in a town by herself with, as far as Hattie could tell, no means of getting home and, besides, they were only here because of Fraser. Which meant that, like it or not, she had to look out for her cousin.

'Hattie, the last thing any of them want is a bloody audience. If they think we're together, they'll take their hook.' She thrust a hand in the air and, with her thumb jutting out, swept it angrily over her shoulder. 'Either that, or they'll offer us a price for a group deal.'

'Oh no. Now you've lost me,' Hattie snapped back. 'Not a chance. Do you hear me?' Pushing her chin defiantly outward, Hattie once again pulled at the leather-look skirt. She could still hear her mother's chastising voice. The way it had reverberated in her ears for most of her life: 'Your skirt, young lady. It needs to be below your knee, not so far up your leg that I can see your underwear. And, before you say it, I really don't care what the other girls in your school are doing or that you'll be a laughing-stock, you're still not going out looking like that.'

Hattie inched into the shadows and watched as her cousin slipped her jacket off her shoulders and, even though the rain still poured, she began to saunter seductively up and down the edge of the road, leaning in and out of cars and pocketing money. It was uncomfortable to watch, a situation that didn't sit well and, after the fourth car slowed and the fourth man passed Louisa money, Hattie became more than suspicious of what was really happening. But, with her heart racing and her mind willing Louisa to call it a night, she chose to take a step back, and she did all she could to zone out of what she could see right before her. Louisa wasn't selling sex; she was selling drugs and, with her mind screaming out that she had to step in, she had to stop her from making the biggest mistake of her life, her body froze and she stood hidden inside the bus shelter, peeping through a small square hole in its side, where she did all she could to zone out and concentrate on the noises of everyday life that surrounded her.

They were all sounds that came from the town, from the traffic that passed by and from the party goers that were visiting the pubs and clubs nearby. They were noises that on a normal night out she wouldn't have noticed, but on a night when it was cold and dark, and when she was holding her breath waiting for the sound of police cars to fill the air, every sound felt emphasised, making the road feel much quieter, darker and more dangerous than normal.

Closing her eyes, Hattie thought about Alice and about the times she'd seen her at the house. She'd been young and, even though she was dressed in her short skirts and low-cut tops, she came across as being nervous and, on the odd occasion that Hattie had seen her, she'd stood in the hallway drumming her fingers against the wall while summoning up the nerve to knock on the door and go into her appointment.

The fact that Alice hadn't been seen since her last appointment made Hattie uncomfortable. It was supposed to be a place where the girls were safe, her mother had said so herself. Yet, in between her entering the office and going back home, something had happened and Hattie tried to think of all the reasons she'd have walked as far as the river but couldn't. It would have been a strange place for the prostitute to go. Most would stand on a street corner, just as Louisa was doing right now. This gave Hattie a jolt and fearfully she wondered what the chances were that, this time next week, the whole village would be out searching for her or Louisa's body too and whether they would be found.

Taking a step forward, Hattie had every intention of insisting that they both go home, but immediately recoiled and turned away when it became more than obvious that Louisa had found herself a client and was currently knelt down, in the rain, in front of the man.

'Lou, we really need to go,' she shouted hopefully over her shoulder. She once again closed her eyes and gritted her teeth with disgust as she heard the man's obvious groan. 'Actually, do you know what. Show's over.' She spun around and stared at the man who looked to be no older than Adam and had the look of a rabbit in headlights. 'Pull up your damned trousers. Pay the woman. Then, do yourself a favour. Get the hell out of here,' Hattie yelled as she stamped her foot against the pavement and cursed as a puddle of cold icy water splashed up and onto her legs.

'What the hell are you doing, sending him away?' Louisa protested. 'He'd have gone again, and he'd just promised me fifty for some roofies.'

'So, that's the answer, is it? Go for the ones that are pissed, sell them some drugs so they can go and rape women? Is that the plan, Lou?' With the rage building up within her, Hattie could still feel Fraser's hands inside her, could still feel the bruising and the invasion and had no idea how far it would have gone if he'd given her some kind of drug to make her a little more compliant. 'Do you know what, Lou, I'm freezing. I don't want anything to do with your get-rich-quick scheme that could land other women in the river right next to Alice. I'm going home and you, you can't stop me.'

'You can't.'

Standing with rain now thrashing against her face and her hands shaking uncontrollably with the cold, Hattie looked up at the dark, ominous sky. More than anything in the world, she wanted to sob. She had no idea how her life had fallen apart or how she'd ended up stood by the side of the road and assisting a drug dealer. Her whole body shook with anger, with fear and, because of her own stupidity, she only had herself to blame. All she needed now was for someone to recognise her or for her to get arrested and have to phone her father to come to her aid.

'Do you know what my dad would do if he found out I'd been here, with you, doing this? Do you have any idea how many times I'd hear about it and the lecture I'd have to constantly listen to?' she shouted. 'And do you know what, Lou? I wouldn't even be able to say a word because I'd have to admit that he was right.' She pushed her hands angrily through her wet, shoulder-length hair. 'Seriously, Lou, it's alright for you—' Hattie was going to say that her cousin had no one to answer to, that there was no one to give her a lecture, but stopped herself mid-sentence.

'Is it...?' Louisa stamped towards her. 'Is it really okay for me, Hattie? Well, good for you. At least you've still got your parents. Someone who gives a damn. Well, I'll tell you what, they're not the people you think they are. They have secrets too. Big secrets. Ones that would blow your whole fucking world apart.'

'What the hell are you talking about?' Confused and angry, Hattie stood in front of Louisa and pushed a hand against her shoulder. 'They did everything for you, Lou. They gave you a home, a place to be when you had no one and nowhere else to go, and this is what you say about them?'

Lifting her hands up to rake them through her hair, Louisa bit down on her lip. 'Well, aren't I the lucky one,' she finally said. 'My life could have been so different, and do you know what,

Hattie, they've played a huge part in my life, but they have no fucking idea what it's really like to be me.' She pointed to the pavement, to the graze that had appeared on the knee of her black leatherette boot. 'I'm doing all of this to save your ass and you have the nerve to stand there and have a go at me.'

'To save my ass?' Standing her ground, Hattie kept her eyes fixed on Louisa's and the heat rose to her cheeks. 'Do you know what, Lou... that is really unfair. And you know it is.' She didn't know whether to argue or sob. She couldn't imagine for a minute that a man would ask for the money back just because he didn't get laid, or that he'd send the heavies around to rough up a girl and, for some reason, Hattie took a step back and thought about the alternatives. 'What's really going on, Lou, because, quite honestly, I don't fucking believe you.'

Looking down, Louisa stared at the pavement while her hands fidgeted with the zip on the small bag that hung across her. 'It's Rohypnol. I'm charging double street price to get back enough money to pay him for the ketamine I lost.' She undid the zip, pulled out a small paper packet. 'In each pack, there are three tablets and the guys that have been pulling up, they're the guys I normally sell the Special K to...'

Staring, Hattie stood open mouthed. She lifted a hand and with her palm held towards her, tapped it against her forehead. 'Oh my God, what possessed you?' Hattie screamed. 'Are you crazy, stupid or both?' She turned around and began to walk away. 'And how the hell did you manage to lose a bag full of ketamine?'

'Hattie, don't leave me.'

Standing with her back to Louisa on the busy road, Hattie watched the cars that sped past her, listened to the comments that some shouted from their open windows and kept an eye on the road ahead, always looking for the flashing blue lights that she felt sure would come. 'Why, why should I stay, Lou? You made me believe that this was all my fault. That me turning down a prick with an ego meant you had to do this. When, in reality, you've dug yourself a hole... and now you're a fucking drug dealer? Jesus, Lou! Look around you. Can't you see what they do to people?' She pointed to a man who was sat in a doorway, his clothes dirty and torn, his head slumped forward, as he leaned against a wall with vomit covering the front of his coat. 'That!' she shouted. 'Do you see the state of him? Do you see how out of control he is? That's what drug users do.'

'Hattie, I swear I don't take them. I've never taken them.' She faltered, looked down. 'Well, okay, I did take them just a couple of times, but, if I'm honest, I didn't like it.' She held on to Hattie's shoulder, looked her directly in the eye. 'So, I just move them on, let those who want to take them do just that.'

'Face it, you're a drug dealer?'

'Hattie...' Letting go of Hattie's shoulders, Louisa moved and pressed a hand against the brickwork, before stumbling awkwardly backwards. Her legs suddenly went from beneath her. She fell to her knees, slumped sidewards, and landed in a heap in the same spot where half of Northallerton had previously urinated.

'Lou?'

'I don't... I just, don't... feel...' Leaning forward, Louisa rested her head against her arm. She began to retch repeatedly. Her face had turned blue. Her eyes flickered and, suddenly, she was silent.

'Oh my God. Lou. What the hell did you take? Don't do this to me.' Running out of the shelter, Hattie held her arm out toward the road and watched as a driver swerved to avoid her. A horn blasted, making her jump, and another passing car purposely drove into a puddle, to send a large splash of water flying up in Hattie's direction. 'Urgh, stop the car. My...' She waved her arms in the air, tried to gain some attention by shouting that her cousin needed help. But it was clear to see that all the motorists saw was nothing more than a pair of hookers, one who looked to be so intoxicated that she'd taken to sleeping on the floor, and Hattie realised for the first time in her life that no one was coming to help her.

16

NINE YEARS BEFORE – HATTIE

In the darkness, Hattie threw herself down onto the cold, hard pavement and, with as much effort as she could, pulled at Louisa's cold, semi-conscious body until her head and upper body rested across her knee. Her face was pale, her eyes flickered and Hattie wished that just one of the cars would stop.

'Please God, let there be just one person that stops. Help me... Please, I need some help over here.' She waved a hand around in the air. 'Okay, Lou... it's okay,' she whispered through teeth that were chattering so violently she could barely think. 'You hold on. Do you hear me?' She looked anxiously around her and grabbed for her bag and the phone within. 'I'm... I'm going to phone an ambulance.' It was the right thing to do but the doubt crept into her mind as she looked down at the way they were dressed and could only imagine the look on her father's face if they got to the hospital looking like this.

'No am... bu... lance. No hospital...' Louisa suddenly managed to groan. 'I don't... I can't...' She gripped hold of Hattie's jacket and kept her glazed, distant eyes on Hattie's face. 'Phone Griff, he'll come.'

'Oh no. I'm not phoning Griffin; you need a bloody ambulance.' Hattie once again waved her arms in the air and tried to attract some attention. 'God damn it, why won't they stop? The bastards can surely see we need help here, that you're...' she sobbed. 'That you're a human being, just like they are.' She tried to imagine what she'd do in their place. How she'd feel if she was driving past and saw two woman, dressed like prostitutes, lying on the ground. 'I'd stop,' she cried. 'I'd stop and I'd help. No matter who they were or how they looked,' she shouted angrily, but then she thought back to the way she'd judged the man who lay in the shop doorway further up the road and the men that had approached her cousin just a short while ago. She hadn't exactly rushed across the road to check that the man was okay and the others, she'd seen them as 'nasty' and unworthy and now, she now regretted those thoughts.

'Phone Griffin, he'll...' Louisa whispered. 'Hattie, he's training to be a doctor, he'll know... what to do.'

Closing her eyes in thought, Hattie felt torn. She wanted to get Louisa the help she needed, but she really didn't want Griff to see her dressed like this. What she'd wanted was to impress him, to turn his head and create a situation where he'd once again want to kiss her, like he had before. But it had to be on her terms, and this time it had to be different, this time she didn't want him running off to university or to anywhere else, not when she knew that together they would have had a chance of being happy and seeing her like this was hardly the lasting impression she wanted to give. But what choice did she have? Desperately she searched through her phone for the last message Adam had sent to her about Griff.

> Hattie. You need to give Griff a call. He talks about you non-stop and, if I'm honest, he's doing my head in. So, if you haven't already, put the man out of his misery because you'd be doing my ears a really big favour xx

The message had been followed by Griffin's number and, after a moment's hesitation, Hattie held her finger over it and took in a long, deep breath before clicking the button and waiting for him to answer.

'Griff... it's Hattie. Hattie Gilby,' she said nervously as he answered. 'This is a big ask, but... I really need your help...'

17

PRESENT DAY – DECEMBER 2023 – SOPHIE

Feeling annoyed and frustrated that she'd allowed her jealousy to get the better of her, Sophie cursed herself for the way she'd run out on Finn. And now that her foot throbbed every time she touched it against the floor, she realised that it wasn't worth the pain, the discomfort or the embarrassment she'd caused herself.

The sudden fall, followed by Finn's expert opinion, had meant that she was now sat in an over-crowded waiting room waiting for an X-ray that could literally take hours and, only by sheer chance, Noah was gurgling happily. He was sat on her knee staring happily at the man who sat next to them. Unlike Sophie, who had no wish to smile happily at anyone. What she really wanted was to grumble at the other patients that surrounded her, most of whom seemed to be constantly knocking, or kicking the chair that she was trying to use as a footrest.

'Charming, isn't it? How some people think they're entitled to two chairs.' A gangly, acne-covered teenager mumbled. He was sat, with his legs spreadeagled next to his very young and impressionable girlfriend who giggled softly and clung tightly to the arm of his bright yellow puffer jacket.

Feeling the colour rise to her cheeks, Sophie shuffled in her seat and, protectively, pulled Noah as close as she could, kissing him on the top of his head. Sitting around was the one thing she hated the most and, after reading the same poster for the fourth time in as many minutes, she gave out a sigh, before glancing at it again. It was a poster that pointed out the risks of unprotected sex, the disease and discomfort that could happen as a result, along with an image of a big pink telephone and a phone number that Sophie felt sure she could now repeat verbatim. It was only after the last time of reading the poster that Sophie noticed the way the teenager had been watching her every movement, mimicking the way she'd tipped her head to one side and creating a joke at her expense with his girlfriend.

'Maybe that's why her foot's in the air. Maybe she's preparing herself for going up in the stirrups,' he said childishly. 'Or maybe her husband will be giving her a right good sorting out, you know, while she's in there.' He stood comically with his legs wide apart, laughing hysterically.

'Oh, there you go, young man. You think you're being all big and clever, well let's all have a chat about why we all think you're at the doctors, shall we?' The sound of an Irish woman's voice rang out, loud and clear, making Sophie cringe inwardly as she recognised it as Finn's gran. Frieda Alexander was the loudest person Sophie had ever known and, suddenly, her presence seemed to take over the waiting room, making Sophie close her eyes and clench her teeth as the wet, slobbering, nicotine-enhanced kiss landed on one side of her face. 'Our Finn told me you were here, and that you might need a hand with the little 'un, you know while you pop in and see the nurse.'

'Oh, I see...' Glaring across the room, Sophie caught sight of the brass plate that had been stuck to Finn's door. He was barely six feet away and angrily she wondered why he couldn't have popped out and told her about the call to his gran himself or that she was on her way down. 'I... Well, I just thought that Finn would pop out and hold him, you know, when I went in.' She smiled through gritted teeth, and watched as Noah was whisked out of her arms, spun around, and kissed repeatedly. It was an action that Noah seemed to enjoy and, with a burst of enthusiasm, he filled the room with loud baby-like giggles. 'I didn't realise he was going to call you.'

'Oh, it's fine. I was coming down anyhow and, when Finn told me you were sat here waiting, I thought I'd come along early, so I did.' She pointed to Sophie's foot, gave her a look of concern. 'Besides, I don't need much of an excuse to come and see this little man. Do I?'

Frieda looked over her shoulder at where at least half a dozen other patients were listening intently to their conversation before she leaned forward and whispered. 'Go on, then, what did you do and how come Finn didn't stick a bandage on you himself?'

'Oh, he's probably annoyed with me.' Sophie dismissively waved a hand in the air. 'I was out with Jasper and... well, the fire alarm went off in the house next door and Finn turned all superhero on us and practically broke the door down to save that Hattie woman.' She rolled her eyes at the teenager who continued to stare in her direction. 'Anyhow, there she was stood at the top of the stairs wearing the smallest towel ever made...' She paused and closed her eyes for a blink. 'And Finn was looking upwards, all googly-eyed.'

'So,' Frieda said between giving Noah kisses, 'she's back, is she?'

'She is and, because I wasn't going to stand there and watch the way they were making eyes at each other, I left the house and promptly managed to turn my ankle on her broken driveway,' she hissed. 'I'm so bloody annoyed, and now I'm waiting to see the nurse because apparently my husband's diary is full and it isn't up to him to work the X-ray machine. I wouldn't mind, I'm sure that I'd have been perfectly fine if he'd thrown a bandage on it himself and I'd stayed at home, but he insisted I came here and waited.' Shaking her head, she clapped her hands in front of Noah, hoping he'd lean forward and jump back into her arms and she felt a huge sense of disappointment when he didn't. 'In fact, I don't think I really need to be here at all.' Realising that Frieda wasn't listening and that she'd already diverted her attention back to Noah, Sophie slumped back in her chair. Even with the commotion that was happening in the room around them, she still somehow managed to overhear what the receptionist was saying over the phone to another patient.

'I'm sorry, Doctor Alexander's gone out... he had an emergency visit, I'm afraid, and his diary says that he'll be out tomorrow morning too.' She listened again. 'I know, it's unfortunate, but... nothing I can do I'm afraid.'

'Have you had your breakfast, my cheeky boy?' Frieda said in a loud and animated voice. 'You tell your granny what you had?' She rubbed Noah's tummy, brought on a new excited gurgle. 'Mmmmm, let me guess?' Again, there was a poke, a squeeze and a giggle. 'I think I can feel some... banana... yes, I can, and what about... Ohhh and some lovely, yummy yogurt. Is that what you had? Is it?' She leaned back, held a hand up to cup her mouth. 'Finn told me what happened with the breakfast and that he'd ended up with most of it down his shirt. It's in my washer as we speak.'

Spinning in her chair, Sophie looked through the front doors of the surgery at the space where Finn's car had previously been parked. 'Finn's been back to your house? This morning? When? I didn't even know he'd gone out,' Sophie queried and immediately felt herself bristle in the knowledge that, not too long ago, Finn had done his laundry at home. Even during the weeks after he'd first left, he'd still brought his shirts home, even though she did have to admit that some of the shirts would be waiting to be ironed for a good few days. But she had always made sure that there were a selection of shirts ready to wear in his wardrobe.

Lifting her phone, Sophie looked at the screen and checked the time. 'I specifically remember him saying that he had a really busy surgery today. Back-to-back patients, he said. He even took a sandwich with him because he wouldn't even have the time for a lunch break.' Sophie furiously tapped her foot against the chair and winced with the pain before thoughtfully returning her mind to that morning during the one-hour visit Finn had made to his son. It had ended the moment Finn had heard the fire alarm sounding off in the house next door. The way he'd whispered Hattie's name in horror under his breath and had run for the front door, and without any thought for himself or others, he'd barged right in. The panic had been more than obvious; the blush of colour that had rushed to his cheeks and the awkward conversation that had followed. It was the first time she'd ever seen Finn almost lost for words, leaving her with no doubt that the relationship between him and Hattie had been far from platonic.

'So, the two of you. You were close, were you?' Sophie had shouted up the stairs, just a few moments after Finn had helped her inside and disappeared up to the nursery with a wriggling Noah. 'Because, I have to say, the two of you looked mighty cosy, when I walked in. Hattie stood there, wrapped in a bath towel, and you, well, you stood there with a stupid grin on your face.' Annoyed with herself for being so jealous, Sophie had stared across the room and gazed at the wedding photograph that stood on the windowsill. It had been a day when they'd both been happy and now she was sat wondering who the woman next door was and what trouble was about to come hurtling into her life now she'd returned.

'He's just drank half of his milk while I changed him,' Finn had said as he'd walked back into the room with Noah perched in his arms. He held on to a white, fluffy teddy bear by its ear, and he carried a half bottle of milk that was immediately dropped when he saw her. 'We needed our nappy changed, didn't we, smelly bot?' Finn smiled and pressed a kiss firmly to the top of Noah's forehead. He lifted a hand to touch his cheek and then, with a deep, wistful look, he'd followed Sophie's gaze towards the picture. 'Look. Why don't you go and change, I'll look after Noah and then I'll get one of the nurses to take a couple of X-rays down at the surgery and if they show anything of concern, we'll drive through to Friarage this afternoon?' He'd pulled a face. 'I'd do it myself, but I have a really busy surgery this morning. Back-to-back patients all bloody day, but, obviously, I'll have some time to take you in later, if you need to go.' He'd looked at her with what she'd thought was a genuine smile and, after he'd leaned forward and dropped a kiss on her cheek, she'd felt herself soften with the need to please him.

Only now, just a few hours later while sitting in the surgery listening to Frieda kiss and blow raspberries at her son, Sophie realised just how easily Finn had managed to deflect her question away from Hattie. He hadn't answered her at all, which made her wonder what the hell he was hiding.

18

NINE YEARS BEFORE – HATTIE

Sitting in the back seat of Griffin's car with the only light in the darkness coming from a brightly lit dashboard, Hattie looked down at where Louisa's head was resting on her knee and nervously pressed her fingers against her cousin's cold, clammy back. The position Louisa was lying in meant that, by doing this, Hattie could feel each time she took an inward breath but, the longer the journey took, the shallower the movement became and the more Hattie began to panic.

'Griff, I'm scared. Do you think she took something because she just dropped like a stone, and I screamed, and I shouted, and no one would help her... I mean, what kind of animals are they if they won't come to the aid of another human being?' Hattie ranted. 'I have no idea what I'd have done if she'd stopped breathing.' She'd said the words as calmly as she could while continually scanning Louisa's face for any kind of movement.

'The worst thing you can do is panic,' Griff replied with a confident smile. 'We're just ten minutes from home and, if anything happens, I'm here to help you, so...' He looked at her through the rear-view mirror, caught her eye for a moment too long and, even in the dimly lit car, Hattie could see the way he eventually looked away with a shy, bashful half-smile.

'I'm so grateful that you came,' Hattie whispered. 'I don't know what I'd have done.' She kept pressing her cold, trembling hand against Louisa's back and, for a few brief seconds, she held her breath fearfully. 'What if she's stopped breathing already, what if I don't know?'

'Okay, try this.' Griff glanced over his shoulder as they pulled up at some traffic lights. 'Pinch the lobe of her ear. She won't like it and will twitch or pull away from you.'

With another sense of relief, Hattie watched the way Louisa wriggled. Her lips twitched and then, with a deep intake of breath, a loud grunt of a snore expelled itself from her.

'It's alright, Lou. We're nearly there,' Hattie whispered reassuringly while all the time she continually rearranged Griff's coat that had been draped across Louisa's body in an effort to warm her because, even though the car's heater was on, Louisa still felt unbelievably cold.

Tipping her head to one side, Hattie watched as the rain lashed against the window, causing rivulets of water to run around the edges as a mixture of windscreen wipers and streetlights made it difficult to see. 'We're almost there, Lou... Just hold on, we won't be long now, Griff, will we?' she questioned hopefully, as the sound of the indicator made her sit up a little further and check the road ahead.

It would be the first time she'd ever been to Griff's house and inquisitively she took in a deep breath as they turned into a small side road that led off to her right. It was a lane she'd once walked along a few years before and, because she couldn't remember seeing any houses down there, she furrowed her brow in question. Large, overgrown bushes and hedgerows grew to each side, with dark, ominous silhouettes of trees scattered between them. They were trees that had long since lost their leaves for the winter and Hattie rolled her eyes uneasily as the tree branches hung across the width of the road and eerily reached out towards the car, like long, wizened fingers.

'There you go, we're just about here...' He pointed further up the road to where Hattie could easily see the bright amber flashing lights of the train line. The barriers that were currently blocking the road and a single car in front of them that waited patiently for the barriers to open.

Sighing, Hattie prepared herself for the wait, and for the train to pass. But she gasped as Griffin took a sharp left and pulled his car to a stop right outside the signal house. 'And we're here,' he whispered and turned in his seat. 'How is she?'

'You live in a signal house that's miles from anywhere?' Hattie questioned. 'Seriously. How come I didn't know that?' Reaching for the door, Hattie wrenched at the handle, but the door didn't move and, in her panic, she wrenched at it again. 'Griff, the door, it seems to be... I mean, I think you've got the child lock on...' She scowled, once again checking on Louisa.

Jumping out of the driver's seat, Griff headed towards the house with his hands rubbing anxiously together, just as the front door was flung open and a large, rotund woman appeared in the doorway. It was a woman Hattie recognised from the church. Frieda had often helped her mother with the flowers and, from what Griff had said, she used to be a nurse, which meant that Louisa would be in very good hands.

Standing with the door held open, Frieda was dressed in a dark-coloured dressing gown that had been tied haphazardly in a knot at the waist, right below where her arms were arrogantly crossed. Her hair was grey and tousled and, if it hadn't been for the cigarette clenched between her teeth, Hattie would have presumed that she'd just climbed out of her bed and that the dressing gown had been thrown on in a hurry.

After a few brief words, Griffin nodded anxiously before turning back to the car where, after a moment's hesitation, he threw open the back door and reached across Louisa until he located her wrist and pressed his fingers firmly against it.

'There you go, Lou. Let's just... That's great, your pulse, that's feeling much better, isn't it?' He looked up and caught Hattie's eye. 'I'm just going to get her inside.' Lifting a hand, he ran it across his chin as though carefully choosing his words. 'You might want to stay in the car. My gran, I know you've met her before, but she's not too fond of visitors and...' He looked down, fixed his gaze on the footwell where his rugby kit had been untidily dumped. 'I've just explained that Louisa was taken ill at a fancy dress and that I got a call to come and help. She seems to have bought the story and appears to be okay with that, but...' He took in a deep breath. 'Other than that, I have no idea what else to say and, if you come in too, it might just get a bit too complicated.' He paused, caught her eye. 'You don't mind, do you?'

Sinking back into the seat, Hattie felt her whole body deflate. It was more than obvious that Griff didn't want his gran to see her and when she was dressed like a prostitute she could fully understand why. It was just another reason to form another regret, another way of making her feel remorseful for having ever agreed to help Louisa in the first place.

'Hey, don't look like that,' Griff said with a tentative smile. 'I'll spin a good story once I've got her inside.' He reached forward, looked up, caught Hattie's eye. 'It's up to you, and I understand if you'd rather not, but there are some joggers and a rugby top down there. They're clean, I didn't wear them yet and well... It might be a good idea to change, before you get home.'

The words jolted Hattie back to reality. Her mind went back to her father's face, the lines of worry that had been etched into his forehead when he'd told her that Alice was still missing and, right now, she realised that Griff was right, the last thing she wanted was to add to her father's worry. Obediently she pulled the rugby shirt out of the bag and slipped it over her head with a satisfied sigh.

'Where am I?' Louisa suddenly asked in a panic as Griff took hold of her hand and pulled her towards him. 'What are you doing?'

'Don't worry, Lou. You're safe,' he answered reassuringly as he hooked her arm over his shoulder and swung her up and into his arms with ease. 'You're at my gran's. She was a nurse. She's going to look after you.' His words were calm and soothing, which was enough to make Louisa relax into his hold and, anxiously, Hattie watched as he stepped away from the car and carried Louisa in through a front door that was quickly closed behind them.

Once alone, Hattie slid out of her skirt. Abandoned it in the footwell and pulled Griff's joggers up and over her hips. They were a good few sizes too big and, in the darkness, Hattie fiddled with the drawstring waist and pulled it as tight as she could before pulling Griff's coat tightly around her shoulders and snuggling down to stare aimlessly out of the car window at the red-brick two-storey house. It looked odd and, oddly, it had mismatched windows – the ones downstairs were small and brightly lit and gave the house a look of being homely and full of warmth and character. In direct comparison, the upstairs windows were large and went along the whole width and breadth of the house, giving it a panoramic view of the train line, something that would have been useful when a station master had lived there. Although, from what Hattie could see, some of the windows had been boarded over, leaving the upstairs of the property to look lost and uncared for.

'Gran says she's going to be absolutely fine,' Griffin said as he jumped back into the driver's seat and then, with a look of apology, jumped back out, ran to the side of the car where Hattie sat dressed in his clothes, and finally pulled the rear door open. 'Sorry, do you want to sit up front?' He swept a hand to one side, and surreptitiously Hattie wiped away the tears that had begun to form in her eyes and gave him a pensive smile. 'She's told Gran that she hasn't eaten for days,' he continued, 'which is most probably the main reason behind her hitting the pavement. So, my gran is now on a mission to force-feed her some chicken broth, which I know from experience will cure all of her ills.' He laughed cheerfully, held out his hand towards her and gipped her fingers in his. 'Hey, you suit my clothes but, Jesus, you're cold,' he grumbled. 'Come here, let's get you warm. Doctor's orders.' Pulling her into his arms, Griff encircled her body with his and pulled her close.

It was a moment Hattie had hoped for since the night Griff had kissed her. She'd often thought about once again being alone with him, sinking into his hold and feeling the warmth of his body. What she hadn't thought was that it would be on a night like tonight and for the first time in days she felt a genuine sense of reassurance, or she would have if her stomach hadn't been bubbling with a nervous excitement that just wouldn't stop. In Griff's arms, she felt safe. The past two years slipped away and, once again, she was happy to be back in his arms, with her face buried in the nape of his neck, breathing in the smell of his aftershave until it overwhelmed her senses. 'You smell so good,' she whispered as she leaned back and looked up into his eyes. 'I'm so pleased you came. Seriously, I have no idea...'

Holding a finger tenderly to her lips, Griff continued to stare. It was as though he were looking at her for the very first time and she found amusement in the way he pouted as he spoke. 'Jesus, Hattie, I've waited two whole years to hold you again and...' Running his fingertips lightly down the side of her face, Griff cupped her chin and gently lifted her mouth towards him. 'And I'm sure you said you needed a lesson in mouth-to-mouth resuscitation.'

In a split second, his mouth grazed hers in a movement that wasn't rushed or felt demanding and, for a moment, she wondered if it would be right to allow Griff to kiss her, without telling him the truth of what she'd done and why. She needed him to know that the escorting hadn't meant a thing, that it had only been the once and that Lou had tricked her into going to stand on a street corner and sell stolen drugs. But, as she stood there and looked up into his eyes, she couldn't. To do that, she'd be selling her cousin out and, even though Louisa had been in the wrong, it was a conversation she needed to take up with her and not with others.

'Griff, I need to tell you something...'

Smiling while shaking his head, Griff wrapped his arms protectively around her. 'Hattie, can you tell me later? Because, right now...' He took in a breath but, as he did, he lowered his mouth until it hovered sensuously above hers. 'Right now, I really want to kiss you.'

19

PRESENT DAY – DECEMBER 2023 – HATTIE

The continuous sound of bleeping equipment, the movement of machinery and raised voices, reverberated through the air as Hattie slowly sauntered behind Louisa through the hospital corridors. This was a walk she was in no hurry to make as she walked down corridors she'd walked along on numerous days before. They were all tiled and cleaned and nothing had changed since the last time she'd been here, but today they felt very different. Very clinical. Today, there was a looming sense of dread, mixed with a nervous energy that surrounded her at the thought of seeing her mother. She wasn't sure what it would be like to hear her speak and she had no idea what she'd want to say in response.

From what Louisa had said, her mother had indicated that she had something important to tell them and, in her mind, Hattie had already gone through all kinds of scenarios. All manner of role play, where she'd tried to practise a set of perfect answers. But, still, there wasn't a scenario that could explain why her mother hadn't spoken before.

Vaguely, Hattie thought that there must have been at least a hundred occasions when she'd sat by her mother's side. Times when it had just been the two of them and she'd been rambling on about her life to her mother. There had been the days when she'd told her all about Charlie. About what it was like to live in Yorkshire, and about the fears she'd had over coming back to the village. All without her mother ever responding or giving her opinion and it was this that hurt her the most as she walked past all the same doors, the same signage she'd read a thousand times and the clearly visible exit doors, where bright green signs showed her which way she should go to find the way out. For a split second, she thought about running; about leaving the hospital and never coming back. After all, if her mother hadn't wanted to talk to her for the last nine years, what could she possibly want to say now? But Hattie resisted; making a fast exit would have been the coward's way out even though doing that would have been a whole lot easier than looking into her dying mother's eyes and listening to the words she suddenly had the urge to say.

Faltering, Hattie leaned against the wall and held on to the long length of plastic trunking that ran across its middle. She felt lightheaded and nauseous, and to alleviate the symptoms she closed her eyes and wished that she'd had a good night's sleep rather than the tossing and turning that had kept her awake. In her mind, she'd gone over and over what she should and shouldn't say and whether or not she should apologise for any part she may have played in her mother's attack. 'What if it had been...' she whispered. 'What if it had all been your fault, what if...' She thought of Fraser, of the men who'd gone after Louisa, of the money and the drugs and the late-night escapade in Northallerton.

Taking in a deep breath, Hattie tried to clear her mind of the questions that were whizzing around in turmoil. They were, of course, all the questions she could no longer ask her mother, because by all accounts they wouldn't be alone. All the family would be there. Which meant that the guilt would continue, unless, of course, her mother said something to rid her of those thoughts.

Checking the time on her phone, Hattie sucked the air into her lungs and gagged as the sweet smell of antiseptic filled her nostrils. It was a smell that clung to her throat, and it took her a few desperate moments of trying not to vomit before she found herself pinching her nose and glancing inquisitively in and out of the four-bed bays, looking for where her mother might be.

It was only then that she noticed where Louisa was heading and, with her legs trembling beneath her, she slowly followed her toward the single-bedded rooms that were all situated at the far end of the ward.

For years, Hattie had always presumed that these rooms were kept for the dying. It was where she'd often seen the seriously ill patients taken, after which a constant stream of relatives would visit. All eventually leaving with tears rolling uncontrollably down their faces. And, now, she was the one being led to one of those rooms and, as she fearfully walked past the nurse's station, she nodded an acknowledgement to the one or two nurses she recognised and took note of the way they looked back at her with pitiful eyes and solemn but knowing smiles.

'Lou...'

For the first time in years, Hattie heard her mother's voice. It was weak, breathless, and sounded desperate.

'Where is she?' Her mother's voice trailed off as she spoke and was followed by a long, agonising groan. 'Where's... my... Hattie?'

20

PRESENT DAY – DECEMBER 2023 – IMOGEN

Imogen Gilby lay back against the pillows of a hospital bed that dwarfed her tiny, wasted frame. There had once been a time when the smell of antiseptic would have irritated her sense of smell. The rattling of trolleys, constant ringing of a telephone and shoes clicking against the corridor floor would have set her nerves on edge, and the sight of hospital staff dressed as though they were about to go out for a jog would have annoyed her more than anything else, but, now, all of those things paled into insignificance and simply gave her the reassurance that she still had the time to say all the things she needed to say.

Lying there, she looked around the room and pulled each breath into her body with a lot more effort than she'd have liked. It was more than obvious that her days were limited and she prayed for her heart to keep beating, just long enough for her family to arrive for the meeting she'd asked for. Although, she wasn't sure whether or not to feel annoyed that Louisa had included herself in the meeting. Her presence shouldn't have really surprised her at all. Not when she'd seemingly always been there, and, with an inquisitive gaze, Imogen watched the way Louisa busied herself around the room. As always, she tidied the bedside cabinet, went through a small collection of dirty washing, and placed the items in a large plastic carrier bag ready to launder and tomorrow, without doubt, Imogen knew that the clothes would be returned. Even though the time was running out and her chances of wearing them was diminishing quickly.

'Where's... my... Hattie...' Once again she groaned as her eyes fixed themselves on the door and, annoyingly, she could feel her temper growing as, for the third time since she'd walked through the door, Louisa held the back of her hand across Imogen's forehead – a constant repetitive habit she seemed to have acquired, as though, by constantly feeling her temperature, she'd make everything better.

'You feel cold, today, my lovely,' Louisa whispered. 'Maybe I should get you another blanket, or how would you like me to find you a nice hot-water bottle? That'd warm you up, wouldn't it?'

Moving as sharply away from Louisa's hand as she could, Imogen closed her eyes in annoyance. She knew she was cold. She knew that her circulation was failing. She didn't need Louisa or anyone else to tell her that her time was running out. Nor did she believe that a dozen blankets or water bottles would change how she felt. Without saying a word, she rolled her eyes towards the ceiling. It was all she could do to keep herself calm, to stop her mind and her body from going into panic over what she was about to do and, with a slight wave of a hand in Louisa's direction, she shooed her away, and then rested the same hand back down beside Adam, where, with eyes that looked wide and fearful, he patiently sat beside her.

'I've... always... loved you,' Imogen whispered as she moved her hand to cover his. 'Don't forget, will you?' She sighed and closed her eyes and thought of all the days and nights he'd recently slept in the chair beside her. He'd barely moved, not even for food, which for Adam was momentous. Eating was something he'd always done, and now aged twenty-six years he was tall, muscular and strong, stoic to the extreme, and totally unflappable, just like his father. Even when he'd been a very young boy, Imogen had quickly realised that he wouldn't be one to show his emotions. Yet, lately, he couldn't look at her or speak, without his eyes filling with tears and his hand reaching for hers. It was the one sign that told her exactly how bad things had become and how important it was that she should tell them the truth. Even though it was a truth she'd never wanted to give.

Moving against the pillows to make herself more comfortable, Imogen felt the urge to cough and, in readiness of the pain that she knew would come, she held her arms tightly around her chest in a hug. It was an action that brought back a memory of that night she'd spent crawling through the garden when she'd thought her life was over. The night she'd been left for dead with her life hanging in the balance. Some would say she'd been spared, yet, in truth, she wished she'd died rather than living a life where she'd undergone one operation after another. Each operation had been intended to give her some normality. But the life she'd had was gone and now she'd become a recluse, both in her mind and in her body.

'Mum...' Hattie's timid, whispered voice came from just inside the door and, with a slow, but definite movement, Imogen turned towards her. 'It's me, Hattie. Are... are you okay?'

Tears filled Imogen's eyes as the relief of seeing her daughter again swept over her like a large, comforting blanket and, even though her vision was now blurred from crying, Imogen simply stared at Hattie and took in every detail of her face, her clothes and the shine of her hair. With a satisfied nod of her head, she watched the way Adam jumped up to greet his sister.

'Hattie, I'm so pleased you're here...' Adam said as he jumped up from his seat, scraped the chair legs across the floor and quickly threw an apology in his mother's direction. 'I was so worried you wouldn't make it.'

'Well... I would have come over last night, if only you'd let me...' Hattie's voice sang out in a way that sounded light and overly jolly, which Imogen knew to be false. It was her daughter's way of masking how she really felt, but, still, she felt pleased that at least two of her children were together and that, for now, the feud between them appeared to be over.

'Hattie,' she eventually whispered more breathlessly than normal. 'Let me see you.' Looking longingly towards her, Imogen held out her hand and, even though her grip was weak, she took pleasure in feeling her daughter's fingers intermingling with hers. The fact that she was here, in this room, meant the world to her, even though she'd known that, by bringing her back here, she was potentially putting her in danger. But, selfishly, she'd wanted nothing more than to see her just one more time. She knew that the victory would be small and short-lived given what she was about to say; it would shatter her children's hearts into a million tiny pieces. Their lives would change immeasurably and, after today, everything that had gone before would suddenly be different. The good family home they all thought they'd grown up in would take on a whole new meaning and every room would be tainted by the past.

With her hands shaking uncontrollably, Imogen let go of Hattie's hand and patted the side of the bed until Hattie did as she wanted and perched on its edge. 'I'm pleased you're here...' Looking into her daughter's eyes, she could see the way she was searching her own for answers, and wished wholeheartedly that she could change what had gone before. But, the truth was, she wouldn't have done anything differently. If she had, she wouldn't have had the many happy years with her family. The Christmases and the birthdays. And, yes, she'd had to put up with the preaching and the sermons that Gerald had given, but she'd loved her husband, and she couldn't have had one part of her life, not without the other. And now, in his absence, it was up to her to ask for their children's forgiveness.

Going over the words that she'd practised at least a million times, Imogen hoped she'd got them right. Although now that it was time to say them, she no longer knew where to start, and was already pre-empting the difficult questions that would surely follow.

'Hattie... where...' With her eyes flickering heavily with sleep, Imogen looked around the room and counted her flock. She had Hattie, Adam and even Louisa. But Luke was still missing and, without him, she knew that she couldn't begin. 'Where's Luke?' she finally managed to say. 'I... I need... Luke.'

'He messaged earlier. Said something about a box and that it had taken some finding and that he wouldn't be long.' Adam coughed and moved to sit by the window. 'You should know what he's like, Mum,' he sniffed with emotion. 'He'd be late for his own damn funeral... if he got the chance.'

'Adam?' Hattie muttered as she reached forward, picked up the water jug and poured her mother a drink. 'Here you go, sip this.'

'Hey, don't have a go at me,' Adam responded. 'He *would* be late, it's no secret. He's always late.'

'Luke... has... to be here,' Imogen whispered impatiently. She'd ignored Adam's comment about the funeral, knowing that hers would be next, and, true to form, she was absolutely sure that Luke would be late attending that too.

Patiently, she lay back against the pillows, but found herself twisting her hands together in anguish and then she took a corner of the bed sheet and turned it around and around until she could twist it no more. Alarmingly, her breathing suddenly slowed. Her eyes grew heavier, and she fought to keep them open, but she was determined not to start, not until Luke was there.

'Look, whatever it is you want to say, Mum, why don't you just start without him?' Hattie stood up, walked to Adam's side, and hooked an arm around his waist. 'You could catch him up later or... we could tell him for you.'

'No.' Imogen snapped. 'He... he has to be here. I need... for you all... to hear this together.' She then looked directly at Louisa who had begun to inch towards the door. 'Lou... this... I suppose this involves you too.'

'What involves Louisa?' Standing in the doorway with his feet spread wide apart and his hand resting on the door-frame, Luke sauntered in, and looked towards where Adam and Hattie stood, clinging together.

'I brought the tin, Mum, just like you asked. Although it wasn't where you said. I found it in your office, in a drawer, so I'm hoping I've brought the right one.' He walked to Imogen's side, where he lifted her hand in his and placed a gentle kiss against her darkened, bruised fingers.

The words were enough to make Imogen sit herself up against the pillows and, with a look of defiance, she took the tin in her hands and held it tightly against her chest. Then she looked down at the box and ran her fingers tentatively across its handle. 'It's the right tin,' she muttered, as her hand went to reach for the bedside cabinet. 'I need... my purse,' she said. 'Get me... my purse... there's a key. I need the key.'

Stepping forward, Hattie pulled open the bedside cabinet,

lifted her mother's large, leather purse out of her bag and passed it to her. With her hand on the leather, Imogen could remember a time when everything of importance had been kept in her purse and why she'd always chosen a big one, with multiple pockets and areas where her driving licence and credit cards sat. Nervously, with a long, shaking, spindly finger, she pulled open the wallet and pulled at the press-studded pocket.

'First... I never... meant to hurt you,' Imogen whispered to everyone in the room. 'You have to know...' She placed the purse back down on her knee and moved her hand slowly upward until she touched Luke's cheek. 'I really didn't...' She blinked repeatedly, tried to remember exactly what she should say and, more importantly, what order she should say it in. 'It wasn't...' She paused and looked around at her family, who were currently hanging on to every one of her words. 'It wasn't meant to hurt any of you.'

'Look, maybe I should go and...' Louisa shuffled past the bottom of the bed. She picked up the small bag of dirty washing and headed for the door. 'I'll leave you to it and I'll come back tomorrow.'

'No...' Imogen snapped, breathlessly. 'Louisa. I've said, this... this affects... you... too.' Imogen took in a deep, painful breath. 'I wish it didn't... but... it does.'

Pointing to the door, Imogen waited for Luke to close it. She knew that she only had one chance to speak. That time was running out fast and that whatever she said next would define her life forever.

'I didn't... know what he'd done. You have to believe me...' Imogen continued between long, painful gasps. 'He told me... they couldn't cope. The women... they could barely look after themselves. Some of them... they had other children... and I thought... we were helping them...' Pausing, Imogen looked from Hattie to Adam. 'And this—' she pointed to the machines that monitored her heart '—I got what I deserved...' Pulling at a tissue with hands that were covered in paper-thin skin, Imogen lifted the tissue up to her face and took a swipe at her tears.

'Is anyone getting any of this?' Luke grunted. 'Because I'm totally lost.' He leaned against the wall, shoulder-bumped Louisa and then looked at each of his siblings in turn. 'Mum, we're all a bit lost so... you know, you might want to spell it out.'

'They were young... they couldn't cope... your father... he said... it was God's will. That we were helping them...' Pulling an oxygen mask onto her face, Imogen sucked heavily on the air. She could feel that the words were being forced out of her in a desperate and sporadic manner. Her breathing had slowed even more than it had before and, with tension cutting into the atmosphere like a knife, she closed her eyes and tried to come up with the words she so urgently wanted to say.

'Mum. You're frightening me...' Hattie said as she spun around and looked to her brothers for support. 'Do you have any idea what's happening, because...'

With exhaustion overtaking her body, Imogen stared down at the bedsheets. She could no longer bear to look her children in the eye, knowing that what she was about to say would break their hearts. She pushed the small silver key she'd dug out of her purse and held tightly between her fingers into the lock of the box and quickly turned it.

'It's all in here,' she said, 'all the details, all the women, the truth and...' Breathing the oxygen in as deeply as she could, Imogen looked up at the bedside monitor where green, yellow and red lines made their way across the screen. When she looked down again, with eyes that were wide and fearful, she saw that the box was empty of all the documents she'd previously kept there. Her eyes shot from one of her children to the next and then to Louisa. Someone had been in her box, which meant that one of them already knew the truth.

'Hattie, take me home, I...' She grabbed at Hattie's hand, pulled her towards her, 'Promise me...' Pulling the oxygen mask off her face, Imogen threw back the bedcovers and, with a strength she didn't know she had, she tried to climb out of bed. Wires that had been attached to her body became detached and, as the alarms rang out and the nurses burst in through the door, Imogen let out a long, visceral scream.

21

NINE YEARS BEFORE – HATTIE

With her heart palpitating heavily in her chest, Hattie almost stumbled out of Griffin's car the moment it pulled up outside her house and it wasn't that she thought for a minute that Griff would treat her in the same way that Fraser had. She knew of old that he hadn't been the sort to push his advances and that two years before, when he'd previously kissed her, it had been him that had taken a step back and slowed the situation down. When she really thought about it, he had acted like the perfect gentleman almost to the point where she'd been disappointed that he hadn't taken things further and, every day since, she'd hoped it would happen again.

'Hey, what's the rush?' Pressing the key fob, Griff smiled as the car flashed its hazards.

Slowing her pace, Hattie leaned on the wall and smiled coyly to herself as she waited for him to approach. This was the night she'd waited for. The night Griff had once again come to her and, even though the situation hadn't been ideal, Hattie thought back to the way Louisa had said that, to get them together, they'd need a bit of a push and, deep inside her, Hattie wondered if Louisa had manufactured a little of what had happened that night, especially when, even though she'd looked as though she needed medical help, she'd insisted that Griff was called.

Closing her eyes, she tried to imagine what it would be like to invite Griff to her room, whether she could sneak him up and down without her parents knowing. Of course, she'd make sure that the room was cloaked in a soft, almost dim amber lighting, a bed that was covered in crisp, white sheets and, for a while, all she'd see would be Griffin's eyes looking into hers as he slowly made love to her. But then there'd be the creaking of the door and, before she knew it, her father would be stood in the doorway, glaring directly at her and, just like the sermon he'd delivered the week before, his voice would bellow loudly across the room.

'The Bible celebrates sex and love as a gift from God, but what you need to realise is that it never separates the two,' she could envision him saying. 'And I don't know a single bride who sat before me who didn't blush when I said it. I know it happens. You just have to make the right choices and only allow it when the moment is right and this, my girl, isn't the right moment. Not under my roof.'

Moving to the back door with Griff close behind her, Hattie stood on her tiptoes, reached up and slid her fingers into a hanging basket that had always hung by the door. Even though it was the middle of winter, it had been filled with artificial flowers – bright pink begonias that would have looked more natural in the summer, with the long lengths of trailing ivy that hung over the edge. It had been her father's answer to maintenance-free gardening. And even from a distance it looked wrong. 'I think it looks welcoming,' he'd once said. 'And it's the perfect hiding place for the back door key.'

'Dad's always put it up there for safekeeping,' she said to Griff. 'He didn't like Mum working at the front of the house and the back door being wide open, he said that just about anyone could get in,' Hattie explained. 'So he put the key up here, so none of us could lose it somewhere between a sports lesson and maths and, once we left school, none of us saw any reason to change things.' Turning into his arms, Hattie felt her stomach flutter with nerves. Her cheeks became flushed and her hand dropped onto his shoulder, where cheekily she pulled him towards her.

'Do you know what?' he mumbled the words while tenderly dropping butterfly kisses across her mouth and cheek. 'It makes perfect sense and I'm so glad he did.' Then, with a self-assured smile, he took a step back, fumbled the key out of her hand and slid it into the lock. 'Let's go in, 'cause—' he wrapped his arms around his own body '—I don't know about you, but I'm freezing.'

'Sorry we're going in through the back door.' She closed her eyes for a blink, took in a deep breath and stepped over the threshold, held a finger up to her lips and listened to the sounds that came from the house. There were the normal clanks and bangs that came from the pipes and the creaks of the roof beams, but the house itself and the sound of people were missing. Which wasn't a surprise. After driving home through the village, she'd noticed that the search was still ongoing, and the men were still walking the fields looking for Alice. The church hall windows had been brightly lit. Which was where her mother would be, making tea and coffee, and handing out biscuits to half the community, including her brothers who always seemed to congregate wherever there was food. And as for her father, he would be right where he should be – in the church and praying with anyone who needed him to stand by their side. Which meant that, right now, the house was empty of others and that she and Griff would be the only people in it.

'Griff,' she whispered, timidly. 'The kiss, was it real, because last time...' Her mouth turned towards him in a questioning smile, her breathing deepened, and she did all she could to keep her eyes fixed to his. 'Last time you left and...'

'Hey, last time was different. I was going back to university and to get into a relationship back then... well, it wouldn't have been fair, would it?' He shook his head decisively. 'You have no idea how difficult it was for me to walk away, to leave you behind. But now, now it's different.' He smiled, pouted, and his eyes sparkled with a seductive mischief. 'Besides, after being away from you for the last two years... I'm not doing that again, Hattie. Not ever...' Then, without any further encouragement, Griffin pulled her in close, teased her lips with his and flicked her hair away from her face before tipping her head backwards and, with a deep, meaningful passion, took her mouth with his.

'I love kissing you,' she whispered, 'In fact...' Without warning, his tongue began to flick in and out of her mouth and, unexpectedly, she heard herself moan as he moved her backwards, until she felt his body press against her to make his arousal more than apparent. With her heart beating wildly, she allowed his mouth to take hers.

'You're beautiful,' he whispered. 'I've thought about you every single day...' He caught his breath, looked down to where her breasts poked seductively out of her top and, with his lips pursed, blew slowly outward. 'Do you know how many times I've dreamed of this moment, of taking you as my own...' Catching her gaze, Hattie could see the sparkle in his eyes and, with shaking fingertips, she began to slowly unbutton his shirt. It was an act of provocation, one she knew would lead to sex and, seductively, she allowed her mouth to move across the firm, chiselled muscles of his chest.

Then, in a movement that was both fluid and intentional, Hattie felt her feet leave the floor. Her legs had somehow become hooked around Griffin's waist and, as though she weighed nothing at all, he carried her across the kitchen to the furthermost corner, where he lay her down on the banquette that stood to one side of the breakfast table. 'I want to make love to you, Hattie,' he whispered. 'You have no idea how much I want this.' Pressing his body against hers, Hattie felt the breath leave her body. She could feel his arousal, the way he moved against her and, with a gasp, she closed her eyes as his lips moved slowly down her neck and onto her breasts and the strong contours of his body pressed down heavily against her. Then, gently, he lifted himself up, hovered above her and searched her eyes with his.

'Are you sure?' he asked.

It was a simple question, one that Hattie hadn't expected, and she wasn't sure how to respond. Instead, she moved a hand downward, gave him a slight nod of her head and, in a single, silent answer to his question, pulled at the button of his jeans and then at the zip.

'I want you so much,' Griffin muttered between kisses. 'But only if it's right, Hattie. I can only do this if...' His hands suddenly skimmed her hips as his eyes once again locked with hers and, without saying a word, she gave him all the permission he needed, as her breathing accelerated and, instinctively, she felt herself arch towards him. The joggers she wore were hurriedly dragged out of the way and swiftly, with his mouth moving passionately with hers, he began to explore her body. His hands and fingers worked fervently against her until she could feel herself wanting to moan, scream and shout with pleasure. As her feelings heightened, his mouth pressed heavily against hers, and only when she'd surrendered herself to him completely did he momentarily pull away and look down at her with deep, sparkling eyes that shone back at her in the moonlight.

'Tell me you're sure,' he whispered through breaths that were fast and sporadic, and, with a final nod of her head, Hattie felt him push deep inside her and, with the slightest feeling of pain, she felt the rhythm of their bodies begin to move in unison. Griff's mouth took hers again and, with his hands under her hips, he pushed himself deeper until violent explosions tore through her and a long, surrendering moan escaped from her lips.

22

NINE YEARS BEFORE – HATTIE

With the heat of lovemaking coursing through her, Hattie felt the colour rise to her cheeks as she suddenly became aware that they were still lying on the banquette, that they were still partially naked and that, at any given moment, her kitchen could be full of both her parents and her brothers. It was a thought that made her quickly move out from beneath Griff and hurriedly reach for the joggers and, with her breaths still heavy and laboured, she pulled them back on.

'I'm just going to pop up and, you know, clean myself up.' Walking towards the small door that was hidden in the panels, Hattie smiled timidly as Griffin furrowed his brow. 'Don't worry, I don't walk through walls – it's a secret staircase. I can get right up to my room this way, without anyone seeing.' She smiled coyly. 'It's a staircase that the servants would have used, you know, back in the day.'

Fascinated, Griffin followed her to the door and looked upwards as it opened. 'Oh wow... and it leads straight into your room. How come no one showed me that before?' he asked with a comical raising of his eyebrows. 'But, then, it's probably best that they didn't, otherwise I'd have probably been sneaking up there.' Inquisitively, he took a step forward, scanned the old wooden steps where a thin strip of carpet could just be seen going up the middle of the treads. It was a piece of carpet surrounded by boxes that were covered in the years of dust accumulated on top of them.

'You'll have to excuse the clutter. It's where my mum puts all the things she no longer deems worthy of hanging in our wardrobes. She leaves it all here ready to send to a charity and, each time one of those plastic bags falls through the door, with a time and a date for collection, she comes here and fills it up.' Hattie leaned forward into another passionate kiss.

'I could kiss you all day,' she whispered as she took a step upward and began to weave in and out of the clutter that covered the stairs. Ever since she'd been a very small child, her mother had made piles that went up and down the staircase and now she watched in amusement as Griff followed her upwards. He took a step at a time and picked random items up as he went.

'I'm amazed that some of these boxes can balance.' He pulled his phone out of his pocket, brought up the torch and lit up the space to show how piles of books had been placed on each step, to make ledges wide enough to balance the boxes. 'What is it all?'

'Oh, it's nothing much, just junk, mainly,' Hattie said thoughtfully and pointed upward. 'Apart from that pile at the top. They're all the things father doesn't want in the office. He doesn't want them where our mother's clients could see them and none of us are allowed to touch them, not even our mother.' She laughed but meant every word. 'Adam once tried to go through it all when he was looking for tombola prizes.' And she could clearly remember the anger that had crossed her father's face and the constant lectures that had followed.

Cautiously, Hattie ran a finger under the Sellotape that went across the top of a box. After she'd made a small slit, she used her phone to light up the area and peered inside the box to see that it was full of files and paperwork and a small blue metal cash box. 'I don't even know why he even keeps it all,' she said as she glanced back at where Griffin watched her with interest. 'Do you know what, it's none of my business and I shouldn't be poking around. Dad would be furious.' Once again, she looked down at the rugby shirt and joggers and smiled. 'Look, I'm going to...' She pointed to the door at the top of the stairs. 'I'm going to get changed and make myself look more like me. So why don't you go back down to the kitchen and wait down there, just in case they all come back.' She took a step back towards him, pressed a firm, sensual kiss against his lips. 'Why don't you pour us a drink? There's probably a bottle of wine in the rack and, once I've changed, I'll come back down.'

In her bedroom, Hattie set to work wiping the make-up off her face before stripping off her clothes, throwing them into the bottom of the wardrobe and, in their place, she pulled on a pair of pale blue jeans, a fluffy white jumper and a pair of big, thick woollen socks.

'Hey,' she whispered as she stepped back into the kitchen. 'Did you pour the wine?'

Smiling, Griff gave her a hesitant nod. 'Well, I did pour a drink. But I poured some juice, one of us is driving,' he said with a laugh. 'And, if I'm not mistaken, our timing was perfect. I'm sure that I've just heard the front door and, by the sound of it, I'd say that one of your brothers came home.' He looked at the time on his phone and gave her a cheeky, playful smile. 'Let's just be happy he didn't come home about twenty minutes earlier.'

Blushing, Hattie picked up a tea towel, flicked him with it and then, after staring at him intently, she sauntered across the kitchen and, with a cheeky smile, pressed her body into his and began to tease his mouth with her tongue. 'What, aren't you ready for round two?'

Sliding his hands under the edge of her jumper, Griffin smiled. 'Seriously, Hattie.' He paused as he stared longingly into her eyes. 'Next time, it'll be somewhere special. I don't regret what just happened but you deserve to be made love to in the right environment, not—' he pointed to the banquette '—not on there.' Taking a step back he raked his hands through his hair but then reached forward, hooked his hand behind her neck and, with a passion she'd come to expect, began to move sensually against her, his mouth tracing a path along the nape of her neck as slowly he worked downwards until his mouth was close to her breast. It was enough to heighten her senses, and for her to respond eagerly until a sound echoed through the house and she felt forced to take a step backwards.

'Jesus Christ, Griff...' She laughed nervously, took in a deep breath, then looked down and away. 'There's someone in the house and there's nothing I want more than to go again but we have to slow down, for both of our sakes.'

'Hey. I get it. But, just for the record, I could literally spend a whole twenty-four hours making love to you and I'd still want more, I just...' Reaching out, Griffin smiled before brushing the hair away from her face. Deep inside, she could see the passion within. There was a hunger within him that took her by surprise and, as he moved forward, he once again began to tease her with his mouth, his tongue and his fingertips. Each touch was even more urgent than it had been before and, with his hands pulling her close to his body, Hattie could once again feel his arousal pressing against her.

'Oh boy, you really could go again, couldn't you,' she giggled, but, with a sharp look in the direction of the hallway, she shook her head. 'But we have to stop... If one of my brothers is home, then my parents, they won't be far behind... and the last thing I want is for them to catch us mid flow.'

Taking a step back, he flashed her a look of apology and held his hands up in the air, palms outward. 'I'm sorry, I...' He shook his head. 'I'm sorry, and of course you're right. You deserve better. You deserve to be made love to... and properly, but Hattie, promise me something?'

'What?'

'Promise me that it's just the two of us in this relationship.' He paused and gave her a coy, pensive look. 'The thought of you going out like you did tonight and all those other men...' He took a step backwards, closed his eyes as though he were trying to think of the words, 'The thought of them going anywhere near you, it kills me...'

Griffin's words caused an explosion to erupt in her mind and, in her temper, she stamped down the hallway, and made her way to the front of the house as she tried to comprehend what he'd just said. She wanted to ask him if he really believed that she was a prostitute and that she'd sold herself to others and, most of all, she wanted him to know he'd been her first. But now she felt the anger tear through her. She was more than embarrassed and, now, she couldn't find the words to explain.

'Do you really think I did that?' Making her way angrily down the hallway, Hattie looked in each of the rooms as she passed, listened intently for any sound that would tell her where her brother could be and, eventually, she took a step upwards and used the stairs as a platform. She wanted nothing more than to put some distance between her and Griff but felt an involuntary sob rise up from her stomach. 'I didn't. I wouldn't. I was going to tell you that, back at your house. I was going to explain how I'd ended up being there, but you didn't want to listen. You asked if it could wait and then, then you kissed me.' She knew that the words were falling from her mouth at speed, but she also knew that, if she didn't tell him the truth, she'd always regret it. 'And now, now I don't know whether you kissed me because you thought...' A sudden thought occurred. Had Griff only kissed her because he'd seen her as a sure thing? Had he seen her as an easy lay, as someone who'd give it up for money, or in his case for free? 'You need to ask Louisa what happened. Ask her about how she begged me to go with her and talked me into wearing those stupid damn clothes.' Sitting down on the step, Hattie let out a loud sob. She could feel her body trembling with annoyance as her stomach turned and her eyes filled with unshed tears. 'I was only there to watch her back. I had to drag her away if any of them looked nasty,' she whispered 'Well, I'll tell you now, Griffin Alexander, they all looked nasty, and I'd rather die than let any one of them go near me... and now...' She looked over his shoulder and at the front door. 'Now, I wish I hadn't let you near me too...'

'Hattie...'

Shuffling higher up the steps, Hattie buried her face in her hands. Griff's words had wounded her more than he'd ever know and, for a moment, she felt the urge to run to her mum. She wanted to tell her everything that had happened but knew she couldn't. Not while she was at the church, surrounded by members of the congregation. 'We're part of the church, a community,' her father had once told her. 'And the congregation, they look up to us. They expect us to show them the way and everything we do or say is listened to, analysed and, worst of all, it's what they judge us on. Which is why, no matter what happens behind closed doors, we keep it to ourselves. Do you hear me?' It had been just one of his rules. No matter what tensions were running high in the house. They were all expected to conduct themselves in a certain way in public, which included the way they dressed. It was a thought that made Hattie hurriedly look down at the clothes she now wore. They were a lot different to the ones she'd had on earlier but, still, she knew that her father wouldn't have liked them. He didn't like them to do anything that would have caused others to form a judgement or for them to give an opinion. Yet, on a night when the whole community had been out looking for a young girl who they presumed to be dead, she'd taken it upon herself to go out and walk the streets, dressed like a hooker.

Leaping up the stairs towards her, Griffin squeezed himself on the step beside her. Immediately, he pulled her into his arms and tenderly rocked her back and forth until her sobbing subsided. 'I'm so sorry. What I said, it all came out wrong. I believe you. Honestly.' With the lightest of fingers, he tipped her chin upward and gently touched his lips against hers. 'And I do want you,' he muttered. 'The truth is, Hattie, I've always wanted you, us, this. Jesus, I fell for you the first time I saw you, the first time I kissed you in my car and now...' He pulled away, touched the end of her nose with his finger. 'I don't want anyone else to go near you other than me, and yes I'm probably going to be one of the most jealous men you ever met, but it's only because...'

'Now then.' Adam's voice suddenly burst out of his mother's office, where he stood leaning against the door-jamb with a hint of amusement crossing his face. 'Can I just say, if you two finally got together, then thank the Lord 'cause Hattie, he never stops talking about you. Seriously, he drives me insane and at least now I know he'll shut up 'cause the last thing he'll ever want to do is share all the gory details with one of your brothers.'

23

NINE YEARS BEFORE – HATTIE

'Do you know what, Adam, for once you're absolutely right.' Giving Hattie a wide, disarming smile, and without caring who was watching, Griffin pressed another firm but tender kiss against her lips, then walked down the stairs to where her brother was standing. In a well-practised movement, they clutched hands and shoulder bumped in a form of hello.

'You frightened us both half to death,' Hattie snapped and, even though she'd known that he was in the house, she was still annoyed by the disturbance. Squinting, she turned her face away as Adam flicked a switch and brought a burst of light into the hallway. 'Didn't anyone ever tell you not to creep up on people? It's a wonder you didn't give me a bloody heart attack!' She noticed that Adam was still dressed in his outdoor coat with a bright red hoody poking out from beneath. His boots, however, were missing, which was how he'd unwittingly managed to sneak around the house without her hearing.

'Not as frightened as you're gonna be,' he laughed. 'Mum is gonna proper kick your arse if she finds out that you two have been up in your bedroom. You do know that, don't you?' He paused, unzipped his coat and, with an air of displeasure, strode back into his mother's office and poked at a pile of files that he'd carelessly spread out across the desk.

'Do you know what, Adam, you're absolutely right. If I had taken Griffin to my room, which, for your information, I didn't, I'd get a lecture on morality. Although this is the twenty first century and I am nineteen years old, not ten,' she threw in. 'Admittedly, they might not be pleased, but, ten minutes after the lecture started, it would have been forgotten. Unlike what she'll say to you when she sees this mess.' Hattie poked at the files. 'What the hell are you doing?'

'I'm looking for something,' he replied arrogantly. 'Isn't that obvious?' Picking one file up after the other, he flicked through its pages and, once satisfied that he'd seen enough, he tossed it to one side.

'But they're...' Taking one of the files, Hattie cast an eye across the details. 'What do you think you'll find in her client files?'

'My birth certificate.' He pulled open the filing cabinet and scooped another handful of files out of the drawer.

'What?' Glaring, Hattie wanted to tear the files out of his hands and push them back into the cabinet, but the look on his face was one of sheer determination. 'And why the hell do you think you'll find it in there?' As she spoke, a stack of the files tumbled sideways and teetered on the edge of the desk. After watching them balance for a good few minutes, Hattie made a grab for them, lifted them up and, unable to watch any longer, pushed them back into the filing cabinet.

'Hattie. It's important.' Heatedly, Adam tapped the desk with a long, pointed finger. 'Luke told me about Berni. He said she'd been here last night, and that our mum wrote this on the pad for her to read and I want to know what the hell she meant by it.' He used his finger to draw an imaginary line beneath the words their mother had written. 'It doesn't make sense, why the hell would she write this?'

'They're my children,' Hattie read the words out loud. Shook her head and stared up at the bookcases. 'I... I have no idea.' Scanning the shelves, she looked for her childhood memory box that had always stood on the top of the bookcase, yet, today, for some reason, the box was gone. Her stomach rolled without warning and Louisa's words exploded in her mind. *'Hattie, they're not the people you think they are. They have secrets too. Big secrets that would blow your world apart.'*

'I'm sure they're hiding something.' Adam was saying. 'It's something big and... reading that, it got me thinking. I've never seen my birth certificate and, do you know what, I want to see it.'

Sitting back, Hattie took a moment to think about what he was saying. It was true, their mother's words didn't make any sense and the only person who could explain them was her.

'Let me get this right,' Griffin suddenly chipped in. 'Your mum wrote something on a desk pad and you get the urge to search for a birth certificate?' He walked across, slipped an arm around Hattie's waist, and read the words. 'I don't get it, why would you do that?'

'Last night,' they both answered in unison. 'Berni was here, screaming and shouting about Alice and walking in and out of all the rooms, banging the doors as she went. Mum brought her in here, wrote that down and then offered to go and search with her for Alice.'

Nodding, Griffin smiled. 'It still doesn't make a reason to suddenly doubt your parentage. Think about it, your mum, she's a medical professional, right?'

'Yeah, of course she is,' Adam responded.

'Well then, if Berni was shouting her mouth off, your mum

would have used her medical knowledge to calm the situation down. She wrote something down on the pad, got Berni to walk towards her to concentrate on the words, which would have calmed her mood. When you think about it,' he said, 'it was a very clever tactic. She deflected the situation and, best of all, no one got hurt.' Turning, he flashed them both a satisfied look before he leaned forward, pulled the sheet of paper off the desk pad and tore it into pieces. 'There, now it's gone and you...' He pointed to Adam. 'You can go back to being you and Hattie, well...' He pouted and then winked seductively. 'Well, Hattie and I, we kind of have some unfinished business, Adam, so...' He rolled his eyes until Adam nodded in agreement.

'You're right, I need to get back to the search,' Adam said with a knowing smile. 'If I'm missed, Dad might take me to the church and make me repent at the altar.' He pointed to the front door, to the boots he'd dropped in the hallway. 'I'll just put those on and...' Kneeling on the doormat, he stared through the side-light windows. 'Jesus, what the hell's going on out there?'

'What?' Spinning on her heel, Hattie looked straight towards the front door, where she could see a long stream of blue flashing lights rushing past the house. It looked as though multiple police cars were being followed by an ambulance. All of them were screeching through the village at speed and disappearing into the distance.

'Adam... look...' Catching hold of his arm as the front door was flung open, Hattie held her breath as she saw the crowd walking towards her. 'They're coming this way.' She gasped and felt the acid immediately rise and fall in her throat. 'Do you think they found her?'

Rushing forward, Adam got to the gate, just as the first of the men stormed past with sombre faces, full of devastation. 'We found a body,' he shouted to Adam. 'Worst sight I ever saw in my life, but it wasn't Alice.' He shook his head, remorsefully. 'It was that mother of hers, Berni.' He raised his hand, lifted a thumb to his neck and moved it from one side of his throat to the other. 'Dead as a doornail, in the woods, beyond the river. She was well hidden, though, buried in the undergrowth.' He lifted a hand, drew a line from one side of his neck to the other. 'Looks like some bastard went and cut her throat.'

24

PRESENT DAY – DECEMBER 2023 – HATTIE

Leaving both Luke and Adam to sit with her mother, Hattie frantically made her way out of the room and through the sterile hospital corridors like a woman on a mission.

Seeing her mother had been a shock. The vibrant and glamourous woman she'd previously been had been reduced to a tiny skeletal frame. A woman who'd struggled to string more than a few words together, during a meeting that had left them all feeling confused and disillusioned. Not one of them had been able to decipher what she'd been trying to say, although the words she'd used had made Hattie fear the worst and, without a moment to lose, she set off for the house, determined to honour her mother's dying wish. She would make sure the house was ready for her to be taken home and, while doing that, she had every intention of finding the truth.

'What the hell were you playing at, Mum?' Hattie questioned as the tears sprang to her eyes. 'What were you trying to say and what the hell did you mean by it all?' She felt confused, bitter and annoyed. All the feelings she really didn't want to have, not at a time when her emotions were already bouncing around the walls.

Climbing into her car, Hattie took a final look up at the hospital, at the arrow slit windows as the words her mother had used spiralled around her mind. 'I didn't... know what he'd done... He told me... they couldn't cope... they could barely look after themselves...' And, worst of all, 'they had other children...' Each sentence on its own would have meant something to her mother, but saying them all out loud, all together, had come out like a jumbled mess until her mother had said, 'I got what I deserved...' These had been the words that had sent a chill running down Hattie's spine and her mind immediately flashed back to the night Alice disappeared and those three words she'd written on the desk pad. 'They're my children.'

Pulling up outside the house, Hattie could feel the palpitations in her chest increasing, and she stared up at the house, at the windows and at the door, and tried to fit all the pieces of the jigsaw together. Adam had once been convinced that they'd all been adopted and maybe they had, but there was no evidence to support that.

Slowly, Hattie pushed open the door and stepped inside, where she stood for a few moments, held her breath and, just as she had so many times in the past, she listened to the sounds of the house. The creaking pipes and the movement of roof beams had all been surprisingly soothing during the night. But now she was alone, the nerves and the panic returned, and, in an attempt to ward off a feeling that was becoming all-consuming, she felt a sudden urge to make her peace with the house and walked deliberately from room to room, checked inside and reassured herself that each room contained nothing that could possibly hurt her.

To Hattie's surprise, none of the rooms had looked much different, even though the dining room stood in darkness and had a thick layer of dust covering its surfaces. It looked as though time had been suspended. Just as it had looked the last time they'd all sat down and eaten as a family. Of course, the dirty plates had been taken away. But the salt and pepper pot mills still stood central to the table, the dinner mats were still in the same places they had been and a dark brown stain still marked the tablecloth, where Adam had tipped his plate and the gravy had spilled off its edge. Hattie ran a single finger across the cloth that would never be white again before turning her attention to the photographs that stood on the sideboard. Smiling, she picked up an image of their last family Christmas and then the picture of them all standing side by side at a wedding. It had been a time when they'd been a happy family of five. Although, after what her mother had just said, Hattie wondered if they'd ever been happy, or even a real family.

Pushing the doubt out of her mind, Hattie refused to think about anything other than getting the house clean and ready. No matter what it took, she intended to bring her mother home and, once she had, only then would she think about what to do next.

Determined to make a start, Hattie made her way up the stairs and held her hand to her parents' bedroom door. For a moment, she tried imagining that her parents were home. That they were inside the room, sleeping. Or that they'd simply gone to the church where her father would be practising his sermon. On days like today, it would have been normal for their mother to go with him. She'd often arrange the flowers to decorate the alter or, with the help of one or two of the villagers, she'd sit in the church hall and polish the silver, while eating cake and drinking far too much coffee and then moaning incessantly about the diet she'd have to go on later. It was a thought that made Hattie smile, until she remembered the truth. Her parents were no longer here. Her father was dead, her mother was about to die, and the house needed cleaning.

Digging through the airing cupboard, Hattie sniffed the air. It had that same odd smell that had emanated from her own bedsheets the night before and, with no wish to make her mother a bed that smelt the same, she chose a selection of bedding before going back to her own room and stripping the bedding. 'We'll have all of this smelling better for tonight.' She gave herself a determined nod of her head, and set off down the stairs with every intention of throwing the bedding into the washing machine until a noise on the driveway caught her attention.

Perching on the half landing, Hattie watched Finn's car pull into the driveway and, without thought, she jumped up, opened the window and sat patiently watching in the hope she'd catch his attention. But, from the look of the gesticulating arm movements that Hattie could see through the front windscreen, she could see that he wasn't alone and that an argument was brewing.

'I don't have to explain myself,' Finn shouted as he jumped out of the car wearing a smart, pin-striped suit that was covered with a dark blue overcoat. For a while, he stood and took a moment of contemplation, before walking to the passenger door and, with a reluctant glare, he swung the door open and lifted Sophie up and into his arms. 'It's my job, Sophie. I often have to go out, patients need to see me.'

'I know, but...' Grabbing at her handbag, Sophie kept one eye on the car. 'Finn, what about Noah?'

'I'm going to go back for him, just as soon as I've got you indoors,' Finn said as he looked up, caught Hattie's eye, and gave her a cautious but affectionate smile. 'In fact...' He placed

Sophie down on the footpath, right next to the door. 'I'm sure you could hop from here, I don't think it's so bad that you need carrying everywhere, so I'm going to get Noah.'

Jumping backwards and out of sight, Hattie watched the way Finn walked back to the car and then, in direct contrast to the way he'd lifted Sophie, he reached into the back seat and with strong, gentle arms, lifted a sleeping Noah out of his car seat and close to his body. Even from a distance, Hattie could see the unconditional look of affection that crossed his face and the soft, gentle kiss he pressed down on Noah's forehead.

Hattie took in a deep breath and, for the blink of an eye, she wished that she and Finn had stood a chance. He'd been her first love. The one that had got away and, even though at the time he'd probably seen it as the great escape, she still wondered how her life would have panned out, if he'd been in it.

Picking the bedding back up off the stairs, Hattie headed toward the kitchen. It was the one room she'd purposely avoided and, with her breath caught in her chest, she hovered outside as the memory of finding her father's body lying on the floor flashed before her. It was a nightmare she knew she had to live through, the only way of pushing it out of her mind was to take control and, with a deep intake of breath, she pushed the door open.

Two hours later, Hattie felt satisfied that the cupboards were clean, the crockery that had been in the cupboards gathering dust had all been stacked in the dishwasher, and the bedding she'd washed earlier had now entered the drying stage of the wash cycle, which filled the kitchen with the scent of petals and roses. The tablecloth that had been strewn across the dining room table had been stripped off and, with no wish to try and get the gravy stain out, she'd walked it to the dustbin and thrown it inside.

It was only then that she sank onto the kitchen floor and began the arduous task of scrubbing the tiles while doing all she could to avoid kneeling on the exact spot where her father had died. As she scrubbed, it seemed as though every emotion erupted from her. Gut-wrenching sobs were followed by angry bursts of energy.

'Who killed you?' she yelled out as another sob caught in her throat and, in her temper, she flung the wet, soapy cloth across the room. 'Who the hell did it and damn you, why don't we have any answers?' Pushing herself up, Hattie crawled across the tiles, where she retrieved the cloth before throwing it back in the opposite direction to land in the bucket, causing bleach water to slop up and over the side.

For years she'd thought that their attack could have been her fault, yet the more she found out the more she steered away from that theory. While sat with her back against the kitchen cupboards, Hattie stared across the fields to where the trees stood on the hillside. It was the place where Berni had died, where she'd been murdered and, for some reason, she couldn't get out of her mind the thought that somehow Berni and her parents were linked. Both were unsolved, both happened during the same week and, to this day, no one could explain what had happened to either.

They were the same questions that had always been there. Festering and unanswered and it was this thought that made Hattie close her eyes and pray for a small semblance of peace. For a few short moments she thought she'd found that sanctum, that inner peace she craved so badly. Until the church bells began to toll... and Hattie knew that the only way she'd ever escape the past would be to find out what happened to her parents, even if it was a truth she didn't want to hear.

25

NINE YEARS BEFORE – HATTIE

Holding back the tears, Hattie grabbed Griffin's hand, hooked her fingers through his and trudged behind the long line of people who made their way down the narrow, uneven footpath that led to the Dog and Duck. The pub was the centre of the village, but tonight it suddenly looked a little too jolly with its array of brightly coloured Christmas decorations that had been hung up to decorate the exterior.

Berni had been murdered, the whole village was in shock and, while looking at the illuminated LED lights through tear-filled eyes, Hattie allowed the reality of the situation to fill her mind. The search was over, at least for tonight. The whole area was now a crime scene, Alice was still missing and most of the villagers had congregated in small groups along the road. It was more than obvious that they had a need to be together and either stood deep in their own thoughts, or with others busy consoling the person who stood alongside them.

From where they stood, the crowd looked across the fields and towards the river, where, in the distance, the tree-line glowed with blue flashing lights, leaving it to look both eerie and unwelcoming. Especially when all of the trees stood in what looked like an almost perfect row. They reminded Hattie of soldiers in a film, all stood on the brink of a hill, waiting to stampede and, because the tree-line had always been an image she'd associated with home, she tried to wipe the thought from her mind that, at some point in the last few hours, it had been a place of evil, and a woman had been brutally murdered. Which meant that, without a doubt, she'd never be able to look at the ridge or the tree-line in the same way again and that they'd always be a permanent reminder of what had happened there.

With a lump in her throat, Hattie thought about her father and the way he'd tried to protect her from what the men had been forced to witness. She'd always thought of him as overbearing and strict, especially as she'd got older, but now she felt grateful for the protection he gave, and she felt guilty that he'd specifically asked her to stay indoors. And she hadn't. She owed him an apology, but she closed her eyes in the knowledge that the apology would almost certainly have to wait. For the next few weeks, her father would be totally consumed. His attention would be diverted and his time at home would be limited. On occasions like this, and for the foreseeable future, he'd belong to the community. And rightly so. It was his job to bring the people together. To create an atmosphere that was safe and loving. And, most of all, he had a funeral to conduct.

Squeezing between small groups of people who were congregating along the roadside, and with an anxiety growing inside her, Hattie's eyes darted from one face to the other. There were a few people she knew, but most of them she didn't recognise. With the heat of Griff's hand travelling up her arm, she kept one eye on Adam, then through the corner of her eye she spotted the gangly frame of Luke heading towards them.

'Luke, why aren't you with Dad?' Draping an arm lovingly

around her brother's shoulders, she quickly pulled him towards her. 'I take it you've heard.'

'Someone killed her, Hattie.'

As he looked up, Hattie could see the fear in his eyes. The tormented look that could only come from a child who didn't understand. A child that was quickly growing into a man, right before her eyes. Yet still not quite old enough that she didn't have to worry about him.

'Are you okay?' she asked him, as she nervously looked over her shoulder. 'You don't look okay, in fact...' She thought about returning to the house, to the safety she felt there, and taking Luke with her. 'Luke, I want you to stay close. The person who killed her, they could still be in the area.' She looked at the faces that surrounded her in the crowd. Then, up to Griff, who leaned forward and pressed a kiss against her forehead. 'I'm scared,' she muttered. 'What if it's someone we know?'

With a knowing look, Adam stepped forward and nodded in Griff's direction. 'Look after her,' he said in a voice that had two meanings and Hattie knew that Adam wasn't simply talking about tonight, or even just the next ten minutes. Even though he was her younger brother by a whole two years, he was looking out for her and giving Griffin a warning.

Standing on his tiptoes, Adam studiously searched the crowd. 'Mum and the others... did someone say that they were still at the church hall? Do you... do you think they're okay, you know, being alone?' He turned and began to walk through the crowd. 'I'm going to take a walk up there, keep an eye on them and maybe walk Mum home,' he shouted over his shoulder, 'so if you two have that unfinished business to take care of—' he lifted his phone, checked the time '—I'd say you have about an hour to get it all sorted.'

With a half-hearted smile, Hattie turned to Griff in the hope he'd agree. She wanted nothing more than to walk them back to the house, but took a step back and watched quizzically as he pulled a hand full of the torn-up desk pad pages out of his pocket and threw them in the roadside bin.

26

NINE YEARS BEFORE – HATTIE

With rain clouds covering the sky in a dark grey layer, Hattie noticed that, even though it was only just after midday, the streetlights were already illuminating the pavement where she'd been stood by the roadside with three large carrier bags at her feet for the past ten minutes, mentally going through the shopping list her mother had given her, while waiting for her father to come and collect her.

'Bread, tick. Ham, cheese, tuna, tick, tick, tick. Milk, butter, crisps, tick.' The items were intended to make a sombre, but practical, buffet for those who had offered to resume the search for Alice. Most of which were at the community centre waiting to set off, just as soon as the police allowed it. Until then, they all hovered around, gossiped and came up with theories as to what might have happened to her and to Berni.

Standing with her umbrella in one hand, Hattie kept her eyes on a road that was normally bustling with people. Instead, even the shops looked as though they were ready to shut down and, with Berni's killer still at large, most of the shopkeepers were withdrawn and hadn't really wanted to chat. The friendly atmosphere that Hattie normally enjoyed had dissipated and, in its place, was a dark and eerie feeling that she suspected wouldn't go away, not until Alice was found and her mother's murderer was put behind bars.

With the thought of a killer being in the community, Hattie's father had insisted on driving her into the village and, even though she'd insisted that she'd be fine to walk home alone, he'd told her to stand and wait for him in a well-lit area, until he arrived.

Pushing her free hand deeper into the pocket of her thick winter coat, Hattie tried to stop herself from shivering. The rain continued to drizzle and the temperature had dropped significantly since the night before and was now at an all-time low.

With the darkness pulling in unusually early, the only real light was coming from the row of shops that stood next to the health centre. Each of the shops were decorated with brightly coloured Christmas lights and the sound of carols could be heard each time a door was opened to send a forced joviality out and onto the street outside.

Sighing, Hattie closed her eyes as, in the distance, the church bells tolled. She knew that, even though Christmas was the biggest event in the Christian calendar, this year it would feel very different within this community. Without a doubt, a murder would mean that even the church would dial down the festivities, especially when Hattie knew that her father would be taking care of the funeral. Even though Berni had been loathed by many for the lifestyle she chose, Hattie could imagine that the community would turn out on mass for a funeral that would become tainted by a continuous police presence until the killer was caught.

Tipping her head to one side, Hattie watched the comings and goings of the few pedestrians that were still venturing along the street. One man stood outside the fruit and veg shop, studying a list he held in his hand. Another juggled bags with a heavy box of beers and then, from inside the pharmacy, came a large, rotund woman who was dressed for the weather. She wore a long, wool coat that had been buttoned up the front and what looked like a home-knitted woollen scarf that circled her neck. A hat with a fur edge had been pulled down as far as it would go and, even though the woman was practically camouflaged, Hattie thought there was something familiar about her. She watched the way she pushed a bag full of medication into her shopping bag and then held her hand to her chest.

'Mrs Alexander?' Hattie shouted. 'Frieda, is that you?' Hattie stumbled over the words. She'd met Griff's gran on a number of occasions at the church and wanted to speak to her, but she didn't want to annoy her father by making him wait. 'I thought it was you,' Hattie said with a nervous half-smile. 'I was just wondering, Louisa, is she okay? It's just...' she rambled. 'I've been trying to call her all day and she hasn't answered... and... Frieda, are you okay?' Taking a closer look at the older lady, Hattie noticed how pallid her face had turned. She looked annoyed, flustered and ready to start ranting.

'Ah, so it was you that was sat in the car with my boy, was it?' Frieda demanded in her soft Irish accent. 'Well, let me tell you now. You ought to be damn well ashamed of yourself, letting your friend go out dressed like that and the two of you doing what you did. I'm amazed she survived, she was in a right bloody state,' Frieda scalded. 'It could take her a while before she recovers.'

Shocked by Frieda's tone, Hattie took a step backwards. She felt embarrassed that Frieda had chastised her, right there in the middle of the street and, with a cautious turn of her head, Hattie looked around and hoped that her father hadn't miraculously appeared and heard the berating. Although, if she'd really thought about it, she should have expected the lash of Frieda's tongue and, while she wished for the ground to open up and swallow her whole, she looked down at the floor and tried to think of what she could say in her defence.

Lifting her hand out of her pocket, Hattie held it against her chest and looked directly into Frieda's eyes. 'I'm sorry that we troubled you last night, we didn't know where else to take her, but Griffin, he said you'd been a nurse and...' She looked down and away, and automatically her hand went into her pocket where she dug around in search of a tissue. 'We just knew you'd be the best person to look after her...' Again, she paused, and swallowed. 'It won't happen again,' she said with a half-smile. 'I promise.'

'I should think not,' Frieda snapped in response, but a look of discomfort showed all over her face. 'Now, I have a hospital appointment to get to, so...' She pulled the cuff of her winter coat upward, checked her watch. 'I need to get off.'

Pulling her hand back out of her pocket, Hattie looked up at the sky. The rain had stopped, and the umbrella was now something she'd begun to twizzle around between her fingers. 'If you're going out,' Hattie asked. 'Do you want me to go over and sit with Louisa? I could keep her company, you know, until you get back?'

'There's no need,' Frieda said sternly. 'She's absolutely fine. She needs sleep and rest, and most of all she needs some good home-cooked food and a little tender loving care. Something she obviously hasn't had since her parents passed on.'

Catching her breath, Hattie took another step back. She hadn't expected Frieda's continued wrath, and even though she didn't really blame her she looked over her shoulder in hope of a fast escape. Everything Frieda had said was true. Louisa did need someone to care for her. She needed someone to guide her and, even though she was already classed as an adult, she'd been alone for almost half of her teenage years, which hadn't helped with her knowing what was right and what was wrong.

Hearing her phone bleep repeatedly in her pocket, Hattie pulled it out and looked down at the screen to see a message from her father. He'd already left home and Hattie felt the need to make amends with Frieda before his arrival.

'Frieda, my dad, he's on his way to pick me up...' She pushed the umbrella into her bag, gave Frieda what she hoped would look like a genuine smile. 'If you like, I could ask him to drop you off at the hospital. It isn't that far, he really wouldn't mind, and, as I said earlier, I could go and sit with Lou and keep her company while you're at your appointment.'

Shaking her head defiantly, and with a hand held tightly to her chest, Frieda began to make her way along the pavement. 'Hattie, mark my words,' she snapped, 'it'd do you good to leave well be.'

'But...'

'Hattie. For goodness' sake. I've told you to leave it... Louisa is fine, she isn't alone.'

27

NINE YEARS BEFORE – LOUISA

Stirring from a deep, troubled sleep, Louisa winced with a pain that shot through her body in spasms and a pressure that pressed down on her shoulders and made every breath feel unbearable. For a few moments, she tried to hold her breath and she prayed for the pain to stop, for her life to jump backwards in time to a place where she still had a mother and a father who loved her.

Moving onto her side as slowly as she could, Louisa yelled out as her calf contracted and her leg shot out in a fast and involuntary movement. As quickly as she could, she straightened her toes and pointed them outward, holding her body taught. Pressing her face into the pillow, she dulled a scream and, with sleep doing all it could to overwhelm her, she tried to prise her eyes open, but couldn't. Her eyes felt heavy, painful and, with a furrowed brow, she drifted in and out of what had happened the night before. One memory blended into another. Everything had become a blur and now her most prominent memory had been Hattie's terrified voice that repeatedly infiltrated her mind with the same words, over and over, until finally there had been nothing, but darkness.

With short, sporadic breaths, Louisa suddenly felt the need to cough. Her throat wouldn't clear, and her mouth and lips were dry and tightening. Even the smallest breath made her throat burn with a ferocity she hadn't previously known and, while trying to ease the pain, she held her chest tightly in a hug and moved one limb at a time until she managed to identify each new ache, but quickly realised that each of her limbs hurt with a deeper intensity than the one she'd checked before. Eventually, she managed to find a position where only the dull, incessant cramping that rolled around in the pit of her stomach continued.

Allowing her mind to drift back into sleep, she allowed the darkness to surround her. It took over her body with a feeling of tranquillity that took away all the pain. And, for a short while, all of her plans and worries about who she was and how she came to be here dissipated. Until just a few minutes later when her eyes flew open, and she felt the terror within her. Memories of the night before hitting her like a tsunami, the waves landing with force. A million regrets were followed by the dread of repercussions and, in her panic, she tried to work out whether or not she'd made enough money and whether today she'd be able to pay Fraser off and get him out of her life, forever.

Moving her head from side to side, Louisa tried to search the room. It was dark and gloomy and, through tired, unfocused eyes, she could just about see the shape of a door at the bottom of the bed. Through it she could see the last remnants of daylight brightening up the room and could just make out the edge of a sink, the shiny stainless-steel of a shower and, to her left, a pair of heavy dark grey curtains that shrouded what looked like a window.

From nowhere, the coughing once again erupted and she tried to lift a hand to cover her mouth. It ought to have been a simple action, one that should have taken barely any effort. But even the smallest, insignificant movement seemed to take more of her strength than she wanted to give and she allowed her hand to flop against the edge of the bedding where her fingers slowly began to caress its surface and a congratulatory smile crossed her face as she suddenly realised where she was. She recalled the way she'd convinced Hattie to phone Griffin and how, the moment he'd arrived at the scene, he'd known exactly what to do and had got her here, to the safety of his gran's house.

Smiling inwardly, she could still see the way Frieda had taken her in and helped her undress. She'd hovered over her while she'd stepped into the soft, oversized pyjamas and, overwhelmed by kindness, Louisa had found herself sobbing into Frieda's welcoming arms. 'There, there, my child,' Frieda had whispered. 'You cry if it helps and, once you're done crying, I've got some homemade chicken noodle soup warming up on the stove, that'll make you feel better. One bowl of that and a warm bed will help you no end, at least for tonight.' She'd placed a hand on the top of each of Louisa's arms and vigorously rubbed them up and down. 'You're freezing and we need to get you warmed up, don't we?'

Sinking into the tender loving care that Frieda gave, Louisa realised how much she'd craved that kind of parental love and, even though being in this house had brought on a kaleidoscope of emotions, she'd gravitated towards the woman who helped her. Even when sleep had constantly pulled at her, she'd kept hold of Frieda's hand and, with a contentment she hadn't felt for a very long time, slipped into a dream where memories of her childhood came flooding back. She could see the birthday cakes, the candles she'd blown out, and the numerous gifts she'd opened. 'If she wants it, she can have it,' her mother had often said, much to her father's disapproval. With deep, contented breaths, Louisa had turned in her bed, only to find that the happy memories could easily flip to the bad ones and, as her eyes closed and her mind began to wander, her body began to thrash around as somewhere in the depths of her mind she'd watched her world fall apart. Suddenly, she was back there, in that house with her aunt and uncle stood by her side, listening to the police tell her that her parents were dead. 'For reasons we can't yet explain, your parents' car left the road and I'm afraid that, by the time the paramedics got to them, there was absolutely nothing they could do,' the policeman had said with a solemn look on his face. The days had turned into weeks of devastation and, in her anger, Louisa could clearly remember the way she'd felt. To her, her parents had got their comeuppance. Especially after the admissions they'd made, which had proved to her that her whole life had been a lie. And, for a brief moment, she'd felt pleased that they'd gone.

'You have to realise, we were desperate for a child,' her mother had said. 'And now that you're sixteen, you need to know the truth.' Sitting in the armchair at the opposite end of the room with her arms crossed defensively across her chest, Louisa's mother had told her how they'd adopted her. 'You were just a baby and your mother, she was young, far too young to cope. She was a girl from the church and your uncle Gerald, he arranged it all.'

'Frieda...' Sitting up abruptly, Louisa screamed out Frieda's name but, as she did, her lips tightened and cracked and the silence that filled the rest of the house was suddenly interrupted by a shrill tone she couldn't ignore. The sound of the level crossing was something she should have expected. They stood just a few feet away from the house, but still felt the vibration.

Holding on to the bed Louisa pushed her fingernails firmly into the mattress and closed her eyes, waiting for the moment to pass.

'It's okay, don't panic. I'm here...' A soft, husky voice came from the passage, and Louisa flicked her eyes open as a familiar-looking woman stepped out of the darkness and into the room. She was tall, thin, with long dark hair that hung limply around her shoulders.

'Are you...' Throwing the woman what she hoped would be a welcoming smile, Louisa felt her stomach turn with a mixture of shock and excitement as she realised that the plan she'd begun to put in place the moment she'd met Griffin Alexander and realised who he was had worked. 'Oh my God. You're Mary, aren't you?'

Giving Louisa a questioning look, the woman walked to her bedside and held a hand up to Louisa's forehead before lifting a glass up from the bedside unit. 'Yes, I'm Mary and you... you need to drink plenty of water, you're still a bit warm.'

Smiling, even though there was a glass being wiggled around in front of her face, Louisa couldn't look at anything else apart from the woman. Her face was pinched, her cheek bones accentuated and the oversized clothes she wore shrouded most of her body. 'Do you know who I am?' Louisa asked, hopefully.

'Sure, Mum told me. You're Louisa and, for some reason, my son brought you here to be looked after.' She paused, walked to the window and pulled back the curtains, where, even though the day was fast turning into night, there was still enough light to brighten the room and for Louisa to see the woman more clearly. 'And it's probably a good job he did, you weren't in a good way last night,' Mary continued. 'You were delusional when you first got here, but Mum and I, we looked after you,' she said with a wry, cynical smile.

'You're... you're Griffin's mum?' It was a question that had suddenly fallen out of Louisa's mouth and, even though it had always been something she'd suspected, she felt shocked by the woman's sudden admission.

'Sure I am. Do you know each other well?' she asked.

Louisa thought carefully about her response. She didn't want to give the wrong impression and, slowly, she took the water glass that Mary had offered. 'We have mutual friends and Griffin, he's always kind and I knew he was training to be a doctor, which is why I got my cousin to call him.'

'Well, I'm pleased you thought of him, he's always been a good lad,' Mary continued, while anxiously lifting a hand to push her hair back and away from her face. 'Although his upbringing, it has nothing to do with me. He's lived with my mum for most of his life... 'cause...' She looked down and away and began to scratch at her arms. 'Well, I wasn't the best role model when he was younger and... he was better off without me, wasn't he?'

Overwhelmed by emotion, Louisa choked back a sob. Her eyes went up and down Mary's body and became fixed on the deep red puckered skin that went across both of her wrists. The scars that had become more visible as Mary had lifted her arm, as had the track marks that had previously been hidden by her sleeves.

'Frieda's gone to Friarage. She thinks you've got a water infection, which is why she got you to pee in a jug. She's going to go and see one of the doctors she knows,' Mary said with a smile. 'She'll pretend that the water sample is hers and he'll give her some antibiotics and then... we'll get you better in no time.' Running the nails of one hand up and down her arm, Mary bit down on her lip, thoughtfully. 'I'm under strict orders,' she said, 'to get you some more soup.' She took in a deep breath. 'I have to do it the minute you wake up, so...'

Slouching back against the pillows, Louisa concentrated on breathing out through her mouth. Her throat still hurt, she could barely swallow, and her lips were dry, cracked and painful. 'Please,' she begged. 'Don't go. I... could I have some more water?' It was all she could think to say, to keep Mary in the room, and gratefully she watched as Mary walked back towards her and perched on the edge of her bed.

Leaning as far forward as she dared, Louisa held the glass tightly in her hand and pressed it against her lips without drinking. The other hand gripped Mary's like a vice. 'I knew that if I came here, to this house, I knew I'd find you,' she said as she tentatively took a sip of the water. 'I've looked for you for years, and...'

'What are you talking about?' Mary shouted as she jumped up from the bed. The glass was dropped, the sound of it breaking filled the room and a look of terror crossed her face. 'Who the hell are you?'

'Please... I didn't mean to...' Biting down on her lip, Louisa felt her anxiety rise. She'd waited for this moment since she'd seen Mary Alexander's name emblazoned on her birth certificate. The birth father's name had been missing and, with nothing else to go on, she'd been at a loss until Griffin Alexander had moved into the area. After finding out a little about his family and upbringing, she'd made it her mission to get to know him more.

'Please. Please come back. I'm Louisa, or Lottie as you'd called me. I think I'm your daughter...'

28

PRESENT DAY – DECEMBER 2023 – HATTIE

With frost crunching beneath her feet, Hattie made her way slowly down the garden path with tiny, tentative steps. It was still dark; the sun hadn't risen yet and she was fearful of making any noise. She looked up at the windows at the back of the house where her brothers had only just gone to their beds after a long, painful night where all three of them had made tea, stared at walls, and tried to come to terms with the fact that their mother had finally passed away.

Then, in the early hours Hattie had finally found the energy to climb the stairs but had tossed and turned for what was left of the night and, eventually, she'd made her way back down before dawn, where she'd made coffee and stared into the darkness until the sun had been just about to rise.

Now, for the first time in years, with every emotion flying around in her mind, she stood, leaning against the drystone wall at the bottom of the garden. The breeze blew in her face, and she held her coffee mug tightly in her hands as tears of both guilt and relief began to roll down her cheeks while, more than anything else, she wanted to see the sunrise, the golden glow that would give her the promise of morning, of a new day and a fresh start and she took a moment to savour the peace that only the countryside could bring. Until, in the distance, she spotted the area where the perpendicular tree-line stood. It was the same tree-line she'd always associated with home, the one you could see as you drove through the valley and into the village, yet, since Berni had been murdered there, she hadn't been able to look at the trees with the same fondness that she'd had for them before.

Resting her coffee mug on the wall, Hattie jumped up to sit beside it and, with her eyes closed, she tried to concentrate on the sound of the river as it barrelled down the valley in the distance. She knew that the church bells would toll again soon, as the clock reached the top of the hour, and she braced herself in readiness for them ringing.

'I should have been there,' Hattie whispered through tightly clenched teeth. 'I should have been with you, I should have stayed at the hospital.' For some reason, she focused on the wishing well as though by talking to it and saying the words out loud, her mother would hear her. 'But instead,' she continued, 'I made excuses, and I came back to this house and made a pretence that, one of these days, they'd bring you home.' She picked up her coffee mug and slowly sipped at the contents. 'And I should have known that...' She paused and sobbed. 'I should have realised that it would be a wish too many.' Picking up a small stone, she threw it at the wishing well and heard it plop into the water deep below. 'I should have wished, and prayed and arghhhhh... I'd have even gone to the church if I'd thought it would've helped.'

Shaking her head, she looked down at the wall and traced the space between the boulders with her finger as a loud, distinct sob left her throat and the tears that dropped down her face were wiped on her sleeve as she continued to chastise herself. 'Who are you kidding, you left because you didn't want to be there. You couldn't do it, all that hand holding and waiting.' Hattie knew that it was true, and that the thought and guilt would stay with her for a very long time. The truth was that she'd had to get out of there, she'd had to try and work out what her mother was wanting to tell them and inside her the curiosity had burned and she'd known that the box was the key. Whatever documents had been in there were now gone and she had to find out why.

'You scared me, Mum,' she muttered. 'I wasn't sure what you were going to say and...' She swallowed hard. 'I was just sure that it wouldn't have been something I really wanted to hear.' She paused, but knew that deep down she'd been most fearful of sitting there, and waiting, just in case her mother had opened her eyes and had finally revealed her truth and, even though Louisa had assured her that the attack couldn't have been her fault, or Fraser, she still hoped that her mother had never found out what she'd done. To find out now that she'd always known would fill her with guilt and shame and, remorsefully, Hattie had hoped that, if her mother had known, she'd remain unconscious for just long enough to take her secret with her.

Closing her eyes against the breeze, Hattie could feel the soreness of her eyelids. They felt raw and full of gravel each time she dabbed at them with a tissue, or the sleeve of her top. 'I should go to the church, shouldn't I?' she whispered to the wishing well. 'I should go to Dad's grave and tell him what happened, although...' She looked up at a sky where the clouds had turned a gunmetal grey and the chance of a picturesque sunrise was looking less likely. 'You're already up there, with him, which means he should already know.' She held her hands out in front of her, twisted her fingers tightly together, sighed and lay back against the wall.

Then, with her thoughts being broken into, Hattie heard the turn of a lock, the click of a door and the hurried patter of feet that flew across the path towards her.

'Jasper, noooooo,' was the yell that followed the three-second jumble of noise. 'I'm sorry, I'm so, so sorry...' The shout was enough to make Hattie quickly move to one side and spin to look at where Sophie was frantically hopping across the path, with Jasper's lead being waved around in the air.

'I meant to put him on the lead and... Jasper don't do this to me... come here!'

The crash of ceramic hitting the concrete path made Hattie freeze on the spot. The warmth of the leftover coffee soaked into her trouser leg and a loud list of profanities fell out of her mouth. 'Ouch... You need to keep your damn dog under control.' She glared at where Sophie stood with a look of horror all over her face and immediately felt sorry for shouting. 'Look, I'm sorry. He just scared the bejesus out of me. And I'm having a really bad day. I shouldn't have shouted...'

'Jasper, come...' Watching in despair as Jasper jumped the wall, Sophie hopped on one foot until she reached her. 'I'm so sorry, I didn't see you. I'm not used to anyone being there, and yes, I know, I should be more responsible and put him on a lead. But he's so fast and my ankle, it hurts so damned much.' She choked back a sob. 'And I didn't think, and, before I knew it, he'd leapt the wall...' She pointed a long, slender finger at the cup that had smashed all over the path. 'I don't know why he does it, every time he gets the chance, he's jumping over and sniffing around your garden and...' With her shoulders drooped, Sophie set off to hop along the path. 'I'll just...' She pointed to the gate and headed towards it.

'No, don't...' Sitting up, Hattie leaned forward and took the lead from Sophie's hand. 'You've already said that your ankle hurts,' she swallowed hard and tried to surreptitiously swipe at her eyes with a sleeve. 'Let me get him for you.'

Hopping closer, Sophie leaned heavily against the wall but then looked up at Hattie's face. 'Are you okay?' she asked. 'You look as though you've been...' She lifted a hand up, indicated the tears that still rolled down Hattie's face. 'You're crying,' she finally added.

There was a silent truce that passed between the two women and, with eyes that just wouldn't stop crying, Hattie swallowed, pressed her lips tightly together and looked at the way Sophie fidgeted nervously by the side of the wall.

'It's my mum,' Hattie said as she took in a deep breath and looked back at the family home, the place where her brothers were sleeping. 'Sorry, it's *our* mum,' she corrected. 'We lost her last night... and I don't know whether to feel sad or relieved,' she admitted. 'That's awful, isn't it?'

'Well, from what I can gather, she had been poorly for quite a long time and the stress of having someone in your life that's so ill can be overwhelming. So I kind of get why you'd feel that way,' Sophie said as they both turned, watched the way Jasper sniffed frantically around the area of garden in front of the wishing well. It was a part of the garden that was now overgrown, and weeds and grasses grew where her father had always intended to plant vegetables. But his interest was more than disturbing, and Hattie immediately jumped from the wall.

'Here, boy,' she shouted while patting her leg, and inching towards him. A game of chase went from one side of the garden to the other until eventually Jasper succumbed and flopped on the floor with his nose pushed hard against the ground. 'What have you got there, boy?' Ruffling his ears, Hattie clipped on his lead, pulled him back towards the wall where she continued to speak. 'Mum's been ill for years but last night she really wanted to speak, she had something to tell us and got part way through saying that there was something she'd hidden from us all. A big family secret and now... now she's gone, and the chances are we'll never find out what she was going to say...' Pausing, Hattie tugged at the lead 'Oh God, never mind, I'm sorry, I don't know why I'm telling you this. You barely know me and I'm sure you've got better things to do.'

Overwhelmed by her own feelings, Hattie raked her hands through her hair. She looked up to the sky and then, embarrassed that the tears that had once again begun to fall, she pushed her hands up and over her face as the sobs erupted from her. Her whole body shook with an emotion she couldn't identify and once again she tried to decide whether she was sad or relieved. The past nine years had been hard on them all, but especially on her mother, who'd been reduced to someone who'd lost everything including her dignity and now Hattie had to try and take comfort in the knowledge that her mother's daily struggle with life was over.

While she held her head in her hands, Hattie heard the neighbour beckon Jasper away. The sound of hopping went from the wall to the door, that was opened and closed, and then suddenly Hattie felt Sophie's arms surround her. She pulled her into a hug, rocked her like a baby and held her against her.

'I'm sorry I wasn't nicer, you know, when we first met,' Sophie whispered into Hattie's ear. 'I let my jealousy of Finn cloud my judgement and it was wrong of me, I shouldn't have judged you.' Once again, her arms tightened around Hattie and, for a few precious moments, they just sat in silence with a calmness surrounding them both, looking at the fields, trees and houses that stood in the distance, and then in unison they looked up at the church tower that hovered above them.

'Do you see those,' Sophie said contemplatively, 'those houses and all the people in them. I can honestly say that there isn't a man or woman in any of those houses who doesn't have a few secrets. And your mum, she's no different. She'll have her secrets too.' Pausing, Sophie leaned back. She took Hattie's hands in her own and gave them a gentle squeeze.

'You're right,' Hattie said after blowing her nose and sniffing loudly, 'I'm just confused. Whatever the secret is, it's one she managed to keep forever. Which means it's something she really didn't want us to know. Not until now...' She shook her head and stared at the house. 'And now, I don't know where to start looking for the answers.'

Sighing, Sophie tipped her head from side to side and pondered the question. 'For what it's worth, do you want to know what I'd do?' she asked, and saw Hattie nod before she continued. 'I'm married to someone who works in medicine, right?'

'Right.'

'Well, from what I can gather, your mum was medical too, wasn't she?' Pulling her phone out of her pocket, Sophie clicked on an app and Hattie watched as she quickly glanced at an image of Noah, sleeping soundly in his crib. 'Sorry, I thought I heard him cry.' She pointed at the upstairs window. 'I left it open so I could hear him and, when I can't, I can look at the camera to see what he's doing.'

Hattie jumped down from the wall, sauntered towards the wishing well, where she wondered if she should toss a coin and ask for one last wish. Sophie shook her head as the sound of Finn's car pulled up on the drive. 'Your mum,' she quickly filled in, 'she was a psychotherapist, right? She had clients and files and, if there's one thing I do know, it's that medical folk are super organised. Their notes are absolutely on point and if your mum had a secret, she'll have documented it. All you have to do is find it.' She lifted a hand and pointed to Hattie's house as she walked towards her own back door. 'I can almost guarantee that all the answers you're looking for are all in there. I can help you look, if you want me to?'

29

PRESENT DAY – DECEMBER 2023 – HATTIE

Hattie dabbed at her sore eyes with a tissue and took a deep breath as she stepped into a kitchen. It was the kind of room that during the winter always looked gloomy, with dark shadows tormenting the corners.

After sidestepping the spot where her father's body had been found, she headed down the long and narrow hallway. She skimmed the dusty dado rail with her fingers, while making a mental checklist of all the things that she'd need to take care of. There would be a funeral to arrange, which meant walking in through those big wooden doors of the church and meeting a vicar. A man or woman who was now in the role her father used to do, which she had to admit did feel strange. And then she'd have to make a list of her mother's friends and associates. All the people who'd want to attend and, with a sigh, she closed her eyes in despair. 'I don't know who they are, I wouldn't know any of them, not any more. So how the hell do I do this?' As she whispered the words, she could feel her legs getting weaker by the second and she held on to the banister to gather her thoughts.

Sophie was right. Her mother *had* been fastidious, her records *would* have been carefully written. In fact, Hattie could clearly remember watching the way she'd written her notes, then updated her records on the computer and, finally, at the end of each day she'd write in her own personal daybook, a journal she'd always kept for as long as Hattie could remember. Which meant that, to Hattie's knowledge, everything had been recorded in triplicate.

With her mouth dry to the point that she could barely swallow, Hattie leaned against the door-frame of her mother's office and stared into the gloom. Reaching forward, she switched on the light and slid her feet across the floor, which made her feel awkward and as though she were intruding. With each step, images of her childhood flooded her mind, and she found herself fighting a sudden, internal battle as she tried to make sense of what her mother had said. 'Which of the memories were real?' she asked herself out loud. 'Especially if our dad was doing something she hadn't been aware of.' She tried to think back to her mother's exact words, something about not knowing what he'd done, and she could still clearly see his face, the sparkle that came and went in his eye and, for a moment, she smiled as she remembered the day he'd told her that she was about to become a big sister. 'In the next few days, the baby will come and your mummy, she's going to be so very happy.' He'd smiled boastfully. 'She's going to need your help; do you think you can help her for me?' And then, her mind went to the night she'd found Adam in here, searching through the filing cabinets, looking for a way to explain what their mother had written on the desk pad.

Shaking her head in an attempt to release her from the trance-like state she'd fallen into, Hattie closed her eyes for a blink and suspiciously wondered if any part of her life had been real and whether or not anything her parents had ever said to her was true. 'This is the problem with secrets, they build mistrust,' she whispered out loud while all the time her eyes were scanning the bookcases. 'And, in the end, now you're gone I can't decide whether any of it was true and if it was, which version of your truth I was told.' She paused and, with her eyes twitching, looked away from the bookcase and stared at the desk. 'Or was the version of the truth I was told simply the one they wanted me to believe.'

Flicking her eyes from the desk to the settee, Hattie could clearly remember the day her father had been sitting there with a Bible resting against his lap, his left hand patting the book continually as he spoke and told her the tale about the day she'd been born. He'd painted a vividly clear picture, just as he had the day that Luke had been born. Her mother had a new baby, one that would be coming home that day to join their family. And now, after what her mother had said, she began to doubt everything her father had ever said, along with every part of her childhood and the main thing she couldn't be sure of was whether or not he'd simply told the same story so many times that in the end he'd actually come to believe them himself.

With a thoughtful gaze, Hattie followed the line of the bookcases that were full to bursting with encyclopaedias, motivational books, novels and box files stacked neatly in rows. There were ornaments and pictures perched in front of the books, along with a pile of dust-covered Bibles.

Pulling open the desk drawer, Hattie searched inside but, other than a ball of elastic bands that stood beside the normal pens, pencils and stapler, the drawer held nothing of significance and, with a roll of her eyes, she turned to the filing cabinet, pulled it open and flicked through the contents. Patient records were all neatly filed and had been conveniently placed in alphabetical order.

'All the files that begin with M,' Hattie chuntered. 'That's what it says on the tab and that's exactly what's in the file.' She lifted one file out after the other and nonchalantly flicked through the pages. Some files were just a few pages thick, while others were almost too big to lift with one hand and, after leafing through them to find absolutely nothing of interest, she considered going upstairs and asking both of her brothers to come and help her. She had to admit that she had absolutely no idea what it was she hoped to find and the idea of searching through her mother's things and files wasn't something she really wanted to do.

'What were you trying to tell us, Mum?' Staring at the desk, she flicked through an old diary that stood on the top. 'What was so important that you kept the documents hidden in that box, with the key in your purse?' She paused, walked to the next filing cabinet, and pulled open the drawer.

'What are you looking for?' Appearing in the doorway, Luke leaned against the architrave. He held his hand up to rub his chin and sighed. 'She'd be furious with us if we poked around in her things, you do know that, don't you?'

Slamming the drawer to a close, Hattie spun round on the spot to give her brother an irritated growl. 'Jesus, Luke, you scared me.' She pointed to the files. 'I was looking and hoping for a clue. I need to know what she was talking about.' She emphasised the words. 'Don't you want to know what she meant? Why she called us all there? Because half of me really does and the other half wishes I hadn't come back at all...' She threw both hands up in the air. 'Her words keep going around my brain and I'm absolutely sure that it's the only thing I'll ever remember about the last time I saw her.'

With her eyes once again filling with tears, she noticed that Luke's eyes were surrounded by dark shadows. His eyes were bright red and his cheeks looked to be flushed with the cold, which made her wonder if he'd been out for a walk.

'So?' he asked. 'You just thought you'd go through it all, did you?' He paused, unzipped his jacket and, with an air of displeasure, he strode toward the desk. 'Go on then, enlighten me. What did you find?'

'Luke, don't be angry. Not today.' Sitting down in the chair that stood behind the desk, Hattie leaned back and closed her eyes. 'Think about what she said – they couldn't cope and we thought we were helping. What did she mean?' She stared at the floor and furrowed her brow. 'And the comment about getting what she deserved.' Her hands went up to her face and, for a few moments, she took pleasure in the darkness. 'No one deserved that, Luke.' She paused and looked out from behind her hands at where her brother stared at the floor.

'Maybe Adam was right all those years ago, when he got it into his head that we were all adopted, just like Louisa. That'd be the easiest answer, wouldn't it?' Luke picked up a file that had been stood on top of the filing cabinet. 'This was probably the last file she'd have been working on...' He blew the dust from the top of a manilla file and began to read the content.

Thoughtfully, Hattie flopped forward to lean on the desk, ran a hand through her hair and gave Luke a look of confusion. 'That can't be true, can it?'

'Would it matter if it were?' Angrily, Luke slammed the filing cabinet closed. 'Even if we were adopted, Hattie, it wouldn't change anything. We'd still be us and she'd still be dead.' He closed his eyes sorrowfully, as a tear dropped down his cheek, and moodily wiped it away. 'Look, I'm sorry, but I don't get what digging up the past will do for us now.'

For the first time in years, Hattie looked up to see Luke crying. His face was contorted with anger and, once again, he reminded her of the teenager who'd climbed into her bed full of fear as a kid. 'Luke, you're right,' she acknowledged, 'it wouldn't change a thing, not between us. But, on the other hand, it would maybe change everything.' She struggled with the words, but knew that knowing the truth had become more than important.

Standing up, Hattie made her way across the room and slid onto the settee where, even though the leather felt cold against her skin, she lay her head back against the cushions and waited for Luke to sit beside her. Tentatively, she held out a hand, took his in hers and threaded her fingers in between his. 'Luke, can we start again, because I know I haven't been around for a while and I'm sorry. But this constant anger you seem to have, it isn't like you.' She looked again towards the bookcases. 'Whatever happens, we have to promise, right here and now, that we'll always be there for each other, because...' She felt her lower lip quiver with emotion. 'Because, no matter what happens, or what we find, we're all we have left.' She squeezed his hand in hers, 'And it's important that we stick together, isn't it?'

'Oh, nice, a family get-together,' Adam's voice bellowed from the other side of the room and the tender moment Hattie was sharing with Luke was lost in the turmoil. 'Make way, it isn't a get-together without me.'

Taking a deep breath in, Hattie couldn't help but smile as Adam launched himself across the room, stuck his elbows outwards and practically jumped between them.

'Now then.' He pushed his bottom in between Luke and Hattie and, on a settee only made for two, they both sat forward to make him some room. 'What were we talking about?' The comment was typical of Adam. He was always the one who turned every situation into a joke and, even when people talked about death, he was the one to always lighten the mood.

'We were talking about Mum,' Hattie filled in, 'and about her revelation, the one she didn't quite get around to saying and...' Hattie pointed to the box files in the knowledge that she'd already looked through the filing cabinet. 'I was going to start a search, try and find clues as to what she was talking about, but the thought of going through all of those...' She sighed, sniffed and, once again, dabbed at her eyes. 'It's the old needle in a haystack, isn't it? The only thing we have to go on is what she said, especially when we have no idea what we're looking for.'

Standing up, Luke stared out of the window and stifled a sob and, with both of his shoulders slumping in despair, he slowly shook his head from side to side. 'She did say something that we're all overlooking,' he said with a nod. 'The box, she'd said that she'd hidden it in a cardboard box that was stood at the top of the old staircase.' He paused thoughtfully and pointed upwards. 'But, when I went to look for it, it wasn't there...'

Again, he stopped speaking and sighed. 'Which didn't make any sense. Mum always knew where everything was, which means that someone must have moved it.'

'Okay,' Hattie muttered as she thought back to the night, after she'd first made love to Griffin, the night he'd followed her up the staircase and inquisitively shone a light on all the boxes that stood there. 'I remember seeing it, it was inside another box. One that had been taped up with Sellotape.'

'Exactly, that's what Mum said,' Luke responded. 'So, why did I find it in the spare bedroom and, if Mum kept the key in her purse, how had someone opened it and removed the content?'

30

PRESENT DAY – DECEMBER 2023 – SOPHIE

Walking back into the house, Sophie immediately caught her breath as she spotted Finn pacing back and forth at the bottom of the stairs with a screaming Noah held tightly in his arms. He was dressed in his suit and looked ready for work and it was more than apparent that Finn was doing all he could to keep the suit clean.

'Couldn't you hear him?' Finn demanded. 'I could hear him screaming the minute I pulled onto the drive.' Marching from the front of the house to the back, Finn hovered in front of the dining table and, with a finger and thumb of his spare arm, he lifted Noah's breakfast dish into the sink and sighed as he rolled his gaze across the floor, where at least a dozen Cheerios had scattered and even Jasper was sniffing them suspiciously.

'You want some toast?' Sophie asked calmly as she went into autopilot, pulled open the bread bin, pulled two slices out of the bag and pushed them into the toaster. 'I have some of that plum jam you like.' She gave him an over-apologetic smile, kept her eyes on Noah and took in a long, deep breath. 'I was talking to Hattie.' Pausing, she watched the way Finn turned and immediately took interest in what she was saying. His brow furrowed and, inquisitively, he went to look over her shoulder and towards the house next door. It was a reaction that made Sophie purposely stay silent. She'd wanted to see what Finn would do and, with a wry smile, she plucked the toast from the toaster, spread a layer of butter across the top and reached for the jam she'd promised him. 'Here you go. Do you want me to take Noah, before you end up needing another clean shirt?' She pushed the plate across the table, held out her arms to Noah, clapped her hands in encouragement and smiled as Noah immediately stopped crying and launched himself towards her. 'Ahhhhhh, there you go.' She turned away and, even though her ankle was painful, she hopped down the hallway.

'Soph...' Finn shouted. 'Don't go, did... did you say that you saw Hattie?' He threw the question at her as he picked up a slice of toast and chewed on a corner. 'Is she okay?'

Sighing with the satisfaction that Finn had given her the exact reaction she'd expected, she slowly made her way back to the kitchen, where she leaned nonchalantly against the door and patted Noah on the back. 'She wasn't great, if I'm honest,' she said. 'Her mum died yesterday and she was upset, hence why I couldn't just leave her.' She kissed Noah on the forehead, ruffled his hair and kept her eyes on the way Finn sat: he'd stopped eating the toast and was currently sitting silently.

'Her mum...' Picking up Sophie's mug of cold coffee, Finn took a long slurp. 'Imogen's dead? Are you sure?'

'Of course I'm sure,' Sophie replied. 'Oh, and Noah wasn't crying, I'd literally just checked him on the camera, less than two seconds before you pulled up. So the next time you want me to feel guilty, don't use our son in your mind games.'

Spinning around to walk down the hallway and away from the glare of her husband's eyes, Sophie bounced Noah up and down on her hip. 'It's quite pathetic to do that, Finn, don't you think?' She pushed her tongue firmly into her cheek while looking through the hallway mirror, to see Noah looking back at himself with a broad, toothy grin.

It was all she could do in an effort not to look at Finn; the last thing she needed was to see his concern for the woman next door, however, it did confirm her deepest fears. Whether she liked it or not, Finn still had feelings for Hattie. What she didn't want to know was how deep those feelings went. Finn was her husband. Hers. And if it killed her, she'd make sure she found out why he and Hattie were no longer together. With a final look in the mirror, she tenderly pressed a kiss against Noah's cheek and looked up at the clock.

'Finn, you're going to be late for work, so...' She smiled contentedly. 'And while I was being such an awful parent, I made you a sandwich. You might want to take it with you.'

31

NINE YEARS BEFORE – LOUISA

In a room where dusk was surrounding them fast, Louisa stared at the way Mary had taken a physical step backwards. She now stood by the door and shook uncontrollably, her eyes wide open with fear.

'Who the hell are you?' she growled through gritted teeth, frantically dragged open the door and threw herself into a room beyond. 'I want you out of my home and I want you out now, do you hear me?' A loud bang was followed by a scream. 'You were only here because I was trying to help you, because my mother agreed to help you and then you sit there and start telling your lies. How the hell dare you?'

Shocked by Mary's response, Louisa scrambled forward in the bed, her foot caught in the bedding and, while trying to free it, she could feel the wave of nausea sweeping across her. Every part of her felt weak and perplexed and her heart was beating so hard, she felt as though her chest could easily explode as Mary's footsteps could be heard swiftly moving further away. In her confusion, Louisa held her breath, tried to listen to the sounds of banging, hammering and grappling that Mary was doing with a door that didn't seem to open.

'Mum... open the door, please God, I need you, please come,' Mary yelled. There was more banging, and more screaming in a loud, yet pitiful voice. 'Griff... Griffin, be a good boy, you need to let your mummy out... it's an emergency.' It was the sound and yell of a woman much younger than her years, a pitiful sound that tore at Louisa's heartstrings but also sent a surge of fear coursing through her. Shaking with fear and uncertainty, Louisa moved as slowly as she could. She felt sure that her legs wouldn't hold her, that they'd buckle beneath her and, with a trembling inside her that just wouldn't stop, she dropped to the floor with a painful thud. After a few seconds of uncertainty, where she checked herself for injury, she began to crawl across a threadbare carpet until she reached where Mary was almost cowering in the doorway.

'Mary. Please. You did hear me, didn't you?' Louisa pleaded. 'I think I'm your daughter. I found proof... I found some paperwork with your name.' She paused, and gagged as the strong, musty smell of damp hit the back of her throat and for the briefest of moments she felt as though she'd stepped into a different universe. The chintz and the ornaments were gone. The room was stripped bare of furniture, apart from an old chair and a threadbare carpet that only partially covered the bare wooden floorboards. 'Where the hell are we?' Louisa asked in her panic as she noticed the windows that had been haphazardly boarded over, as though they'd been done in a hurry. 'What is this place? I... I was at Frieda's house, she was looking after me, but this...' With eyes that were wide and fearful, Louisa pressed her back against the wall. 'Where the hell did you take me?'

Shuffling around the perimeter of the room, Mary banged

on each of the windows in turn, her voice now little more than a murmur as she constantly muttered the same words, over and over. 'It isn't real, she isn't here, I can't do this.' She gasped as she spoke and, with the flats of her hands, she worked her way around each of the walls and windows until she came back to the door.

'Where's Frieda?' Louisa calmly demanded. 'I want to know where I am.'

'Out. Frieda's out. I already told you that.' Standing with her face now pressed firmly against the door, Mary kept hold of the doorknob. 'She didn't want to leave you. Not on your own. So they brought you up here.' Turning, Mary pressed her back against the door and continually shook her head from side to side. 'I was doing okay, my meds were working and all I was supposed to do was give you soup,' she said breathlessly while pointing to a small table and to a bowl, spoon and flask that stood on top. 'And I could have done that. She trusted me to do that.' Lifting her hands to her head, Mary threaded her fingers through her hair where she dragged painfully at the roots. 'And now you're telling lies and...' She looked over her shoulder and once again she grabbed at the doorknob. 'Damn door's locked,' she sobbed as she slid to the floor in a crumpled heap. 'It's always locked.'

'Please... I swear, I'm not lying. I've always wanted to meet you.' Louisa could feel her mind swimming with confusion, she was sure she'd got this right. That this woman was the one she'd been looking for, but, now she was here, nothing seemed right and her body and mind turned heavy and lethargic. There wasn't a single part of her that didn't ache and, with the deep desire to escape, she pulled herself slowly across the floor and closer to Mary. 'I thought you'd be pleased,' she heard herself sob. 'I thought you'd want to meet me too.'

'You can't be her,' Mary screamed as she curled herself into a small, terrified ball. 'You just can't be.' Mary's body trembled violently, her eyes grew wide with fear and her hands began to twist around each other in an aggressive and brutal manner. 'You're lying...' Mary sobbed. 'You just have to be lying. They told me she'd died...' She shook her head from side to side and punched out at the floor and petulantly she began to run her fingernails up and down her arms where she scratched at her scars. 'They told me... she was dead, and they took her away.'

'Who told you that?' Louisa's voice cracked as she spoke, her fingers clawed at the remnants of the carpet and the tears began to roll down her face with frustration. 'I don't know who told you that, but it isn't true, look, I'm here and I promise... I didn't mean to scare you, and I'm not lying, I just...' She watched as Mary pushed herself further into the corner of the room and into the darkest of the shadows. 'I just want to know you.'

'Well, I don't want to know you.' Mary immediately snapped back. 'I want you to go, I want my house back and... I... I don't want you to come back.' With a fist curled, Mary reached out and punched the door. 'Mum... open the door. Mum...'

'Mary...' Louisa fearfully looked from the woman to the door. She was confused, hurt and she couldn't understand how she could have got things so wrong. Coming here, finding Mary and being reunited with her hadn't gone the way she'd expected. She'd hoped for a happy reunion. A mother and daughter moment where they'd run into each other's arms. A life where they'd finally be together in a happy and contented existence. What she hadn't expected was the vitriolic response, the almost psychotic behaviour, and all in a house that had boarded-up windows and a door that appeared to be locked.

Looking over her shoulder, Louisa hoped to see her clothes hung over a chair, or at the bottom of the bed, but, with the darkness pulling in, she could only just see the room she'd come from and, quickly, she flashed her eyes up at the walls and looked for a light switch, or a lamp, and, as though her prayers had been answered, the monotonous tone of the level crossing filled the air, red flashing lights lit up the room and for a moment Louisa braced herself for the trembling that would come.

'Mary, Mary, look at me?' Louisa whispered through the noise. 'Do you know where there's a light switch, we need some light, I need you to see me.' The sound of a train whizzing past at speed cut through the air, the room shook with vibration and time stood still as her eyes connected with Mary's. 'You must have noticed,' she whispered, 'you must have seen it,' Louisa yelled passionately. 'We have the same hair, the same face, the eyes. Can't you see your eyes in mine, because I can.' Once again, she held out a hand. 'Look at me, even my hands are the same as yours...'

'Why... why...' she bellowed. 'Why are you doing this...?' Frantically, Mary kicked out in her rage. Her legs connected with a small mahogany table, and she gasped out loud as it crashed to the floor. The small makeshift jam jar vase that had stood on top had broken as it landed on the hard, wooden floorboards, its small winter flowers were now scattered and broken, making Mary curl up into a tighter ball where she rocked herself back and forth with her eyes fixed on the broken shards of glass.

'Mary, let me help you...' Scurrying forward, Louisa began to pick up the flowers, but stopped abruptly as she noticed the way that Mary was staring intently. It was a look that sent a shudder running up and down her spine and, with every ounce of energy Louisa had left, she carefully held a hand out towards Mary, but recoiled quickly as Mary jumped backwards. 'I'm sorry,' she muttered. 'I just wanted to know you, to hold you and... and I know I shouldn't have just blurted it out but I couldn't help myself...' Louisa added through the tears. 'I've wanted to meet you since I found out you existed...' She sighed dramatically, and once again she held her arm out towards where Mary had curled up. 'I wasn't even sure I'd found the right Mary, not until I saw you and then...' She nodded. 'Then I knew it was you... I knew I'd found you.'

'Don't touch me,' Mary yelled back. 'Mum, Mum, where are you? Get me out of here...' With eyes that were dark, wide and fearful, Mary stretched out, reached up and, with her fingers twisted around the doorknob, shook it violently. 'I don't know who you think you are, but...' She leaned into the wall, banged persistently on the door. 'Mum... Mum, please, you have to come...'

'Please, I can prove it.' Looking down at the floor, Louisa thought about her words. She had no idea where to start, or how to stop the situation escalating further. All she did know was that she had nothing left to lose.

Lifting her hands up to her face, Louisa swept her hair backwards. 'There was a photograph. It looked as though it had been taken on the day I was born. It was in a room that looked white and stark and the bed, it was a mattress that lay on a floor. Please, you must remember having the picture taken?' Studying Mary's eyes, Louisa saw the memory flash across her face and every part of her wanted to scream and shout, and tell Mary how her parents had died and she'd suddenly found herself alone in the world. She'd done her best to navigate, but couldn't, and her last hope had been that her birth mother would find her.

'Mary Griffonia Alexander,' she whispered slowly. 'That's you, isn't it?' Looking at Mary through desperate, pleading eyes, Louisa searched for some kind of recognition and some hope that she believed what she was saying. 'It said your name on the back of the photograph and, after I met Griffin and he told me how he'd been named after his mother, I honestly thought I'd been handed a miracle. After that, I made it my mission to know him, because, by knowing him, I could look for you.' Lifting her hands upward, Louisa held the palms out in the hope that Mary wouldn't see her as a threat and, slowly, she inched across the floor until she could run her fingers slowly across Mary's arm. This time, there was no hurried retraction, no flaying of arms or legs.

'Mary,' Louisa pleaded. 'Who was it that told you your baby was dead?'

Pensively, Mary stared at a mark on the carpet, a place where something had been spilled and left to stain. 'He was a good man, he was there to help me, to rid me of sin,' she whispered. 'He told me that he'd look after me, and that he'd look after my baby, but he didn't.'

'Mary, who was he?'

Looking up, for the first time, Mary looked into Louisa's eyes and, with tears rolling down her cheeks, she took in a deep breath. 'He was a vicar... and, I think, he was called Gerald.' She nodded, slowly and thoughtfully. 'That's right, he was called Gerald.'

32

PRESENT DAY – DECEMBER 2023 – SOPHIE

With a modicum of courage, Sophie pulled a tubular bandage up and over her painful ankle before carefully pressing her foot against the hard-tiled floor as a test. She was in no doubt that the ankle needed support, and that walking on it without support would be a stupid thing to do, but she also knew that the ankle wasn't nearly as bad or as tender as she'd initially made out.

It had been an act she'd put on for Finn's benefit in the knowledge that, if he thought she'd be home all day, with her foot in the air, the last thing he'd do was pay attention to the roads, or to who was following him. Even though Sophie felt as though it was the oddest thing to do, she knew that she had no choice if she were to ever work out what Finn was up to. Of course, she knew he often went on domiciliary visits, and that he often left the surgery during the day. But the Finn she knew would have never left a waiting room full of people, which was why it all seemed a little odd and why Sophie had assumed that his disappearance was connected to Hattie. Or she had, but now, after meeting Hattie that morning, Sophie had doubts. After all,

Finn had been acting oddly for a very long time, causing one argument after the other and, even though she'd needed him at home with her and Noah, he'd made excuse after excuse as to why he couldn't stay and why he'd gone back to live at Frieda's. Something didn't add up and, angrily, she reached across the table, picked up her coffee mug and took a long drink. 'Urgh, that's cold,' she grumbled before slamming it down, watching as the cold, milky coffee spilt over its edge and all over the shiny, clean worktop.

'Damn it,' she growled, before taking in a deep breath. She picked up a cloth, wiped the worktop clean. It was a breakfast bar where she and Finn would sit to eat and where, during dinner every night, he'd often talked her through his day. There would often be tales about the staff shortages, the constant struggles he had with the building, the issues with the car park and the patient visits where he'd recall the funnier parts of his day along with the issues that had shocked him the most. 'Do you know what, Soph, when a patient walks in through my door, I'm never sure whether I'll be looking at their arse or their elbow.' It had been something they'd often laughed about. So for him to miss out something so critical that had happened during his day, especially when he'd had no choice but to leave a crowded surgery behind, and on a day when she'd been sat in it, did feel quite odd. Which made Sophie suspicious.

'Come on, Noah, let's get a move on.' After pulling Noah's winter coat around him, she gave him a warm, loving smile. Felt her whole body melt at the way he curled his lip as he ate a rusk she'd given him, the sparkles that filled his eyes full of mischief and the way he lovingly held the biscuit towards her.

Zipping up a pair of knee-high boots over the tight tubular bandage, Sophie once again pressed her foot to the floor. She did it cautiously at first. And, even though there was a little pain, she knew that all she had to do was get to the car and take Noah to nursery and then, as soon as she could, she'd follow Finn, find out where he was going and who he was seeing. But that was where her plan fell down. 'He's going to recognise the car, isn't he?' She bit down on her lip. 'Finn is far too observant. He'll spot you a mile away, you fool.' She paused, and thought. 'Which means, that you, Mrs Alexander, have to come up with a better plan, don't you?'

33

PRESENT DAY – DECEMBER 2023 – HATTIE

'It's just a sketch,' Hattie murmured miserably as she looked down at the small piece of paper that Luke had found. It was a plain white sheet that had been folded in half and tucked inside the Bible that her father had always carried around with him.

'The numbers look as though they're in his handwriting.' She took in the scrawl, and the numbers that were barely recognisable. 'He was probably planning a garden party, or some kind of fundraiser. I mean, look, it's clearly our garden.' She pointed to a small circle that stood in one corner, the gate that stood by its side. 'That's the wishing well and that's the gate and this dark line here, that shows where the house is, and the walls that surround the garden. And these...' Once again, she used a finger to draw a line across the drawing. 'These are... I don't know, maybe a place where he planned to put the stalls, but why he'd number them without a key? It could mean just about anything.' Once again, she picked up the piece of paper, turned it around in her hands and couldn't help but think that her father would have been the last person to touch it. 'The numbers are weird and don't make any sense: ninety-seven, one, three, six and eleven, all written inside these boxes. It could mean just about anything.'

'Well, I don't remember any garden parties,' Adam grumbled as he stood up and paced around the office. 'And I really don't care about his scruffy drawing, what I care about is finding the documents that Mum was going to show us.' He pulled a book off the shelf, began to leaf through it. 'They just have to be here somewhere.'

'Maybe they're here, somewhere, just waiting to be found,' Hattie replied dreamily as she walked to the bookshelves and ran a finger gently along the spines. 'Maybe we have to look in every book to find them.'

'And maybe there's nothing to find.' Luke screwed the piece of paper up and tossed it towards the bin, where it landed on the floor and rolled back towards him. 'Have you even taken into consideration that the documents are gone? That someone took them, or they could have been taken by the police and, right now, they could be sat in an archive box, in the police dungeons.'

Sitting back and closing her eyes, Hattie thought of how the police would have searched the house. Nothing would have been left unturned, which made Hattie cringe, and her thought went back to the box. Whoever had opened it must have had a key and the only people with access to that key had been at the hospital the night before, in that room when she opened the box. Which kept bringing her back to the same conclusion: one of them already knew what their mother was trying to say. After cautiously opening her eyes, she looked between her brothers suspiciously before picking the picture up from the floor, flattening it out and staring at it.

'He always threatened to plant vegetables,' she finally added. 'Maybe he needed a plan?' It had been a standing family joke that each year her father would get the plot ready for planting but had never followed through, which had always seemed odd.

'Sophie made an interesting point this morning, because Finn is really meticulous with his medical notes. She thought Mum would have been quite particular too.' Once again, her gaze went to the filing cabinets. 'And now I come to think about it, she always said something about creating records in triplicate. Which meant that she would have had her notes, and her files, and then...' She rolled her eyes around the room. 'Where's her laptop?'

For a time, the silence was deafening. Even the pipes and the roofbeams stopped making a noise and Hattie couldn't help but notice the way Luke paced, his feet almost dancing with a nervous tapping reaction, and his cheeks seemed to turn a bright fuchsia, right before her eyes.

'She asked me to hide it. That night she was attacked, I ran out behind Adam and we both found her, down at the bottom of the garden, right next to the well. We phoned for an ambulance and, knowing that time was critical, Adam went to the gate to look for the paramedics.' He paused and anxiously ran a hand through his hair. 'And in those few minutes, she made me promise to hide it.'

'So the police never saw it?'

'No...'

'Luke, why didn't you say something before?'

Trudging down the hallway, Luke's shoulders physically rose and fell in a sigh. 'Because she didn't want anyone to see it, so I respected her privacy and I left it where it was and, to be honest, I'm glad I did. Bloody vultures were all over the house as it was, the last thing she'd have wanted was for them to go through her laptop.'

Following him, Hattie and Adam stood at the bottom of the

old Victorian staircase and watched as he walked halfway up and forcefully began to throw the bin bags that were still full of clothes out of his way.

'Do you know what he's doing?' Adam questioned, but Hattie had already become bored of watching and had turned around to flick on the kettle.

'Do you think I should wash the best china, just in case anyone calls?' she shouted over her shoulder as a loud grating sound was heard and she looked back up the stairs to see Luke lifting a stair-tread to reveal a huge void right under the step.

'I saw Mum lifting it one day. She told me off for sneaking up on her and then, that night, she told me to hide the computer and to never tell anyone where I'd put it and I didn't... but now she's gone and...' With the laptop held tightly in his hand, and his lip wobbling with the emotion, Luke held it out towards them. 'I didn't mean to hide it for so long, but I guessed that one day she'd ask for it back and I wanted to know exactly where it was when she did.'

With her mind doing somersaults at the sight of the secret compartment, Hattie walked back to the office. If her mother had a secret stair box in the house, then she was in no doubt that she'd have had other places to hide things and Luke was right, they'd all respected her mother's privacy while she'd lived but, now, she was gone... and, even if she had to lift every floorboard, she would.

'Listen,' Hattie said as she picked up the pile of Bibles. 'I'm going to take these to the bin, unless of course either of you want them.'

Shaking his head, Luke walked to the coat rack. 'Not me. I've nipped the laptop upstairs. I've plugged it in to charge and...' He tipped his head on one side. 'If you're up for it, we'll have a good look through it the minute I get back from the farm.' He paused, thoughtfully. 'No matter what happens, I still have to work. Animals still need feeding.'

Giving Luke a wave, Hattie walked to the dustbin, lifted the lid and, with a satisfactory smile, dropped the Bibles inside just as the church bells began to toll. It was a sound that once again made her catch her breath, and with a look of remorse she glanced over her shoulder towards where the church tower stood. 'Maybe,' she whispered, 'maybe it's the church's way of telling me that I should have taken them in there.' She took in a deep breath, knowing that on one of the days later in the week she'd have to go. But the thought of walking inside felt like a step too far.

34

PRESENT DAY – DECEMBER 2023 – SOPHIE

With Jasper's lead tied to the tree, and Noah sat in his stroller, Sophie paced up and down the driveway with an exaggerated limp. The bonnet of her car was up; for effect she'd set the indicators flashing, and with the phone held up to her ear she waited until she heard the back door of the vicarage open and the sound of Hattie's feet on the path before she began her performance.

'You're going to be how long?' she growled as loudly as she could into the phone. 'Are you serious? I've hurt my ankle and I need the car to get my son to nursery.' She lifted the phone away from her ear and looked at the screen with a frown. 'There's no way I can walk.' She paused, listened intently as the man on the other end of the phone apologised profusely. He was more than sorry but had to prioritise cars that were stood on the side of the motorway and, unless the recovery man could fly between Bedale and Ugathwaite, there wouldn't be a chance of arriving anytime in the next two to three hours.

Crouching down, Sophie fastened the straps on Noah's

harness. 'Well, that's just great. I'll walk it on an ankle that feels like I just broke it, shall I?' Stifling a sob, Sophie stabbed a finger at the screen, thrust her phone into her pocket and tugged Jasper's lead free from where it was tied.

'Hey. Are you okay?' Walking through the gap in the conifers, Hattie gave Sophie a quizzical smile. 'I'm sorry, but I couldn't help but overhear you.' She glanced at the car and pulled a face. 'That doesn't look good. What's happened?' she asked as she walked to the front of the car, looked under the bonnet and studied the engine.

'Oh, I don't know. I got in, turned it over and nothing. It's days like this that I could really do with Finn being at home.' Sophie pulled a small white blanket up to cover Noah's legs and pushed his bright green octopus into his hands. 'It just seems to be one thing after the other. The man on the phone said it could be something to do with the timing belt, whatever one of those is.' Sophie moved to the front of the car and dropped the bonnet with a loud, vibrating slam. 'I don't normally get emotional but I could have really done with Noah going to nursery today.' She closed her eyes for a blink. 'My ankle is really sore, and I really want to get to Friarage at some point today to get it X-rayed, but now... this...' Sophie impatiently pulled a small plastic bag out of her pocket, and ran her hand down the front of her jeans. 'Come on, Jasper, at least you could hurry up and do what you need to do for me...' Sophie said as she rolled her eyes and impatiently pulled a small plastic bag out of her pocket, running her hand down the front of her jeans. 'He hates going in the garden, but there's no way that I can take him for a walk.' Sophie leaned over the buggy, wiped Noah's mouth with a tissue and, with her foot held up in the air, she slouched against the car. 'I'm sorry, I shouldn't be moaning. Not today, it'd be the last thing you'd need.' She looked over her shoulder. 'We could go inside, I could put the kettle on, and make us some coffee?' Reaching out, she placed a hand against Hattie's arm and tipped her head to one side. 'I mean, that's if you want to, 'cause it's not like I'm going anywhere, is it?'

'Not for me,' Hattie replied with a rueful smile. 'If I'm honest, I've drunk more tea and coffee this morning than I can stomach, but, if it helps, I could run you through to Friarage?' She held out a hand, took Jasper's lead from Sophie. 'Or I could take this one for a walk and you could...' She pointed to where her car was parked on the drive next door. 'It's still full of my junk, but, if you don't mind that, you're welcome to borrow it, that's if...' Furrowing her brow, Hattie looked up and down to Sophie's foot. 'That's if you're fit to drive?'

'Hattie, if that's okay, you'd be a lifesaver and yes, I can drive, look...' She lifted her foot higher up in the air and wriggled it around as though she were trying to prove a point. 'You'd be absolutely saving my life. I mean...' She patted the top of the buggy. 'I love my boy more than anything in the world but an afternoon of him being at nursery is exactly what I need, and it's only if I put too much weight on it that it hurts.'

Looking from Sophie to the car and back again, Hattie began to laugh. 'Saying that, it's automatic, isn't it?' With her foot held comically in the air, she waved it around. 'Now I think about it, you only need the right foot and, as far as I can tell, that one looks okay.' Reaching into her pocket, Hattie pulled out a key, and held it up in the air. 'You're welcome to it and, if I'm honest, I was planning a walk, so if you want I could take Jasper with me, and we'd both be doing each other a favour, wouldn't we, boy?'

'As I say,' Sophie said. 'You are a lifesaver.' It was all she could think to say as she gave Hattie a wave and studiously knelt down beside Noah and gave him a smile. 'Isn't your mummy just the cleverest mummy in the world?' Sophie whispered with a giggle as, through a corner of her eye, she watched Hattie and Jasper disappear out of sight. 'The plan worked perfectly and now mummy can follow daddy in a car he won't recognise and he won't have a clue that it's me, will he?'

35

PRESENT DAY – DECEMBER 2023 – HATTIE

With the breeze howling in from the river, Hattie tugged at her coat and, even though its leaves had long since fallen, she sheltered beside one of the larger trees and with her gloves held tightly in her hands she tried to make sense of the overwhelming and chaotic night she'd just been through.

Every minute since being back at the vicarage had been like an out-of-body experience and she felt as though she'd been caught in the middle of a strong, powerful tornado that had come to earth with a bang the moment her mother had died. Since then, every part of her felt as though she'd been slowly dragged through mud, where everything she'd done had taken twice as long as normal, every movement had felt slow and painful, with much more effort than humanly possible, which was ironic because right now and in complete contrast she was looking up at the way the winter had changed the trees and listening to the birdsong that came from a robin sat in the branches above her and, miraculously, she was feeling more at peace than she had in years.

Sidestepping a large, muddy puddle, Hattie once again

began to make her way along the lane with Jasper in tow while all the time trying to put her life in context. Her mother's battles were over. She'd seemingly found a truce with her brothers and, much to her surprise, her first love now just happened to live in the house next door, at least on a part-time basis and somehow, in the middle of all these things happening, she'd managed to find a new friend in Sophie, Griffin's wife, which, if someone had told her would happen, she'd have placed a very large bet against believing them. Even so, she had to admit that meeting Sophie had helped her. It had been the first time she'd chatted so openly to anyone in years. Not long after moving away, she'd made a point of avoiding new friendships. It had made life easier to avoid the awkward questions that new friendships brought. In the few months after her parents were attacked, she'd lost count of the times she'd been asked the gory details of what had happened, either that or by mentioning what had happened had shut the whole conversation down to a point where no one knew what to say, and in the end all parties would stay silent. However, for some reason, Hattie felt that a friendship with Sophie would be different. Presumably, she already knew about her past, and about what had happened, which gave Hattie an instilled confidence that she'd be a little more respectful about digging into the past.

'Come on, boy, time we were getting back,' she grumbled as Jasper once again aimed for a bush and took great pleasure in sniffing almost every leaf and then proceeded to pee on most of them. It was only as they rounded the corner that Hattie noticed a difference in his behaviour. Suddenly, he lurched forward, lifted himself up and onto his haunches and began to yap, in an unusual bark. Looking up, Hattie noticed the man walking towards them, and the German shepherd he held on a lead. 'Oh no you don't, Jasper,' she whispered under her breath as, once again, he pulled and Hattie felt the anxiety rise inside her as the dog and its owner walked directly towards her.

'Don't mind us,' the tall, stocky man shouted. He was dressed for the Arctic with his thick blue quilted coat zipped up until it met his chin and his hood covering his head, with the bungee cord tied in a bow. 'He looks all rough and tough but he's friendly enough and he likes to have a sniff of his fellow doggies as he walks right past them.'

Giving the man a nervous look, Hattie wished that he would do just that and walk right past but, instead, he took another step towards her and allowed his dog to stretch his neck forward until his and Jasper's noses were just about touching.

'Oh, I'm sure he's fine, but Jasper's not my dog, I'm just walking him for my neighbour and... well, I have to admit, I really don't want to get him to get eaten before we get to take him home,' she grumbled with a half-smile and a laugh. She desperately wanted to come across as being cheerful, but the skewed smile while her stomach was turning over in somersaults was as much as she could manage.

'Oh,' the man replied, 'you soon get used to who are the friendly dogs, and who aren't... It's a bit like people – some are nice, some, not so nice, and if you're wondering, I'm one of the nice ones.'

'Oh, okay,' Hattie shouted back nervously but pulled at Jasper and took another step in the opposite direction. 'Sorry, but I'm on a losing battle already with this one, he's already filthy and I keep trying to keep him out of the puddles, but he just loves jumping in them so much and my neighbour's already going to have a fit when she sees him, last thing I need is to end up getting him bitten too.'

'Oh, Tyson wouldn't bite him.' Leaning forward, the man rubbed his own dog's ears before tugging his lead. 'And, as for the mud, it's nothing that a quick few minutes under the hosepipe wouldn't cure. My boy loves a dip under the hosepipe, don't you, boy?'

'Isn't it too cold?' Again, she unconvincingly turned the corners of her mouth in an upward direction and, with another definite step backwards, she gave out an exasperated sigh. 'I'm sorry, but I have to go, and I know you say that your dog won't bite, but I'd really rather not put it to the test, you know, if you don't mind.' It was a sentence that marked the end of the conversation as, with an undignified huff, the man turned at speed, and continued his walk, leaving Hattie to take in a guarded breath of relief.

Turning to see Jasper jump into a ditch, Hattie held her hands in the air, submissively. 'I give up, I absolutely give up,' she said as she sniffed at the air and noticed the smogginess that was drifting towards her. Without thinking, she turned in the direction of where she thought the smell was coming from and, through narrowed eyes, she could just make out the church spire, with the river in the distance. It was a view she'd had for most of her life, and a lane that she'd walked down at least a thousand times before, yet today she felt as though she were seeing it all for the very first time. Of course, there was still the place where the trees were lined up on the hillside, it was a sight that Hattie knew she'd never be comfortable with, and unsteadily she pulled Jasper to one side of the lane as the sound of fast-moving footsteps jogged towards her. After the confrontation she'd just had with the man, she froze and defensively turned with her arm held protectively outward.

'Oh, sorry, I came up on you a bit fast there, my lovely, didn't I?' The voice came from a woman who was dressed in the brightest dayglow running clothes. Her black Lycra leggings had flashes of orange down each leg and were matched with a bright orange top that had been stretched over her more than ample bosom. It was only then that Hattie glanced up at her face and realised that the woman was much older than she'd have expected, a similar age to her mum, and had the same crow's feet that formed lines at the side of her eyes, the same soft ripples that surrounded her mouth.

'Oh hello, puppy, it's little Jasper, isn't it? I'd recognise you anywhere,' she said with an enthusiastic smile while leaning over and ruffling Jasper's ears. 'He's the young doctor's dog, isn't he?' As she asked the question, the woman stood upright, placed her hands on her hips and pulled deep breaths into her body. 'He's always out and about, aren't you, boy? I often see him out with one of his owners.' Pulling at a water bottle that was attached to her waistband, she took a long, slow slurp, wiped her brow with a wristband. 'Looks like you've got yourself a new friend,' she said directly to Jasper and, with her hand unexpectedly reaching out towards Hattie, she looked up to meet her gaze. 'I'm Patsy.'

'Oh, hello, Patsy, I'm pleased to meet you, but I'm not new, well, I guess I'm new to Jasper but I'm not new to the village.' She stopped, closed her eyes for a beat and gave the woman a friendly smile. 'I'm Hattie Gilby, I live at the vicarage.' As the words left her mouth, Hattie knew they'd been a terrible mistake as Patsy's face dropped, her face went pale and almost instinctively she took a huge step backwards.

'You, you're the vicar's daughter, aren't you, the one who...' She fumbled around with the water bottle and, in her attempt to push it back into her waistband, she missed and yelped as the plastic container rolled through the mud and came to a stop beside Jasper, who saw the whole thing as a game and looked as though he was ready to pounce.

'No, Jasper, don't do that.' Doing her best not to show how

much the woman's reaction had offended her, Hattie twisted Jasper's lead tightly around her hand, stopped him from lurching forward and leaned forward to pick the bottle up. 'I'm sorry,' she heard herself saying. 'Yes, my dad was the vicar. I take it you knew my family?' She closed her eyes for a blink and gave the woman an apologetic smile. 'Actually, don't answer that, I'm just going to...' She pointed to the lane, then back down to Jasper. 'Me... him, we'll be on our way.' It was all she could think to say as she turned, looked back at the trees that just ten minutes before had looked idyllic. The calmness she'd previously felt had gone and now, with her eyes filling with tears, she wanted nothing more than to return to the house and lock the doors and hibernate until the winter was over.

Just a few seconds later, Hattie heard the woman following, her footsteps grew louder and louder as she splashed through the puddles to catch her up and, once again, Jasper began to pay a lot of attention to what was happening behind him.

'Hattie, did you say, look... please wait,' Patsy shouted. 'I'm so sorry. I reacted quite badly, and I shouldn't have, it's just...' She closed her eyes, meditatively. 'I did know your parents. Although —' she shook her head contemplatively '—they probably wouldn't have remembered me and I was distraught when I heard what happened to them both, still am and...' Tipping her head to one side, she looked into Hattie's face and studied it with a smile. 'Do you know what, now I've got over the shock, you do remind me of her, of your mum. You've got the same shape lips and cheekbones, they're high, just like hers.' Patsy said as she held out a hand and gently placed it against Hattie's arm. 'I didn't always live around here, I lived in Northallerton, and that's where I met them. Your dad, he used to come to our church. He did the odd sermon and quite often he'd stay for coffee in the church hall after, which is where I met him.'

Looking up, Patsy stared at the trees, blinked repeatedly as though she was trying not to cry, and, for a moment, Hattie feared the words she'd say next and quickly interjected.

'You don't have to explain.'

'Oh I do,' the woman quickly replied. 'What happened to them both, it was such a tragedy and I still can't believe it happened, not without an explanation as to the who or why.' With a deep groan of despair, the woman once again leaned over and rested her hands against her knees. 'I mean, who would do that to two lovely people? People who never hurt anyone in their lives?' She closed her eyes, shook her head. 'I never heard anyone say a bad word against them... I mean, all those people they helped, including me.'

Smiling, Hattie felt the relief wash over her. Patsy's words had brought some comfort to her. She'd liked her parents. They'd helped her and others, which was not what Hattie had been expecting her to say. 'Thank you,' she said, 'I'm pleased that they helped you.'

'Helped me?' Patsy continued. 'I guess that help is such a small word in comparison to what he did, because your lovely dad did more than help me. He gave me the ultimate gift: he gave me my Henry and for that I'll be forever grateful.'

'Sorry, I'm not quite following. Who's Henry?' Hattie questioned apologetically, but looked over her shoulder to where Jasper had become bored of waiting and, as though under protest, had made his way to a puddle and lay in the water. 'Oh, for God's sake, Jasper, get out of there,' she shouted. 'You really do need a bath now, don't you?'

'Henry, he's my son, of course,' the woman replied with a furrowed brow. 'Your wonderful parents, they were angels of mercy and, without them, I'd have never got to adopt my boy, would I?' she questioned. 'And do you know what, last year, he had a boy of his own, which makes me an old and fuddy duddy grandma.' She held a hand up to her mouth, formed a cup and leaned forward as though she were telling a secret. 'Which is why I'm out jogging. If I want to keep up with the little one, I need to get fit. Don't I?' Laughing, she turned, and with an exaggerated trot, she began to jog away in the opposite direction. Her ponytail bounced up and down comically and, as she moved away, she gave Hattie a friendly wave over her shoulder. 'Next time you see your mum, you remember me to her, won't you. Tell her Patsy, Patsy Arnold, was asking about her and that I sent my love from the whole of my family.'

Automatically, Hattie nodded and waved. It was the right thing to do. Word about her mother's death would soon hit the village grapevine without her actually saying it and, with a heavy heart, Hattie wished she'd have come on this walk yesterday and that she'd have still had time to pass the message forward. At least then she'd have been able to ask her mother about the adoptions, about Louisa's adoption and, finally, she'd have had the chance to ask her outright as to whether she or her brothers had also been adopted.

Dragging Jasper out of the puddle, Hattie realised that there were as many puddles ahead of her as there were behind. Although she noted that Jasper couldn't get much wetter if he tried, for a second, she wondered which way she should go. Whether it was easier to go back the way she'd come or whether she should carry on regardless.

Lifting her phone from her pocket, Hattie glanced down at the time. She was sure that Sophie wouldn't be back for at least a couple more hours and, as the screen lit up and Charlie's name flashed up before her, she quickly closed the phone down, pushed it back in her pocket and realised that talking to Charlie right now would be more than she could bear. She didn't need another argument, nor did she want to spoil her walk by having to explain about her mother and break down in tears while she did it.

Instead, Hattie picked up her pace, and pulled a soaking wet Jasper behind her. She was in a rush to get home. She needed to talk to her brothers. She wanted to tell them about the conversation she'd just had with Patsy, and the revelation about the adoptions. Of course, they had all been aware that their parents had been instrumental in Louisa's adoption, but now that circle had widened in the knowledge that they'd arranged many more and, with a confident smile, Hattie felt liberated in the knowledge that at least now she had some idea of what they should look for.

36

PRESENT DAY – DECEMBER 2023 – SOPHIE

After hurriedly dropping Noah off at nursery, Sophie pulled Hattie's car to the side of the road and parked it next to the kebab shop that faced the surgery. Her positioning gave her a clear view of Finn's car, the road and the front door to the surgery. Now all she had to do was wait for her husband to emerge and, for her own reassurance, her thoughts went back to the phone call she'd overheard the day before. 'I'm sorry, Doctor Alexander's gone out... he had an emergency visit, I'm afraid, and his diary says that he'll be out tomorrow morning too.'

Drumming her fingers impatiently against the steering wheel, Sophie hoped that the appointment would be at the same time as it had been the day before and impulsively, while waiting, she cast an eye around Hattie's car. It was more than obvious that it had been packed in a hurry and, like she'd said, she'd only managed to unpack some of her things and a good portion of her life still remained in the car. There was a duvet and a pillow that took up half the back seat along with half a dozen pairs of shoes that had been dropped behind the driver's seat, giving the car the unpleasant, musty odour. In the front footwell were bags of books and, with her gaze dropping into the bag closest, Sophie pulled at a book from inside. '*Tess of the d'Urbervilles*. Really?' She thought about Hattie and quickly realised how, after their initial meeting, she'd assumed what kind of person she'd be. She certainly hadn't thought she'd be the kind of person to read the classics and now she quickly berated herself for being so mean.

'Let's hope someone prepared you for the ending,' she laughed as she dropped the book back into the bag and then looked up as she saw her husband confidently stride across the car park. His overcoat had been pulled on and a dark pink-striped scarf hung loosely around his neck and, as she'd fully expected, as he did on all of his domiciliary visits, he gripped his medical bag in one of his hands.

'So, let's see what you're up to?' she whispered under her breath as though he'd be able to hear her and automatically ducked in her seat as he looked across the road and in her direction.

Holding her breath, she waited patiently for Finn to pull up to the junction, and for his car's indicator to flash. It was the only way she'd know which way to turn and, even from here, she could see the anxious look on his face, his furrowed brow and the way he continually chewed on the side of his lip. It was something he did during times of high stress, like he had on the day she'd given birth to Noah and had ended up sat beside her, needing treatment.

Turning into the road behind him, Sophie followed at a distance. She did all she could to keep at least one car between her and Finn and felt confident that he hadn't already spotted her, that he wouldn't recognise the car, and that at least for now he had no idea that he was being followed along a road lined with terraced houses, council properties and an odd industrial unit that had been squeezed onto some old, unused land. But the village was small and, in the distance, she could already see that they were about to drive out of the built-up area and onto roads that were surrounded by fields and the valley. While practically holding her breath, Sophie furrowed her brow as Finn unexpectedly turned down an old, winding lane that she'd been down before.

Slowing down at the junction, she waited. She didn't want to turn too quickly and gave it a few seconds just in case Finn had been on autopilot and had driven down the lane in error. It was the only explanation she could think of and for him to turn towards the railway house, in the middle of the day, where both he and his grandmother lived.

'Maybe he forgot something. Maybe he's just calling in before he goes somewhere else,' she whispered as she drove past the dominant, solitary two-storey red brick building. It stood in the middle of an overgrown garden without another house in sight and the only thing for miles that spoiled the view was the trainline where at least twenty trains a day flew past the house, tooting their horns, and making the ornaments on Frieda's mantelpiece shake with vibration.

With her eyes constantly searching for Finn and her fingers gripping the steering wheel like a vice, Sophie followed him down the lane. Slowing the car, she prayed that, once she got to them, the railway barriers wouldn't be closed. If they were and Finn was stood in the garden, there would be a chance he'd see her, that he'd recognise the car and that she'd find herself having to explain why she was there.

With the house in sight and the barriers open, Hattie crawled along the lane until the moment when the loud, ominous alarm began and, with her mind flying into overdrive and with no time to waste, she slammed her foot firmly against the accelerator, sped across the line and, heart booming in her chest, watched through the rear-view mirror as the barriers dropped right behind her.

Hitting the brakes, Sophie stared into the footwell and took a moment to catch her breath. Her fingers had gone white with the pressure of squeezing the wheel and forcibly she willed herself to let go, but couldn't. Racing across a line wasn't something she felt proud of. The danger had been real and, just a few seconds later, she'd have left her son without a mother and for what? Because she'd believed that her husband had been up to no good, because she'd wanted to catch him out, when, in fact, all he was doing was popping back home. The word 'home' struck her like a punch. Finn had left her. He didn't live with her and Noah any more, he lived with his grandmother, and this house was now his home, and she had no idea if they'd ever be a family of three again. It was a thought that tore her in two. She'd always loved being part of a family and, if she didn't have a family here, in England, then the only route left open to her was to go back to Ireland to the family she had there. But, first, she owed it to herself and to Noah to fix what was broken and, if it killed her, she had every intention of convincing Finn to come back to their home.

Feeling satisfied that she'd managed to park far enough away from the house as she could, without being seen, Sophie climbed out of the car, looked over her shoulder continuously and began to walk the short distance back to the track. While using the undergrowth as camouflage, she peered above the railings in the hope she'd be able to see whether or not Finn was still there.

Standing nervously by the line, Sophie studied Frieda's house from a distance and came to the conclusion that it looked odd. The lower floor with its small, insignificant windows looked very different to the floor above that had large, picture windows that seemed to circumnavigate the building. 'They were built like that because of the trains,' Frieda had told her during one of her few earlier visits. 'Smaller windows help with the noise, not like the ones upstairs. They're big and wide, it's so that the track can be seen for miles and miles.' She'd said the words proudly, while passing her a framed image of her husband stood with his father. 'My Douglas, his father used to be the station master here. He grew up here and would stand upstairs with his dad for hours on end because it was his job to watch the level crossing. To operate the lights and to maintain the gates. And every day, at least twenty times a day. Rain or shine. His dad would run up and down those steps at the back of the house. He'd stop the traffic and manually open and close those gates. It was nothing like today, of course, with their loud sirens and flashing lights.' She'd paused and wiped the tears that were filling her eyes. 'When we got married, we moved away. His parents died and other people took over this house. But my Douglas, he always missed the place and, when he spotted it had come up for sale, he insisted that we packed up our life in Bedale and buy it,' she laughed. 'You should have seen our Finn's face when he heard the first train whizz past, he was horrified.'

'What if his dad forgot to close them?' Sophie had asked. 'What would have happened then?'

'Oh, he wouldn't have forgot. My Douglas, he said that his dad used to know what times the trains were due. He'd watch the line ahead with his binoculars and, as soon as he saw them approaching, he'd get himself down there and close those gates, rain or shine. And don't forget, we only had a few cars going through a day back then. They only went to the farm as they do now.' She'd shook her head as the memory passed and Frieda's voice had faded, making Sophie feel uncomfortable by the silence.

'Why does she still live there? You'd think she'd move now that your grandad has passed, wouldn't you? I can't see any reason for her to stay.' Sophie had said to Finn not long after their first visit. It had been a question that had taken him a while to answer and, after a thoughtful pause, he'd said, 'I don't know. Maybe she has her reasons, maybe she's just grown to like it there.'

Squinting to see the upstairs rooms, Sophie felt puzzled by the woodchip boards that covered the windows. They were boards that, as long as she'd known, had been there, making the upper floor look tired and unused, and she made a mental note to ask Finn why it had been done, and whether or not it made the house feel as creepy as it looked.

Walking as slowly as she could along the side of the track, Sophie looked for movement. Finn's car was still parked in the drive, as was Frieda's, and for a moment she thought about phoning him, asking him about his day and how it was going? But, deep inside, she dreaded his answer. She couldn't bear the idea that he'd lie to her and knew that to entrap him wasn't the answer. The one thing she did know was that Frieda hadn't been sick the day before. She'd been as large as life at the surgery and hadn't needed a doctor. And, according to the receptionist the day before, Finn was out visiting a patient. Which was why Sophie felt confused.

Looking over her shoulder to where Hattie's car was parked, she considered walking back to it, climbing back in and pulling it into Frieda's drive and joining in with the family reunion. But something told her not to. If she did, she'd have to explain why she was there. Why she wasn't at home resting her ankle, how her limp had miraculously disappeared and why she was in someone else's car, when she had a perfectly good car parked on the drive outside their house. A car that she still had to move and hide for a day, in the pretence that, for Hattie's benefit, it had been at the garage.

Feeling exposed, Sophie disappointedly gave up on the voyeurism. 'It's not as though he's meeting up with another woman, is it?' she grumbled and felt almost disappointed that she hadn't found him to be doing something more sinister. 'And I guess that visiting his gran isn't such a bad thing, is it?' she whispered. 'So why do I get the feeling there's something I'm missing, something really important?'

Walking back to the car, she opened the door, threw herself inside and, with her hands banging against the steering wheel, she leaned back against the headrest and rested her eyes. 'Come on,' she said. 'Think of the facts. He lives in this house, so it isn't odd that he's come here, apart from the fact that he's supposed to be working and, if he likes it so much, why doesn't he like taking me here?' It was a fact. Sophie had only ever been in Frieda's house a handful of times. The first time had been on a day before they'd moved to live here and, even though she'd never wanted to eat anything made in Frieda's kitchen, she had always found it odd that they rarely visited, not even on Christmas or birthdays.

'It's just easier for me to come to you, my lovely. Isn't it?' Frieda had often said. 'All of Noah's things are at yours, and besides,' she'd said with her hand patting Noah's head like a puppy, 'you don't always want to be bundling him up, dragging him around in the car and sitting him in a house that's as noisy as hell, now, do you?' She'd shaken her head and picked Noah up. 'Your granny loves you far too much to put you through all those scary noises, doesn't she?' It had been a statement that

Sophie couldn't argue with, and it had quickly become the norm for Frieda to go to them.

Sucking in a long, deep breath, Sophie screwed her eyes up tight. She went over the conversation she'd had with Frieda the day before, right from the moment she'd sat down beside her, and they'd talked about everything and absolutely nothing. It had been a constant round of questions and answers, most of which had been directed at Noah. And even though Frieda had said that Finn had asked her to come and watch Noah, she'd made her excuses and left abruptly before Sophie had been called into her appointment. Which, now that Sophie thought about it, had all seemed a little bit odd. Especially when, today, he was at her house, rather than being out seeing a patient.

37

PRESENT DAY – DECEMBER 2023 – HATTIE

Turning across the square and towards her house, Hattie wrinkled her nose. The smogginess had grown, the air now thick with the smell of the burning and a plume of smoke could be seen coming from behind her house.

Confused and without hesitation, Hattie ran down the drive, pulled Jasper behind her and, with the effort of an Olympic hurdler, she cleared the drystone wall that stood to one side of the house as the black plume of smoke became more apparent. Nervously, she hesitated and placed a hand over her mouth as she caught sight of the files, the utility bills and old, overread novels that were scattered along the garden path, right next to a single copy of the Bible, that lay on its back with its pages pointing upwards and wafting back and forth in the breeze.

Tying Jasper to the tree, Hattie inched forward and, fearful of what was happening, she willed the pup to stay quiet as a loud, ominous bang was followed by a grating noise that made her stop in her tracks. With her back to the wall and her eyes stinging from the smoke, she peered around the side of the house, into the back garden and to where, in the middle of the

The Family Home

vegetable plot, a bonfire raged with fury. The smell of molten plastic and burning wood hit the back of her throat and, while coughing repeatedly, she instinctively covered her face with her scarf, as another plume of thick black smoke travelled towards her. Turning away and with her eyes filled with fear, she looked into the kitchen, where Adam stood, with his nostrils flared, and eyes that had widened to form big dark circles, full of an explosive rage that Hattie didn't recognise.

'Hattie, you need to get out of my way!' Standing before her, he held out an arm full of files. 'I've burned the desk and these, these are next,' he shouted. It was a tone that made her consider her next move and, with her eyes fixed on the files, she took a calculated step back, and held her hands up submissively.

'Adam. Please, please don't do that.' She thought about Patsy, about how she would tell him what had been said and how the files were now more important than ever. But Adam looked determined. He moved fiercely from foot to foot and Hattie held her breath as one after the other case files fell to the floor.

'Adam, this isn't the answer. You do know that, don't you?' she said calmly. 'I need you to stop, to think, and I'm begging you, please don't burn these files.' She fixed her eyes firmly on his and gave him what she hoped would look like a calm, sisterly smile. But his shoulders lifted dramatically, and his nostrils continued to flare until a loud bang came from inside the fire and a flurry of sparks flew upwards. 'I have something to tell you, something important and these files, they could be important too.'

Ignoring her plea, Adam forced his way past, stamped across the gravel and the mud and headed to the edge of the fire. 'It was all a lie,' Adam said with an over-enthusiastic nod that was quickly followed by a sadistic laugh. A sudden wave of unspent emotion washed across his face and his features immediately turned from being handsome and charismatic to harsh and full of resentment. He barked the words and then, as though the mud were swallowing him whole, he slid to his knees, where he began to search through the wet, ruined files and, one by one, he picked them up and with his shoulders slumped dramatically tossed each of the files into the flames.

Shivering with the cold, Hattie felt her heart break in two. She knew that grief made people do the craziest of things, but seeing Adam in this much pain was more than she could bear. With tears rolling down her face, she found herself slipping to the ground, to kneel beside him.

'Adam, please.' The words were followed by a heartfelt sob. The events of the day had proved too much, her thoughts were spinning around in a bizarre and confusing way. It was more than obvious that Adam knew the truth, that he'd found something in his mother's office that had sent him into a rage. She just didn't know what, or how to tell him what Patsy had said or whether it would bring him some comfort. 'Tell me what you found.'

With her body trembling with fear, Hattie held an arm up to shield her face from the heat and squinted through burning eyes as a long, sorrowful howl came from behind her, where Jasper was tied. The smoke was making him howl and he kept going between jumping up and down to lying flat on his stomach in an attempt to get out of the smoke.

'Hattie, it's better if you don't know. If you never know the truth,' he said abruptly and, with his whole body erupting with anger, he picked up a wooden shelf and tossed it fiercely towards the fire, sending a new array of sparks flying angrily upward. Then, because there was nothing left to throw, he began to twist his hands together and, from somewhere deep inside, he let out a long, sorrowful yell and turned towards her with a look of desperation. 'This house,' He paused, thought about his words. 'It's evil. Pure fucking evil and, even though I'd happily burn it all to the ground, we can't, and we're stuck here...'

'Adam, you're not making any sense, what the hell did you find?' With his hands gripping hers, Hattie could feel the uncontrollable way they were shaking, the fear that sat deep within his eyes and the way that, even with the heat hitting him square in the face, he'd gone pale with anguish.

38

NINE YEARS BEFORE – IMOGEN

Dressed in a pale blue cotton shift dress, perfect make-up and with her hair looking as though it had been professionally styled, Imogen Gilby sat at the round oak breakfast table with its lace tablecloth and pretty shop-bought carnations stood in a vase.

After laying the table for her family ready for breakfast, she'd sat back and admired how pretty it looked. Floral bone china cups, with matching saucers, and a teapot stood around the table, along with a selection of toast and croissants that were growing colder by the minute. To finish the table, she'd placed a small dish of butter to one side along with a deep purple plum jam she'd made last summer.

Slowly, she flicked through the pages of a *House Beautiful* magazine and, with a long, pointed, perfectly manicured finger, she carefully tried to study each page and read every article with care, in the knowledge that, if anyone arrived, or looked over the wall at the bottom of the garden, they would think she was simply reading a magazine or planning to redecorate.

In reality, her eyes never left the tree-line that stood in the distance behind the house. It was still early and, being winter, the sun had taken a long time to rise, which meant that the blue flashing lights still lit up the horizon, and the silhouette of a white forensic tent had been placed between the tallest two trees, with a floodlight that showed the silhouettes of the forensic examiners, stood inside, studying a body. It was an immediate visual reminder that Berni's body was still there, all alone, on the frozen ground and surrounded by an array of undergrowth that had been used to hide her.

'Morning, darling.' Walking into the kitchen, Gerald kissed her upturned cheek and, with a cursory glance across the field, sat down beside her. Picked up the teapot and used it like a giant china pointer. 'I see they're still out there,' he sighed, 'doing what they normally do.' He pushed his glasses further up his nose and then made a show of sniffing the air. 'Is that bacon I smell cooking?'

Imogen gave the cooker a glance and pushed him away. 'As you can see, darling, the pan didn't jump out of the drawer and start cooking it for you, nor does it say restaurant over the door, so...' She gave him an audacious smile. 'If you're hungry, I think you might like to cook it yourself.'

While rolling his jaw and trying to think up a suitable answer, Gerald allowed the comment to pass. He flicked his eyes upwards, and to what was happening outside, before turning back to his wife with a thoughtful but knowing look. 'Are the children not up yet?' he asked, as he poured the tea and with a small silver spoon added some sugar.

Imogen waited for him to add the milk before lovingly resting her hand over her husband's. 'Let them sleep,' she said. 'They've had a long night, and... so have we.' Taking in a long, deep breath, she closed her painful, burning eyes. She had the urge to press her fingers tightly against the sockets and relieve herself of the pain, but had no wish to spoil her carefully applied make-up.

'There were loads of them out there earlier,' she whispered. 'They were walking across the field with torches that were really bright and, I swear, they searched every inch of those woods.' She lifted the teacup to her lips and, without drinking, held the cup in front of her face to cover her mouth. 'The police, I'm sure they found some things. They bagged them, and labelled them,' she whispered and pointed to the circumference of the field. 'All the way across, they went. A long row of men, all dressed in those silly white suits.'

'Darling, stop worrying. It's nothing that will affects us, and there's nothing for them to find.' Gerald suddenly barked in a low, disgruntled voice. 'The knife has gone.'

The statement was followed by a moment's silence, until eventually Imogen slowly turned her eyes towards him. 'And Alice,' she asked, 'has she gone too?' With a cautionary look over her shoulder, she threw him an unspoken apology. 'You said you'd let her go, that she wouldn't be any trouble.'

'Immi, you have to realise. All of this changed everything. Her baby was born the night before last and Alice...' Lifting the newspaper, he began to flick through the pages without reading. 'You could say she disappeared.' He took in a deep breath and, with his jaw set rigid, dropped the newspaper, leaned forward and pressed a hand down on her knee until she couldn't move. With a menacing smile, he moved his face close to hers until she could feel his breath on her face. 'You don't need to worry, she held her baby and she died happy.'

'You didn't need to kill her,' Imogen quickly fired back. 'She was my friend. She confided in me and, do you know what, I happened to like her.'

'Don't be so bloody naïve, Imogen. She wasn't your friend.'

He pressed a kiss against her cheek and tightened his grip. 'Once I knew she had family that were coming here, screaming and asking questions, I couldn't risk it. They were going to expose us.'

Tearfully, Imogen kept her eyes on the magazine she'd been so happily admiring before her husband had come down to breakfast. 'She just wanted her child to go to a better home,' she finally said. 'She begged me and I promised her that her baby would be looked after.'

'And you won't break your promise. That baby is already on its way to Suffolk, he'll be brought up by a rich family, with a big house and garden, much like the ones you look at in these stupid magazines.' Gerald slammed his hand against the table, making Imogen catch her breath as the china jumped and vibrated, before coughing into his hand and giving her a firm, questioning look. 'What's done is done. We need to move on.'

For appearances sake, and just in case anyone was watching, he once again pressed a kiss against her cheek. 'And, just for your information, she's at the bottom of old Mrs Stockton's grave. I buried her myself in the last place anyone would think to look. Even the sniffer dogs would struggle to find a body, amongst bodies.' Moving backwards, he once again picked up the teapot, refreshed his cup with the amber fluid. 'It's just a shame we didn't have time to move the mother.' He nodded and slid his hand upwards to touch the clerical collar that hung around his neck, as if by doing so it might relieve him from the feeling of guilt. 'At least then, we wouldn't have this bloody circus going on in the back field and you might have been in a better mood.'

Opening the newspaper, he shook it into position and spread it out on the table before him.

'And Berni?'

'She had to go. She was loud, and she was obnoxious,' he spat the words out with venom. 'She knew exactly who we were. I'm sure of it.' Turning the page of his newspaper, he kept his eye on the door. 'And, if you'd worked out who Alice was before taking her on, you'd have seen the danger. You'd have known what would happen.'

Bruised, Imogen felt her composure slip. But, then she dragged the air in, lifted her chin and looked her husband straight in the eye. 'I'm not the only one to blame, Gerald, you made mistakes too, so don't you dare land all of this on my shoulders.' She picked up the butter knife, held it towards him. 'You're not the only one capable of killing and don't you forget it!'

Leaning to one side, Gerald cupped her chin with his fingers and sensually pressed a long, suggestive kiss against her lips. With a wry smile, he sat back down, picked up his teacup and sipped at his tea. 'Darling, I love you when you're angry,' he said. 'But, you know the sermon, he that is without sin amongst you, let him first cast a stone at her,' he quoted from the Bible. 'When I dragged you out of the gutter, you were nothing more than a cheap, nasty prostitute and I think you should remember that every time you look in the mirror. Or at the children I gave you.'

With resentment building inside her, Imogen felt herself cringe. They were the same words she'd heard him say at least a hundred times before and, each time he said them, she hated him a little bit more and without thought she once again picked up the knife and held it against the side of his leg.

'Well, we both know that Hattie isn't yours, don't we?' she sneered, 'So, you gave me my boys and look at the pain you caused others by doing it.'

'Immi,' he continued as he quickly disarmed her and slammed the knife back down on the table. 'We gave our children a better life.' He shook his head, took hold of her hand. 'After Hattie was born, I saw that look in your eye, the way you looked every time you saw someone with a new-born and, I have to admit, I ached for a child of my own and it was only by the good of God that these women seemed to trust us both. They wanted a better home for their babies and it really didn't hurst for us both to make a profit, did it. People were willing to pay for babies. We have to remember that everyone won from the deal.' He smiled, nodding, and once again looked out and across the fields. 'Apart from the women we disposed of.' He turned, cocked his head to one side as though listening to the house. 'We need to change the subject. The children, they'll be up soon.'

'We're going to go to hell in a handcart for what we did, Gerald. You do know that, don't you?' She held her hand to her heart. Tapped her fingers against it. 'I can feel it. I can feel it right here in my heart.'

For a few moments, the only noise in the room came from the rustling of newspaper while Imogen thought of the woman she'd allowed to escape so many years before, the help she'd given her and the lies she'd told.

'Immi. No one suspects a thing, and you can't crumble. I won't let you. Not today. I need you to be strong... As far as the congregation are concerned, today is just another day at the office. I'll go to the house. I'll see Berni's family. I'll check in on the search party, who are still looking for Alice.' He paused, smiled indignantly. 'We both know that the search will be fruitless and, when you see me on the news, giving a report to the press, you'll be proud of the performance I give. By lunchtime, I'll have held hands with all the grieving relatives and I'll stand there and pray with them, just as is expected.'

Sitting forward in her chair, Imogen flicked at an imaginary speck of dust from the shoulder of his jacket. 'You are clever, aren't you?' she said sarcastically. 'No one would ever suspect the village vicar. Would they?'

Turning to the window, she stared up at the dark rolling clouds. Gerald was right and, even though she hated him for constantly reminding her, she'd been no one when they'd first met and, just like both Berni and Alice, she'd been the one to stand on street corners and happily charge for her services until Gerald had taken her in and had given her a home and a family.

'I can't be found out, Gerald. I just can't. When Berni turned up here, I knew she'd recognised me, in fact, I was sure she had.' She took in a deep breath, walked to the window, and lifted the latch before lifting her chin and dragging in the cold winter air. 'It has to stop, Gerald, I just...' She stopped, thoughtfully. 'I can't do it any more and I know it's lucrative, but I just want a normal life and to be a vicar's wife. I want to be the one who makes tea in the church hall and bakes scones for the congregation.' Jumping backwards, Imogen felt the grip on her wrist and, with force, her whole body moved backwards. It was what he did. The kind, sweet, calm-tempered vicar, that behind closed doors could turn on a sixpence.

'You ungrateful bitch. I did it for you. For us. For my children... If you hadn't messed up your own body, you'd have given me a son and I wouldn't have had to go out and find them, would I?'

'It wasn't my fault...'

'So whose fault was it?' he asked. 'Mine?'

He pushed her roughly to one side and, with an indomitable stride, walked to the worktop, where he took a knife from a large block, picked an apple out of the bowl and with long, sweeping cuts, began to slice the fruit into pieces.

It was an action that made Imogen stare at the knife block

for longer than she should have and, with the anger growing within her, she considered her options. Everything she ever did started and ended with Gerald. He'd made all the rules since she'd been a girl and she wondered what it would be like if he were no longer there and she was allowed to make the decisions, all by herself.

Dismissing the thought as quickly as it had come, she turned back to the window, where she spotted the pair of black and white spaniels. They dragged their police handlers along at speed, their noses already hot on a trail. 'My God. They've brought the dogs in.' Her voice wobbled, precariously. 'What if...'

Walking to stand behind her, she felt Gerald's hand drop onto her shoulders. Flinching, she waited for the pain he'd inflict. 'Don't. Worry. About. A. Thing,' he said slowly. 'The whole field behind us is an ancient burial ground. It's full of dead bodies,' he said as his hands grew tighter. 'The whole damn place is full of cadavers and, from what I know, one smells much like the other.' He leaned back, crossed his arms defiantly. 'They can't excavate them all, can they?'

'Excavate what?' Hattie sauntered into the room. She was still wearing her red-checked pyjamas; her hair was tied up in a high, messy bun that spilled out from its elastic and a towelling dressing gown had been thrown loosely around her shoulders. 'Oh God. Are they still out there?' she asked and moved around the kitchen, slowly opening one cupboard after the next. Searching for food. 'Did they find Alice?'

'No, and there's some bread in the pantry. There's also plenty of eggs or cereals,' Imogen shouted across the kitchen. She looked up at her husband, caught his eye, gave him a short, sharp shake of her head. 'Throw some bacon in a pan, Hattie, will you, darling. Your dad's looking as though he could do with a good start to his day, and I'm already dressed and ready for work. First client will be here just after nine and the last thing I need is splatter marks across the front of my dress from frying.' She pulled a cigarette out of a packet, placed it in her mouth and waited for her husband to light it.

Sitting back down at the table, Imogen smiled proudly as Hattie did as she was asked. Even though she couldn't help herself, she watched Hattie butter the bread. The way she placed it on a plate and added brown sauce with the ultimate care. The sandwich-making routine was all going to plan, until Luke sneaked in from behind and, with a lightning reaction, grabbed a piece of bacon straight from the pan, picked up a slice of her readily buttered bread and, with a clap of his hands, joyfully pressed the two together. 'Ta da. Sandwich.'

'Hey, get off.' Hattie yelled. 'That's for Dad. Mum, tell him.'

'Tell him what?' Imogen picked up the teapot, gave it a shake and disappointedly placed it back down. 'Tell him not to steal bacon when he's obviously hungry or just tell him that I love him,' she laughed. 'Put the kettle on, Luke, darling, will you?' She lifted her face to his, accepted the kiss he proffered and blew out a long white stream of smoke.

'Morning,' he said while pushing the sandwich firmly into his mouth. 'Have they found anything yet?' He pointed to the search team, who were starting at the edge of the field and working their way inwards. It was a question that no one answered. The silence in the room was only disturbed by the continued spatter of bacon as it sizzled in the pan and the constant tapping of Luke's finger as he searched his phone, looking for news. 'There just has to be something on here about it.'

'Put that down,' Gerald said as he lifted his cup to his mouth. 'You know I don't like phones at the table, it's disrespectful to your mother. She spends a lot of time preparing your meals.'

Laughing out loud, Luke pulled a chair out from the table. Spun it around and straddled it, rodeo style. 'Well, if I'm not mistaken, Hattie made the bacon and she didn't even cook it for me, she cooked it for you. Didn't you, Sis?' he joked. 'I was just in the right place at the right time and took full benefit of the situation.' He wiped his mouth free of grease with an over-exaggerated sweep of his hand.

'Don't be facetious.'

'Dad. I don't even know what facetious means. I'm just keeping my sister inside the house. Where she's safe.' Luke ducked as his dad playfully swiped him. 'There's some nutter out there, killing women, and if I were her, well, I'd stay indoors, 'til the lunatic is caught.'

'Why don't *you* stay indoors?' Hattie threw back.

'He isn't killing men. He's killing women.'

'Maybe, if you don't shut up, this woman will be killing you.' With a half-smile, Hattie lifted the bacon out of the pan. Placed it on top of a newly buttered piece of bread and passed it to her father. 'Besides, how do you know it's a man?'

Choking on her tea, Imogen swallowed as hard as she could, stubbed out her cigarette and sighed. She'd always taken pleasure in the bickering that passed between the two children, but today it was different and, with a sorrowful gulp, she waved her hand around as her lip began to wobble. 'Sorry. I'm sorry. It's just all so sad, isn't it?' She threw a look to the opposite end of the table where Adam had sidled in, with his phone held tightly in his hand. He was quiet in comparison to the other two. Less boisterous and, even though he normally had his head stuck in a book or was looking at some kind of device, he was ordinarily the most pleasant amongst them.

'In a three-year period,' Adam suddenly said, 'the majority of people convicted of murder were men. Ninety-two per cent of them, to be exact.' He looked up from his phone. 'So, the probability—'

'Okay, okay, we get it,' Luke cut in. 'But what the hell happened out there last night?' He held his hands out, palms up. 'We were all out searching for this Alice woman, who, just to remind everyone, is still missing.' He leaned against the patio door, crossed his arms defiantly. 'And then we find her mother, in the woods, with her throat cut from ear to ear.' He paused and threw a playful punch in his older brother's direction. 'I mean, what is that all about?'

39

PRESENT DAY – DECEMBER 2023 – SOPHIE

An hour after she'd parked, Sophie began to fidget in her seat. The weather had once again changed. Large, bulbous raindrops fell against the windscreen and, without putting the wipers on to clear her view, she was stuck in the car, unable to see anything that was happening outside and her view of the house at the other side of the lines was now completely distorted.

Periodically, the sirens would blast out with a shrill repetitive sound that told her that a train was coming. Then the gates would drop down to block the road and, twice already, they'd stayed down for much longer than she'd have liked. All the time leaving her on edge, watching and waiting for Finn to leave and hoping that that wouldn't happen, not until she had the chance to follow him back down the lane and hopefully on to his next destination.

As the rain finally began to stop, she looked at the house through narrowed eyes and felt sure she saw a small, but significant movement. The upstairs window that was half boarded over had a section of chipboard missing, presumably to allow some light into the room. But it was here that she saw the old, dirty curtain move to one side, a hand waved frantically and then, a face filled the space and a pair of eyes stared right at her. Everything happened in less than a few seconds and, the longer she stared, the more convinced she became that it might never have happened at all.

'Great,' she whispered. 'Now you're bloody hallucinating.' With the steering wheel tightly gripped between her fingers, Sophie held on to her breath. She couldn't help but keep her eyes on the window and did all she could not to blink. But the movement was gone and now, she convinced herself, as well as everything else, her imagination was playing tricks on her and staying where she was wasn't helping the situation. She came to the conclusion that it was time to go back to the nursery.

With the engine slowly ticking over, she was just about to set off when she heard a door bang in the distance. To gain a better view, she flicked her windscreen wipers on and stared to see Finn, who stood at the top of the steep wooden staircase, with his medical bag held tightly in his hand and his face full of thunder. With her thoughts going back to the face in the window, she shuddered and began to second guess what she'd seen.

'Maybe it was just his gran,' she blinked repeatedly as though, by doing so, she'd be able to replay the scene. 'I mean, who the hell else would it be?'

Broodingly, Sophie touched the accelerator. She was tired of playing detective. Tired of trying to make sense of her husband's behaviour. She leaned forward in her seat, just as the front door of Frieda's house flew open. It was a sight that made her jump from the car and with the engine still running, she eased the door until it was only just closed and ran to the fence, where she crouched, hidden by the undergrowth and peered at the way Frieda pulled an old, long cardigan around her shoulders and grimaced at Finn. Every inch of her large, rotund body stood in front of Finn like a barrier blocking the doorway and without warning, she curled her lip, pointed at the room upstairs and, thrust a hand outward, to slap Finn hard across his face.

Reeling from the shock, and so as not to give herself away, Sophie crouched further down. She knelt into the undergrowth and held her hand up to cover her mouth. She didn't care that the rain was soaking into the knees of her jeans, or that they'd probably be ruined by the stains. What she did care about was Finn and the fact that, right now, he might see her. With a million questions flying around in her mind, Sophie considered running across the track towards him. But, instead, she stayed where she was with her jeans becoming more soaked by the minute and shaking with anticipation, as Frieda slammed the door. Leaving Finn to stand open-mouthed in the middle of the path, drenched from the rain, and glaring up at the window above.

40

PRESENT DAY – DECEMBER 2023 – SOPHIE

Pulling the car up outside Frieda's house, Sophie took in a deep breath and breathed in the scent of crisp white lilies, fresh pinecones and exotic orchids that lay in the bouquet beside her. After following Finn back to the surgery, she'd called at the florist and, with a cunning plan, she'd headed back towards Frieda's.

'Hi, how are you doing?' Sophie said in a voice that sang out an octave higher than normal. She'd parked up and sat outside for a good ten minutes while all the time keeping her gaze on the upstairs window and daring herself to climb out of the car.

'What do we owe this pleasure?' Frieda asked, with her body standing before Sophie like a giant fortress. 'And whose car are you in? That isn't your car, is it, and you're all dirty. What on earth did you do to your clothes?' she reeled off the words without taking a breath.

'It's a long story. I was on my way to see you, hence the flowers, and I got a flat tyre.' She took in a deep breath and gave Frieda a gentle but candid smile. 'I had to change it all by myself, hence the mess on my clothes, but because I'd already bought the flowers I thought it would be okay to still come.' Standing on her tiptoes, Sophie pushed the bouquet of flowers into Frieda's hand and took an assertive step forward, giving Frieda no alternative but to stand to one side. 'And the car, it's my neighbour's.'

'Well... er, come in.'

'They smell lovely, don't they?' Sophie pointed to the flowers. 'The car smells amazing. I can almost pick out each scent of lilies, roses and pinecones.' Casting her gaze around the living room, Sophie tried to think what else she could say. It was the first time she'd been there without either Noah or Finn and, anxiously, she began to twist her fingers around each other and wished she'd thought up a much better plan.

'Oh, this is cosy. I love your house,' she finally said. 'It's a long time since I've been but it never changes, does it?' The lounge was small, and only just big enough for a double settee and a single chair, although there were small side tables scattered all around the edges of the room, as though every inch of every wall had to be filled. Each of the tables were cluttered. Some had small boxes of tissues, glasses of water, spectacles. Others held remote controls and another was covered in a set of framed photographs and a radio that blasted out from the corner. A small bathroom stood to the side of the door, along with a double bedroom and a dining kitchen that only had a sink, a hob and single cupboard in it. These were the rooms where Frieda had lived for the past forty years surrounded by the junk shop ornaments and piles of books, and magazines that lived on the floor.

Cringing, Sophie stood perfectly still as Frieda wrapped her arms around her and planted kisses all over her cheek. It was a show of affection she'd come to expect, although it was the part she hated the most. What she really wanted was to find out who was upstairs, especially when she knew that the only other bedrooms were up there, which included the room that Finn had had since being a boy.

'Oh, thank you, thank you, thank you. What a lovely surprise,' Frieda uttered. 'It's not very often I get bought flowers these days.' She looked around the room expectantly and, with the colour flushing her face, began to shuffle the piles of books and magazines until she cleared a space on the settee. 'I wasn't expecting guests,' she grumbled. 'I'd have tidied up if I'd known you were coming. Now then, you sit down right there and tell me what I did to deserve such a gesture.'

'Well, you're always doing stuff for us and, after seeing you yesterday, I thought you might need a bit of a boost.' Sophie knew she was waffling, and making forced conversation, but what she really wanted was to dig Frieda for information and, with her head tipped to one side, she listened to the house, hoped to hear a noise from above, anything that would start the conversation about who was living upstairs. 'Besides,' she continued, 'I don't see you very often. Not without either Finn or Noah and I thought it'd be nice for me to visit you for a change and for us to have a nice, long chat.' It was the only thing she could say to buy her some time. To look for any sign that would tell her why Finn had been there and, more to the point, why he and his gran had argued. With a grateful, loving smile, she hoped that Frieda would offer her a drink.

'Oh, that's a shame,' Frieda replied and hurriedly looked at her watch. 'I'm just going out, otherwise I'd have put the kettle on.' She stood up, walked through the room and toward her bedroom. 'I just need to get changed. You don't mind, do you?'

Standing up as quickly as she could, Sophie scoured the room. There were so many things lying around, so much clutter and a month's worth of dust that covered each of the surfaces, making Sophie afraid to touch anything in case she left a fingerprint or a smudge. Once she'd given up on finding any clues, she walked to the front door and saw a small key laying on the shelf behind a bright red candle.

'You know Maria, don't you?' Frieda asked as she came out of the bedroom wearing her coat. 'She's the one I told you about, the lady who used to work at the surgery. Well, it's her birthday and I'm going round there with the rest of the women who come to the book club. We're going to have a bit of a party.'

Feeling relieved that she wouldn't have to sit there and drink tea for the next two hours, Sophie hovered by the door and the moment Frieda turned her back, she surreptitiously scooped up the key with a firm, indignant smile.

41

NINE YEARS BEFORE – MARY

'I can't believe it. I can't believe you're here, that you're alive.' Mary's voice was distant, almost a whisper that broke with intermittent sobs as she spoke. 'You were so tiny when you were born, you were so very small, frail and I had nothing for you, no clothes, no nappies, nothing.' She held her hands out and, with each of her palms facing the other, in a demonstration of size she held them just a few inches apart. 'You were just this big and...'

The room was now almost completely dark, the only lights on the railway, a constant light that was distant and backed up by the ones that lit up the whole room every time a train approached. From where she sat, nervously squeezed into the corner of the room, Mary could easily make out the whites of Louisa's wide-open eyes, her profile, the shape of her body and the tears that glistened as they rolled unashamedly down her face. It was a moment of semblance, where she felt a calmness pass through her, although the butterflies in her stomach went into overdrive as she tried to think of all the questions she really wanted to ask.

'I held you,' she continued, 'I held you close to my chest, under my clothes, for as long as I could. It was the only way I could keep you warm in a room that was relentlessly cold. The night air, it was biting and without...' She paused thoughtfully. She wasn't sure what she should or shouldn't say next and still trembled inside when she thought of the chamber, the cold, white, dusty, harsh place where she'd been kept during the days prior to her daughter's birth. Still to this day she had a million regrets about the way she had traded her soul with the devil and the promises she made.

'I'd be risking everything to let you go,' Imogen had spat with venom, 'you do know that, don't you? If he finds out, he'll kill us both, he'll kill your child. Which means, you can't ever come back. You have to disappear. Do you hear me?' Imogen had said cruelly. 'She'll be better off without you anyhow and she'll go to a better home. I have a nice family for her. One where she'll wish for nothing.' Pressing her face close to Mary's, Imogen had looked down at the baby with wistful eyes. 'And, you know, she'll quickly forget you...'

It had been a moment of indecision; Mary had been more than aware that the life she could offer her baby wasn't a good one. She already had a son she couldn't look after. A boy that lived with his grandmother. She was the one he loved, not her. Yet, deep inside, she'd wanted nothing more than to keep tight hold of her baby. To lay her cheek against her head, to take the deep breaths in and breathe in her odour. It had been a look that had obviously transposed in her face and, before she'd realised what was happening, Imogen had pulled a knife out of her pocket and quickly stepped behind her.

'I'm supposed to kill you, like he did with the other one.' The words had echoed around the chamber and, while Mary had stared down and into her innocent daughter's eyes, she'd felt the fear rush through her as the blade of the knife had pressed against her throat. 'She's buried, in a place where no one will find her. In non-sacred ground, like the trash she was,' Imogen growled. 'She didn't even get a proper funeral and her family, they'll never know what became of her.'

'Please,' Mary had begged, 'I'll do what you ask, just...' With the pressure of the knife digging into her skin, Mary could still remember the way she'd so easily handed her daughter's life over in a trade for her own. She hadn't even fought to keep her.

'We had a short time alone together and they promised me, they said you'd be safe, that you'd be looked after... but, then, she told me you'd died. That your birth had obviously been too much for you and that you hadn't even survived the first night. I can even remember the accusing look in her eyes when she blamed me. She told me I hadn't looked after you and that, if I walked away, she wouldn't call the authorities.' Mary looked down at the carpet, ran a finger through the threads that showed in the place where the pile used to be. 'She told me to go home and to look after my son, but I couldn't, could I?' she sobbed. 'I wasn't capable of keeping my own baby alive. I blamed myself every day for what had happened, and I couldn't bring myself to love my son, not when my daughter had died... yet...' She reached out, ran her fingers across Louisa's face as though she were making sure that her daughter was real, that she was actually there, sat before her. 'That didn't happen and somehow you're here. You're alive and... she lied to me... how didn't I know that you lived?'

Shaking violently with emotion, Mary eased herself up from the floor, gripped Louisa's hand in her own and, once she'd convinced herself that her daughter was real, she led her to where a settee stood by the window. 'That's why I live up here. I prefer to be alone, just close enough to watch my son grow but not so close that he knew I was here. For years, he had no clue.' She pointed to the windows and to the boards that covered them. 'Of course, he knows I'm here now and, if I'm honest, I've got used to being up here. I like it.'

With a sigh, Mary ran her hand lovingly across the back of the settee. It was the place where she often sat during the day. From here, she could make the most of the daylight, she could see the traffic coming and going, and she'd even got used to the people who travelled daily along the long country lane, the times they went to work and the time they went home again. But, most of all, from here, she could see when her son arrived home.

Curling her legs up and into the corner of the seat, Mary once again waited until the room had lit up before she took the time to study her baby's face and lovingly gave her a wistful smile. Louisa had been right, they did share the same type of hair, their lip shape was the same, along with the jawline and uncharacteristically she carefully wiped away the tears that fell down Louisa's cheeks in rapid succession. 'Baby, please don't cry...' Mary whispered. 'We found each other and, now we did that, no one can take that away from us, not again. You just need to tell me what happened, I need to know how you came to be here.'

42

NINE YEARS BEFORE – LOUISA

'There's nothing much more to tell,' Louisa confessed after going over her life, the way she'd been brought up and finally she told Mary about how she'd learned of being adopted. 'I don't even know why they told me. They obviously had their reasons, but, before I could ask them, they'd both been killed in a car crash.' Once again, the memory of that night came back, and she could see the police that came to the house and the distress that followed. 'It was horrible, I was all alone, and I kept thinking about what they'd said and I knew I had to find you.'

Lying on her side, Louisa curled her legs up beside her, rested her head against Mary's knee and allowed her hand to rest uncomfortably against the rough material that covered the settee. The smell was unbearable – the cushions smelt damp, musty and had an odour that reminded Louisa of a rabbit hutch that hadn't been cleaned. But the fact was that she didn't want to move, and she found herself smiling affectionately as Mary continued to dab at her tears and took comfort in the way she'd calmed, the gentle nature she showed and, after the initial moments of confusion and disbelief, the way she'd quickly accepted who she was and why she'd come here.

'So, you've known quite a while,' Mary questioned. 'And, if you knew where to find me, why didn't you come sooner?'

'I didn't know where you were, not at first. It was only when Finn came to our school, when I got to know him better. Of course, I was attracted to his surname, knowing that it was the same as yours, and I guess I asked him one too many questions. I asked what his mother was called and then I put two and two together and I got to know him,' she said proudly. 'He thought I was just a friend, but had no idea that I was really his sister.'

Sitting up, Louisa used her sleeve to dry her face and saw the softness that had taken over Mary's face. She looked kind, and loving, but the heartbreak behind her eyes was unmistakable and Louisa knew she still had a tenderness left to give.

'So he doesn't know?'

'He doesn't and I wouldn't have told him. I was just going to savour the friendship, but then another girl went missing. She was a prostitute. Everyone thought she'd gone off with a punter, but her mother was frantic. She told us that her Alice was pregnant and that she wouldn't have gone off, not without getting in touch. The whole village went out to search. They walked the fields and the riverbank and, just a few hours after the search had begun, they found the mother, dead as a doornail, her throat cut from ear to ear.' She lifted a hand and drew a line across her throat. 'And no one knows who did it.'

Within an instant, Mary had shot to her feet. She began to pace back and forth, her hands kept going up to her head, where she ran them through her hair and pulled at the roots and, even in the darkness, Louisa could just about see the harsh line of her jaw that appeared to roll in annoyance.

'The girl...' Mary yelled out loud. 'You said she's still missing?' It was a statement and a question all at once and Louisa fearfully sat upright in the hope that Mary would calm down, that her temper would fade and that they'd go back to the calm semblance they'd found. But Mary knelt down before her, her hands went up to hold Louisa's face in hers like a vice. 'Louisa, you have to think, exactly when did she disappear?'

With her eyes fixed on the door, Louisa tried to remember. All the days had blended into one and right now she willed for the door to open and for Frieda to return and for her to help her put the days back together. 'Two or three days, I can't... I can't remember,' she finally sobbed.

Nodding slowly, Mary stared out through the window. 'You have to help me...' she whispered. 'I think I know where she'll be and you, you need to help me get to her.'

43

PRESENT DAY – DECEMBER 2023 – SOPHIE

With the rain now coming down like stair-rods, Sophie pulled her car to the side of the road and, after looking over her shoulder with a cursory glance, pretended to dig around in her handbag and held her phone to her ear until Frieda had driven past, on her way to the party.

She had just one hour left before she had to pick Noah up from the nursery, before they'd put emergency protocol into operation, making Finn aware that she hadn't shown up. It was a risk. One she had to take and, with her eyes fixed firmly on the road, she watched and waited in case Frieda returned. It was a wait that sent her heart beating wildly in her chest, her stomach turned over in somersaults and, finally, she swung the car around and, with a determination she didn't know she had, she pulled the car back into Frieda's drive.

'You've absolutely lost the plot,' she said out loud as she climbed out of the car and slammed the door closed behind her. Her boots sank into the mud. Her legs began to tremble, and she realised that she was about to enter a property without the owner's consent. It was something she'd never normally do, not without good reason and she tried to come to terms with the concept before convincing herself that it didn't class as breaking in. Not if she had a key. Albeit, she did have to admit, the key had been one she'd stolen.

With her hand held up in an attempt to shield her face from the rain, she swept her hair backwards and stared up at the windows above, where she felt sure she'd seen a face, but, still, she couldn't be sure. She had to admit that her paranoia was getting worse. Her mood swings were off the charts and, regretfully, she did wonder if Finn had been right. If she did need the medication he constantly offered. Because, if Finn preferred the idea of living here, in a house with boarded-up windows, rather than living with her, then all she could imagine was that living with her must have been an absolute nightmare. With a sigh and the rain hitting her in the face, she tried to put herself in his shoes. She tried to understand how bad it must have been for him to leave his son and go and live in a different house. But then, if she'd been that awful or that much of a risk, would he have left Noah with her? Or was that his plan, to get himself settled in a house of his own and then come back for his child?

Looking into the palm of her hand, she looked from the key that lay there, up the steps and to the door that stood at the top and, suddenly, she dreaded the thought of walking through it. It suddenly occurred to her that she might find something she didn't want to see and, once again, her thoughts went back to Noah and the repercussions of her actions for him. She felt sure that whatever she found out today would be the difference between them staying together in England or moving back to Ireland. Both of which would be close to impossible if she got herself arrested.

Climbing to the top of the old, slippery wooden steps, Sophie leaned forward to peer in through the window. It was almost four o'clock and she hoped she'd be able to see enough, that she'd be able to satisfy her curiosity without going in through the door, but the sun had almost gone down and, in a room where boards had been used to cover most of the windows, she struggled to see anything more than shapes and shadows. Eventually, with time running out and a need to get out of the rain, Sophie pushed the key into the lock and, with a nervous but satisfied grin, watched as the door sprang open and the dark, oppressive room she'd seen through the window opened up before her. Cautiously, she took a step forward.

The first thing Sophie noticed was the smell. There was a strange aroma that filled the room and, with her nose wrinkled and her hand patting the cold, damp wall, she felt for a light switch.

'Hello? Is anyone there?' she shouted. Her eyes were wide, and she felt a deep sense of shock by what she saw. Unlike the room downstairs, this one was sparsely filled. There was a single chair, and a long low-backed settee that stood by the window. Old, fusty rugs were scattered around the floor, presumably to cover the carpet and, from what she could see, there was no television, no radio and barely any soft furnishings.

With the rhythm of her heart increasing by the second, Sophie reached for her phone and, with her back to the door, she tipped her head to one side and quickly concluded that something wasn't right. Nothing about the room added up and it certainly didn't look like somewhere Finn would want to live, not if she knew her husband. He'd always been fussy and, even when they'd had barely any money at all, he'd worked in the evenings or on weekends while in medical school to furnish his accommodation, and to make it look exactly the way he wanted. He'd had a big snuggle chair that had been covered in a soft velour material. A matching pouffe the same height as the suite and an eighty-five-inch television that had dominated the room.

Turning her phone around in her hand, she once again thought about going back to the car. Minimally, she needed to phone the nursery. She needed to let them know she was going to be late but, also, she had a nagging desire to call the police. To get them to come and check out the house. But, even to her, her thoughts felt ludicrous. 'What would you say to them?' she whispered under her breath. 'Excuse me, but my husband, he's the local doctor, and I broke into the flat where he lives because he's been acting a bit weird and, now I'm inside, he doesn't have a telly.' She rolled her eyes dismissively, shook her head and began to laugh at her own stupidity. She had to admit that, even for her, and her overactive imagination, this had to be up there with all of the other nonsensical things she'd ever done.

Sighing, she realised that she had no evidence to prove that Finn had done anything wrong. Or, if he actually lived here at all. All she knew was what he'd said. He'd told her that he'd taken his things back to his gran's. That he'd come back to see Noah, mornings and evenings. What he hadn't said was that he was sleeping at his gran's. Yes, he'd called in for food, and to do his laundry, but Sophie felt sure that there was only the one bedroom downstairs, which meant that Finn would have no choice but to stay up here and she just couldn't see it.

The thoughts were all flying around in her mind so fast, she couldn't see which of them she needed to turn next in order that they'd keep on spinning. In an attempt to lighten her mood, she held her phone up in her hand and lit up the room until she reached the small piece of window where she'd thought she'd seen a face looking out through the net curtains that had once been white.

'Hello... is anyone there?' With a single finger, she moved the curtain to one side and berated herself for coming here alone. 'What the hell were you thinking?' It was a comment that made her bite down on her lip. She looked over her shoulder and stared anxiously at the door that still stood wide open. It was time she left. Time she went back to being a responsible adult and a mother rather than trying to be a wannabe detective and, with her hand on the doorknob, she began to pull it to a close behind her. The momentum only stopping as she heard a low, gravelly moan coming from one of the rooms at the front of the house. It was a noise similar to that of a wounded animal, one that lay by the roadside waiting to die and, with her throat constricting to a point she felt barely able to breathe, Sophie's stomach jumped with fear as the sound was repeated, this time even louder and longer than the moan from before.

In her panic, she began to work her way around the room and continued her search for a light switch. Self-preservation told her not to search the house in the dark, not when she had no idea what she was up against and, even though every part of her wanted to run, she couldn't bring herself to do so.

'Hold on there, I'm coming, I won't be a minute!' As the light went on, she blinked repeatedly. Her feet moved with caution, and she tentatively pushed open each door in turn until she came to the bedroom. It was a room that was shrouded in darkness and, as she slowly pushed the door open, she immediately saw the wasted frame of a middle-aged woman lying prone on top of a bed. She wore a pair of ill-fitting tracksuit bottoms, a long-armed oversized T-shirt and a pair of thick woollen socks. The blanket that had been covering her had been tossed to one side and, even from the doorway, Sophie could see the beads of sweat that were scattered haphazardly across her face.

'It's okay, I'm here now. I'm Sophie, I'm going to help you.' Taking in a deep audible breath, Sophie nervously rested the back of her hand against the woman's forehead. It was something she'd seen Finn do for Noah and, even though she had no real idea why she was doing it or what she needed to feel for, she felt sure that the woman was unnaturally hot, clammy and her face was pale. Her breathing came in short, sharp blasts and Sophie glanced fearfully over her shoulder in the hope that Finn might be stood behind her. That he might have returned and would know what to do. Unlike her, who'd gone back to the thought of phoning the police because, no matter how this whole situation looked, something really wasn't right. This woman was being kept here, possibly against her will, locked in a flat and Sophie's husband and his gran just had to know all about it.

'Now then, my darling, can you tell me your name?'

With her head shaking from side to side. The woman reached out, her arm shaking as she touched Sophie's cheek. 'I'm... Mary... I need...' she managed to mumble. 'I need Finn, I need... my boy. He'll help me.'

'Your boy?' Blinking with confusion, Sophie reached for her phone. But, then, she began adding two and two together. The woman had called Finn her boy, she'd said her name was Mary, which... 'Oh my goodness, are you Finn's mother?' Her voice came out as a high-pitched squeal as the pieces of jigsaw dropped into place and the realisation hit her. 'But he...' She wanted to say that he'd only ever mentioned her in the past tense. That, because of everything he'd said, Sophie had believed she'd passed away, that she'd been no longer with them, hence the reason he'd been brought up by his gran. But none of that was true and, once again, she lifted her phone and immediately saw the screensaver flash up before her. It was a picture of Finn holding Noah, just a few days after he'd been born. Their noses were almost touching in a soft, loving look that had convinced Sophie that, no matter what, Finn had and would always love his boy.

'Mary, if I phone Finn, will he help you? Will he know what to do?'

Nodding slowly, Mary turned onto her side, wiped the sweat from her forehead and, with her whole body shaking relentlessly, she stared into Sophie's eyes as though she were begging for help.

Trembling with emotion, Sophie tried to decide what to do. If she phoned Finn, he'd be annoyed that she was there. That she'd broken into his gran's house and that, inadvertently, she'd found his mother. A part of his life he'd obviously wanted to keep hidden. Her only other option was to phone an ambulance. To bring in a medical team and, because she didn't know how ethical it had been for Finn to treat his own mother, she was scared that the authorities would cause him a problem and that inadvertently, that would cause an issue for both her and for Noah.

'Here, let me get you a drink.' Standing up, Sophie kept her eyes on Mary's face and on the beads of sweat that continued to form on her forehead and, with her legs wobbling beneath her, she slowly turned to head for the kitchen as she felt Mary's hand grab hold of hers. With a soft, gentle squeeze, Mary pulled her back toward her.

'Please...' she whispered, 'please, don't go, you need to help me.'

44

PRESENT DAY – DECEMBER 2023 – HATTIE

After making her way through the house, Hattie gulped repeatedly as she saw the carnage that littered the hallway. Her pace physically slowed as she reached the bottom of the stairs and, with an outstretched hand, trembling fingers and a stomach that was twisting with anxiety, she gave the office door a slight push and held her breath as it opened.

The room looked as though it had been the epicentre of an earthquake. The desk that had been there as long as Hattie could remember had gone and, in its place, was the nine years' worth of grime that had been gathered beneath it on the carpet beneath. Empty filing cabinet drawers were open, books had been dragged off the bookcases and all the items that had been on top of the desk now lay strewn across a dust-covered carpet, including the laptop that was leaning against the radiator at a peculiar angle.

Tentatively, Hattie slid her feet between the objects and, with an exasperated sigh, she managed to clear a small space with her foot and dropped to her knees. It didn't take a genius to work out what had happened and, with Adam now sauntering around in the room behind her, she meticulously began to pick each of the items up and, without saying a word, she carefully stacked them up on the windowsill.

'I think this is broken...' Adam whispered sheepishly as he lifted the high-backed office chair out of the way, groaned and then began the task of trying to straighten the spine, which, if the dint in the wall was anything to go by, looked as though it had taken the full force of Adam's frustration.

Turning away and with a small area of carpet now cleared, Hattie reached for the laptop. She almost had to dare herself to touch it. Prayed that it worked and, after the chance meeting with Patsy earlier, she really wanted the opportunity to access her mother's files in the hope she could learn the whole story and finally get to understand who her parents had really been, the people they'd helped and what part they'd played in a life that Hattie had known nothing about.

Hesitantly, she ran her fingers across the keyboard and immediately jumped backward as the screen lit up and burst into life. It was a moment she'd hoped for, prayed for and dreaded all at once, but she felt the tears spring into her eyes as she saw the crack that went across the screen, along with the cables that had been shredded with rage.

'I'm so sorry,' Adam muttered. 'After you went out, I plugged it in and...' Sliding into position beside her on the carpet, he leaned with his back against the settee. Then, after a moment's deliberation, he reached forward, gently placed his hand over Hattie's and, following a gentle nod that assured her that his temper had calmed, he slowly lifted the laptop from her knee to his. 'As soon as I opened the file, I saw the sub-files. The names, including mine, Louisa's and Luke's.' He began to control the mouse, clicked in and out of folders.

'But...' Hattie furrowed her brow; she'd been sure that her

name would have been there too and, now, she felt confused by its absence.

'Your name wasn't there. I was confused too, just give me a minute, I'll show you.' Sighing, Adam opened one folder after the other and frustratingly tapped his finger against the mouse pad, closed them down and searched again. 'I'm sure it was in one of these.' Again there were a number of folders opened and closed. 'Wait a minute, I think...' With a definitive nod, he clicked an icon and pointed to the screen where an array of folders opened up before her. Some had been customised, their symbols changed to being that of a tree, a computer or a picture frame, and Hattie presumed that, knowing her mother, the information in each would be different.

For a split second, Hattie's eyes scanned the names that were written below each of the tree symbols. Six files had names and Hattie heard herself say them out loud. 'Louisa 1993, Adam 1997, Luke 2001, Henry 2004, Amy 2007, Kyle 2011,' she whispered. 'But what does the last one mean?' She stared aimlessly at the final folder. The words 'In progress 2014' were written below it. Turning to Adam, she saw him puff up his cheeks and blow the breath slowly outward before turning to look at her.

'Are you sure you want to see this?' He emphasised the word sure. 'Once you've seen this, Hattie, you can't unsee it and everything will change.' He closed his eyes for a few thoughtful seconds. 'It will define every memory you've ever had.'

Nodding with uncertainty, Hattie placed her hand over his. 'I don't think we have a choice, do we?' she answered truthfully. 'She wanted us to know the truth, she was going to show us the truth, but...' Stopping, Hattie stared out of the window. 'But most of the documents were gone. They're no longer in the box and whatever it says in these files, someone already knows, and they didn't tell us... but who?' Shuffling to rest against Adam, Hattie closed her eyes and allowed her mind to drift over all the events that had happened over the years and all the people who'd had access to the house and that box and, with the nausea turning in her stomach, Hattie bit down on her lip. 'Louisa...' Suddenly, she could see all the happenings during all the years since their mother's attack, and all the things Louisa had said and done. The events came flying at her all at once like a barrage of fast-moving images, and movie clips flashing sporadically. 'She was always there, always in the middle of things and, even when pregnant with the triplets, she kept on going. But, now I think about it, I don't know why? She didn't even like our mother; she'd often said so.' Hattie thought back to the years after Louisa's parents had died, the times she'd rebelled, the way she'd screamed and shouted at her aunt and uncle and the way she'd refused to do anything they wanted. 'Right after the attack,' Hattie whispered. 'She turned into the prodigal child, didn't she?' It was a thought that made Hattie's mind flick back to Fraser, the man she'd been on the date with, and the night that had followed when Louisa had turned up looking bruised and battered. Each happening stacked up like a giant Jenga game and, right now, all Hattie could imagine was that the game was about to fall down and land heavily around her ankles.

Staring, Hattie took control of the mouse pad and slowly clicked in and out of the folders, but watched as Adam began to scroll through his phone, his fingers tapping away at the screen, frantically flicking through pages. 'Okay,' he said, 'this is what I found...' He turned the phone towards Hattie. 'Take my file, for example.' He slid his hand towards the mouse pad and hovered over the word Adam before clicking the folder open. 'This shows that my birth mother was called Camilla Booth, right?' He turned, frowned, and took a deep breath in. 'And here, on my phone, this is what it says about her.'

Taking the phone from his hand, Hattie felt her throat constrict in anticipation as she slowly slid the screen upwards and read the report. 'Desperate search for a young, seventeen-year-old pregnant woman, Camilla Booth, continues...'

'She was just seventeen, Hattie, and as far as I can see she was never, ever found. And, at first, I thought it was just her, but I searched all the others. In Luke's file, Cerise Eveleigh, she was older, but went missing too and, as far as I can see, none of them were ever found. There's only one that I can't find anything on, no missing person, no social media, no nothing.'

'Mary Griffonia Alexander...' Hattie's mind went wild with confusion; her hand flew to her mouth, the nausea worsened, and she quickly grabbed at the waste bin and held it tightly against her chest. 'I think I'm going to be sick,' she announced. 'Isn't... isn't that...?' She kept her eyes fixed to the screen. 'Griffin, his mum, she was called Mary, wasn't she, but I thought she was dead?' She paused, her breathing accelerated. 'It has to be a coincidence, doesn't it? I mean, he barely ever spoke of her, and, when he did, he always spoke in the past tense...' She thought back to those few short days when she and Griffin had been together, the hours she'd lain in his arms and they'd spoken about everything and nothing and, even when she'd asked him directly about his mother, he'd done all he could to avoid the answer.

Standing up, Adam began to pace. 'All of this, it makes me wonder what the hell was going on, Hattie.' With emotion filling his eyes, he searched the walls for answers. 'And, now, I have no idea who the hell I am and if I am the son of Camilla Booth. I need to know where she is and what happened to her.'

Jumping to her feet, Hattie felt the emotion wash over her as she pulled her brother into a hug. She wasn't used to seeing Adam crumble. He was normally the one who made everyone laugh, the one who kept the party going and to see him like this was something she'd have happily lived without.

'Okay. I might be able to help. I have something to tell you. Something good.' She took a step back, waved a hand around in the air. 'I met a woman, out there, on the lane,' she whispered calmly. 'We got chatting and our parents were mentioned, and she suddenly began to tell me how much our parents had helped her. That they'd been her guardian angels. That, without them, they wouldn't have adopted their son, Henry.' As she uttered the words, a sob rose to her throat. 'She said they were good people, Adam. They were helping people and it's what we'd have expected, isn't it? Our dad was a vicar. Helping people is what he did and, by the sounds of it, our mother helped too. So, in my mind, there's no question. You're his son and, no matter how you were born or who to, it doesn't change anything. We... we'll always be family.' Once again, she squeezed him hard but felt the resistance as once again he picked up his phone and began to scroll.

'Hattie, before you come to any conclusions, you have to see it all...' he growled. 'The last file, the one that's called "In progress 2014".' Clicking on the file, Adam turned the laptop and Hattie felt the room begin to spin around her as images appeared on the screen.

'Alice Adams.' She heard the words leave her mouth but couldn't comprehend them. 'Isn't that... Wasn't that...'

Suddenly her thoughts went back to that night, to the way Berni had stamped through the house, the way she'd spoken to her mother and how they'd eventually walked down the street like long-lost friends.

'This is what she was trying to tell us.' Adam paused and

once again looked up at the walls and allowed his gaze to follow the line of the bookcase. 'I don't know what it means, but she obviously knew something...' He stopped speaking, dropped off the settee and onto his knees on the carpet and began to search through the pieces of paper that still lay torn and screwed up by his feet. 'Oh my God, I've just thought of something...' He pulled at one piece of paper after the other, straightened it out and finally he sighed a breath of relief as he found the small piece of paper they'd found in the Bible earlier that day. 'The dates, the squares, they all...' He smoothed out the sheet, lay it on the seat beside her. 'We didn't know what it meant... do you remember? We thought this was a garden party.' He hurriedly pointed from one of the squares that had been drawn on the piece of paper to the other. 'Ninety-three, seven, one, four, six, eleven...'

Then he once again swung the laptop around to face him and, with his face turning pallid, he looked back and forth between the screen and the sheet. 'It's a date. Each number relates to a year. Mine was number ninety-seven, the year I was born and...' He tapped the piece of paper angrily with a finger. 'Hattie, each of these squares... each one is the same as the date and if the women went missing, if they were never seen again, what's the chances that the numbers relate to a grave?'

With her breaths coming in fast, sporadic gulps, Hattie leaned forward. She didn't know what to say, how to react and, with her stomach twisting in knots, she stared at the bookshelves and ran her eyes back and forth along all the few books that still remained. 'Adam. You're crazy... and you're wrong, and you... you just have to be.' Her voice came and went in gasps and, even though she looked back at the screen and could see that the numbers clearly corresponded with those on the sheet, she didn't want to believe it. 'You're crazy,' she finally screamed. 'You are absolutely goddamned crazy and I... I can't do this. I won't listen to this, I don't want to. Not now. Not ever. She only just died and you...' Jumping to her feet, Hattie rushed to the door, swung it open and immediately heard the sound of Jasper's bark, followed by a long, whimpering howl that came from outside. 'Oh my God, Jasper. It's Sophie's dog. I'd tied him up and I forgot all about him.'

Sprinting through the house, Hattie headed for the back door, where she could already see that the lead had been chewed through. Jasper was gone and all that was left was a small amount of lead hanging from the branch where she'd tied him earlier.

'You go one way, and I'll go the other,' Adam yelled out as he ran past and immediately headed toward the front of the house, where the broken front gate stood wide open. With her heart beating audibly in her chest, Hattie watched for a second, hoped that Jasper would come bounding towards her and then, in her anguish, she turned and felt the air leave her mouth in a long, drawn-out scream.

'What is it?' Within seconds, Adam was beside her and, with a long shaking finger, Hattie pointed to where Jasper was happily digging. The hole now wide and deep with Jasper half in and half out, Hattie watched in horror as a perfectly formed human skull was tossed out of the hole and rolled across the ground, towards the bonfire.

45

PRESENT DAY – DECEMBER 2023 – SOPHIE

'Come on, I promise I'll help you.' With an anxious smile and one of her hands helping Mary stand, Sophie used her other hand to secure a blanket around the older woman's shoulders. It was just long enough to tie in a rough knot at the front and all she could find to help keep her warm until she got to the car. 'It's going to be just fine, I promise.' Once again, Sophie reiterated her oath and with her hand in Mary's she slowly pulled her forward. 'We have to go, Mary, we need to get you down to the car, before they come back.'

'But it's...' She stared helplessly at the door, at the darkness outside. 'It's dark, it's...' She began to shiver relentlessly, the beads of sweat still showed on her forehead, her legs were barely holding her upright and, with a terrified gasp, she took a step backward. 'I can't go out there, I'm not... Griffin, he said I'm not allowed to go out there. I have to stay indoors. It's for my own good.'

With tears stinging her eyes, Sophie bit down on her lip and tried to imagine how this woman, Finn's mother, had come to be held captive in this house. She was thin, gaunt and, by the look of the food Sophie had seen in the flat, she looked as though she'd lived on a bland and meagre diet that had been topped up with a cocktail of sedatives.

'Mary, listen to me.' Facing her, Sophie took hold of both of her hands, looked her directly in the eye and saw both the fear and the hope within. 'You need to trust me. I'm going to take you to the hospital, to a place where Finn isn't the boss. He can't drug you there. He can't lock you in a room and it's going to be a place where you'll get some proper care, some lovely food and some sunlight.' She nodded in affirmation and pointed to the windows in the hope that Mary would realise just how much she wanted to help her. 'You can't keep living like this, up here, with the windows all boarded over. It isn't right, is it?'

Pulling her phone out of her pocket, Sophie checked the time. She had no idea how long it would be before Frieda came home, or when Finn would return. The only thing she did know was that this woman had been held captive for a good number of years and for the love of God, she'd taken it upon herself to help her escape.

With fear flooding through her mind, Sophie thought about all the times Finn had offered her drugs for anxiety and depression. The prescriptions he'd offered to write. And, sickeningly, she wondered whether this would have been her fate. For him and Noah to live in the flat downstairs, while she'd rotted on the floor above. It was a scenario she wasn't willing to risk. She had no choice but to get Mary to a place of safety and then, she'd go for Noah and with just the essentials, before Finn got back to the house and found out what she'd done, she had to leave. She had to take her son and go back to Ireland, for both of their sakes.

Taking one step at a time, and with a determined effort she guided Mary through the flat and back to the door. 'That's the way, just take your time, my lovely,' she whispered as she took note of how painfully thin Mary was. How each step was a struggle and the way the shaking overtook her whole body as she moved and she began to wonder just how many drugs Finn had been feeding her.

'That's right, my lovely, keep coming towards me.' Whispering the words, Sophie smiled, nodded and, while taking small steps backwards, she led her out onto the platform, and took a step downward. 'Just go slowly, Mary, and if you feel unwell, or if you need to stop, you just let me know, won't you? We can sit down.' She looked nervously over her shoulder. The steps were steep and slippy and Hattie's car was still a long way from them. 'Let's just take it steady. The last thing we want is an accident.'

While not knowing what else to do, Sophie kept her eyes fixed on Mary's. She held on to the blanket, with the other hand holding tightly to Mary's. It was a slow progression where one step was taken forward, two back and then they'd move forward again. In ten minutes, they'd moved just three feet and with an exasperated sigh, Sophie let go of Mary's hand and reached for the handrail just as Mary quickly pulled away and, with her arms open wide, she spun around on the spot to look up at the stars.

'I'm out, I'm actually outside...' She took in a deep breath, closed her eyes and then she began to laugh sadistically. 'They don't let me out. They never let me out. Not after last time.'

The words hit Sophie like a punch to the gut and with eyes that were wide with alarm, she made a grab for Mary's hand, 'Last time,' she yelled. 'Mary, tell me what happened last time?' It was a question that would get no answer as Sophie felt the unexpected power of Mary's hand catch her firmly in the chest. Her whole body felt as though she'd been hit with a thunderbolt. Her feet lost their purchase. Her hands scrambled to keep hold of the rail and then, she felt nothing but the air all around her as she was launched backwards until she hit the ground, and for just a few seconds while she remained conscious, every inch of her body felt as though it were about to explode.

46

PRESENT DAY – DECEMBER 2023 – HATTIE

Running through the rain and across the mud-covered garden towards the spot where Jasper continued to dig, Hattie felt her feet slip and slide beneath her. The ground felt as though it were moving, like a large, uneven platform on a theme park that tipped erratically from side to side and, within seconds, she found herself falling, landing on her hands and knees and, with the bonfire just inches away from her face, and even though the heat from the embers scorched her face, for the briefest of moments Hattie couldn't move. Her body froze and, with her eyes wide and fearful, she stared into the empty eye sockets of a human skull.

'Adam... Adam... get it... get it away from me...' she screamed out loud, frantically scurrying across the ground and, with an arm resembling a hockey stick, she knocked the skull out of her way. 'For God's sake, Adam, where the hell are you?' she yelled in temper as she heard Adam yell something about going next door and getting a lead for Jasper and although she knew that Jasper needed restraining, the last thing she wanted was to deal with both Jasper and human remains alone. But like always and with no choice but to sort the issue out by herself, and in a rugby-style manoeuvre, she launched herself forward, caught hold of Jasper's collar and with just one of her fingers she unceremoniously dragged him out of the hole and threw him behind her. 'Adam, you need to hurry up and get the damn dog,' she yelled as her hands began to work like shovels. Fear of what was buried beneath made her push the earth back into the hole. She needed to cover it, to hide it, to make it disappear as though it had never been there in the first place. 'Adam, what's taking so long. I need you to help me, we have to...'

'You have to do what?'

It was a woman's voice that came from behind her. A voice that was soft yet menacing and cut through the air in a way that made Hattie's mind and body freeze on the spot. Her first instinct was to hide the skull. She had to make sure that no one else saw it.

'Are you going to try and cover up what your parents did?' the woman's voice tested. 'Well, I have news for you.' She began to laugh in a cruel and sadistic way. 'You can't. The world is about to find out who they really were, what they did and, do you know what else... your lovely brother, he isn't in a position to help you. I've made sure of that.'

With every part of her shaking inside, Hattie felt her blood turn to ice. She closed her eyes; her legs didn't feel as though they would hold her and, fearing the worst, she felt her whole body begin to crumble. 'Adam...' she screeched. 'Adam, speak to me... Where the hell are you?' Apprehensively, Hattie held her hands in the air. She felt as though a firing squad was stood right behind her and, while fully expecting the bullets to hit her square in the back, she began to turn, but immediately dropped her hands when she saw the frail, broken woman who leaned helplessly against the drystone wall and somehow managed to slip downward until she flopped almost comically, with an air of instant defeat.

'Who are you?' Hattie asked. 'And what the hell are you talking about, what the hell did you do?' With a new-found confidence, Hattie moved forward. Her eyes flitting back and forth, looking for Adam, and only once she'd checked the garden path for movement did her gaze return to the woman whose eyes had turned dull, her face pallid and her unbearably thin arms, were covered in blood.

Screaming, Hattie once again moved around the garden, her hands held out, her palms forward defensively, fearful of what the woman had already done to Adam. Her mind flipped into a full-blown somersault. 'No, no, no...' Hattie yelled. 'This can't, this can't be happening, not again. Not now, not today... I can't...'

'Do you know who I am?' The woman interjected calmly. Her voice was weak, her hands shaking. 'I'm Mary, I'm the one they let live. Just so long as I walked away and gave them my baby.' As she spoke, her face turned to stone, her features bland and emotionless. 'I'm Griffin's mum and Louisa, she's my daughter too. They stole her. They told me she'd died. They told me she'd perished. That it was all my fault...' The words hung heavily in the air as Mary began to sob but then tapped her leg knowingly. 'Come here, boy, come on, that's my boy.' Again, she tapped her leg and Hattie watched in anguish as Jasper happily ran towards her.

'Jasper, no don't... come...'

'Oh, don't you worry yourself. Me and Jasper, we know each other, don't we?' Reaching out, the woman grabbed at Jasper's collar and, with a sadistic smile, she pulled a knife out that had been hidden under her leg and with a reaction that Hattie wouldn't have thought her capable of, she held it firmly to the wriggling puppy's neck. 'He belongs to my son, the same son who locked me in a room for the past nine years.' Her eyes searched Hattie's. 'That's right, you're working it all out now, aren't you?' She nodded slowly, 'Finn is my son. Which means I'd happily kill his puppy too.'

Shocked and confused, Hattie could barely speak, her throat tightened, her hands had gone stiff, unresponsive, her legs had weakened to a point she thought they might fail her. 'What the hell do you want?' It was all Hattie could think to say as she stared painfully down the garden, her eyes constantly searching for Adam. 'And what did you do to my brother?'

'I did what I always said I would. I always promised myself that, one by one, I'd take away her children, just like she took mine.' Mary laughed out loud as Jasper struggled, twisted and tried to get away. 'I always said that I wanted to see the pain in her eyes when she found out what I'd done and...' She paused. 'I'm not stupid enough to think I'd get to see that, but at least I'll know the torture she'll go through when all she has left is a grave to sit beside.'

'But you're too late...' Hattie suddenly blurted out. 'She's already dead. She died this morning, she...' Her breathing slowed, the tears continued to fall, and Hattie did all she could not to focus on Adam, who had now come into view and was slowly moving towards them on his stomach, like a caterpillar, partially hidden by the undergrowth.

'You're lying.'

'I'm not lying, I wouldn't, I swear... Now please, let Jasper go. He isn't my dog and...' Hattie had no idea why she'd tried to explain, all she wanted was for the pain to stop, and for her friends and her family to be safe, including Jasper.

'Mum...' From nowhere, Finn leapt over the wall, held his hands up in the air and carefully inched slowly towards where his mother sat, slumped against the wall. 'Mum, what happened and why are you here? You know this isn't right, don't you?' With a voice that was calm, almost hypnotic, Finn moved into a position until his body separated his mother from Hattie. 'You're not going to hurt Hattie; she isn't at fault here.'

'She's one of them.'

'Maybe so, but I won't let you hurt her. It was part of our deal. You know how much she means to me.' Finn moved slowly backwards. Gave Hattie a quick look over his shoulder, waved his hand in the direction of the house. 'Hattie, get out of here. Go and get some help.'

'I won't let you love her...' Mary screamed, 'not her, she's a Gilby.'

'And I walked away on the understanding that the killing would stop, that you'd stay in the flat and...' Suddenly his shoulders slumped in defeat. 'And even though I loved her, I did what you asked, I did everything you asked and now, now you have to do what I ask too. You have to come back to the flat because if they found out what you did, you'd go to prison. You'd be taken away from us and...' He held a hand out towards her but couldn't resist the looks that went from her to Hattie. 'Mum, please... I'm begging you.'

'You still want her, don't you?'

Hattie gasped as the sentence cut through the air. Finn loved her. Finn had always loved her. They were the words she'd always wanted to hear, but not here, not like this.

'You know I do.' Finn replied, 'And I walked away. I did that for you, for everyone's safety, but right now, right here, you'll have to kill me first before I'll let you get anywhere near her.' He paused. 'Now, why don't you let me take you home, let me get you your medication. Let me settle you down for the evening.' As he spoke, he was constantly looking around, checking on

Hattie, on Adam, and with an outstretched arm he did all he could to help release Jasper.

'I don't want your damned medication, you can't make me take it and she...' She glared in Hattie's direction, 'She has to die... or none of it was worth it. Imogen, she has to feel the pain. She has to know what it's like to lose a child and that means her...' With a long, pointed finger, Mary pointed to Hattie. 'I won't rest until she is dead.'

Calmly, Finn held a hand out to his mother. 'Please, Hattie was telling the truth. Imogen, she's dead. She can't feel the pain, not any more, and you need to let me look after you. Like I've always done...' With tears streaming down his face, Finn turned to look directly at Hattie. 'I'm so sorry, I've always tried to protect you...'

'Finn... please, make it all stop. I need for it to stop,' Hattie pleaded and watched as Finn shook his head, sorrowfully.

'I wish I could. But it's all my fault.' He cleared his throat and held a hand to his heart. 'That night, my mum killed your father and, when I ran down the garden to help Imogen, she was there with a knife and...' He glanced back and forth to the wishing well. 'I took it off her, threw it down there.' He paced back and forth. 'I didn't know what else to do. I just wanted to protect you all.'

'But...' Hattie closed her eyes, she could still remember that night, the way Finn was helping her mother when the paramedics arrived. 'I don't understand... I didn't see her, she wasn't there.'

'That's because Louisa turned up just a few seconds later. As you know, Louisa had been at Gran's, she told Mum that another girl had gone missing, and Mum insisted that Louisa took her to the sepulchre. It was the place where my mother had been held captive, the place where Louisa was born.' Wistfully, Finn pointed across the fields, to the next large village in the valley. 'It's at the crematorium and when they got there they found evidence that Alice had been there, that her baby had been born there.' Sinking to his knees, Finn held his hands together. 'I've prayed every day that I could right all the wrongs. But I can't.' He shook his head. Lifted a hand to wipe away his tears. 'Louisa took her home, gave her the right meds and I made a promise that I'd walk away from us, because she asked me to.' Again, he paused. Looked up to the sky, to where the rain once again began to fall. 'I'm her son, it was my duty to protect her... and I know now I shouldn't have, I should have turned her in. I should have had her committed and we...' In a second, Finn's words were drowned out by the sound of the church bells, as was his scream as Mary lurched forward and plunged the knife as deep as she could into his back.

47

PRESENT DAY – DECEMBER 2023 – LOUISA

Even though it was the middle of winter, the sun had surprisingly managed to burst through the dark, ominous clouds that had been lurking in the sky for days, making Louisa smile as she pulled up in the crematorium's car park to see long, ethereal shafts of light landing on the rooftop. It gave the whole building a strange, spine-chilling glow, which, for a place that was surrounded by death, seemed rather fitting.

Even though she came here often to drop Grant, her husband, off at work, attending a funeral was a rare occasion and, out of habit, more than need, she made her way slowly through the building until she reached his office. Following a soft tap on the door, she slipped inside to see Grant thumbing through reams of paperwork that was almost spilling from the sides of his desk.

'Six of them today,' Grant growled angrily. 'Every day we have a new succession of people who walk in through the front door and out through the back. One damn group of snivelling, snotty mourners vacate the building and, like a swarm of wasps, the next moves in and, what's worse, they're even more snivelling and more snotty when they leave.' Looking up as he spoke, he pushed a hand through his short dark hair, disturbing the gel he'd so carefully applied earlier that morning.

'Oh my God, you can't say that...' With a quick look over her shoulder, she sighed at her husband's irritability. 'What if someone hears you?'

Laughing sardonically, he pointed through the door that still stood open and to the cremation chamber that stood at the other side of the corridor. 'They're not gonna hear me now, are they. I've got two from this morning still waiting to hit the furnace.'

Pushing the door to a close with a smile, she padded towards him, dropped her handbag onto a tub chair that stood to one side of his desk and lovingly placed a hand on his shoulder, before leaning in and pressing a kiss against his forehead. 'Think of the money.'

'Lou, I do think of the money... It's the only damn reason I'm here.' He rolled his eyes, picked three sheets of paper up from the desk, lifted them up in the air and let them go, where they fluttered and dropped to the carpet. 'And every day I have to deal with a mountain of paperwork. I mean... what the hell happened to my life.' Closing his eyes, he took in a long, drawn breath that he blew out slowly. 'Sorry, that wasn't meant how it sounded, but when we met... every day, it was different.'

'Of course, it was different,' she scalded. 'First, we didn't have three kids to feed and, second, you spent every day trying your best not to end up in prison.' Unconsciously, her hand went up to his hair and she began to tease the strands of hair he'd disturbed back into position.

'But... I never did go to prison... did I?' He tapped his nose with a finger. 'I'm too clever for that.'

'You mean you never got caught.' Once again, she leaned in

and searched his eyes with her own. It was true, their lives were very different. She wasn't on the game any more, and he wasn't selling drugs or growing cannabis in houses that he had no intention of paying the rent on. Instead, he worked at the crematorium. He dealt with, as he put it, 'snivelling, snotty mourners' on a daily basis. 'For what it's worth,' she said, 'I couldn't do it, I couldn't work here, I wouldn't want to,' she muttered incredulously and, with a downward glance, she rolled her eyes around an office that still looked as though it had been furnished in the eighties. A rectangular desk stood central to the room. Cables trailed dangerously over its edge and a long, rubber ridge had been laid across the carpet tiles, to bridge the gap between the desk and the plug socket. A coffee-and-cream filing cabinet stood in the corner, with as many items of unfiled paperwork stood on top and a pot plant thrown off-centre on the windowsill was looking in desperate need of water.

'Lou, I just...' Standing up, Grant walked to the window, stared at the car park beyond and ran a hand thoughtfully over his neatly trimmed beard. 'I just miss the excitement of the chase. There was always that danger, that adrenaline rush and, yes, I miss the risk...' He paused, turned and gave her a pensive smile. 'But since the kids came along, I've tried to be a good person... I just don't think I am one.'

The sigh that followed told Louisa everything she needed to know. Grant had tried as hard as she had to make their lives normal. They'd both done everything they could. But every day was the same and the monotony of it was killing them both. 'How about we do something exciting, something that will give us the adrenaline we both crave?' She pouted as she spoke, thought about what she was saying. There had to be a way that they could bring up their very young, very needy children and get the adrenaline rush they needed.

'What are you suggesting?'

'I don't know right now.' She laughed and glanced out of the window, where the sound of a car door alerted her attention. Glancing between the bushes, she fixed her gaze on Hattie, who was dressed in black, and tentatively, almost painfully, walked across the car park and towards the building. 'Grant...' she muttered. 'If I could find a way to give us all of that fun back, along with the occasional adrenaline rush, without the risk. Would you want it?'

Within a moment, he was stood by her side, he'd pushed his arm around her waist and, with long, demanding fingers, he turned her face towards him and pressed a long, almost passionate kiss against her lips. 'You're up to something?' he whispered and his eyes searched hers, mischievously. 'And I like it.'

'Do you?' She pulled herself playfully out of his hold and took a step backwards. 'I have to go. The family, they'll be here any minute and... I have a plan, which means I need to go and see Hattie before they arrive.' Picking up her handbag, Louisa rummaged inside, picked out a tube of lipstick, pulled off the lid, wound it up and studied the bright red colour within. 'And now that you've ruined my lipstick, I may have to change it, but maybe...' she said reflectively, 'I should wear something a little more demure...' Laughing, she dropped the lipstick back into the bag and, after another search, she picked out another and, with a final pout at herself in her compact mirror, she applied the lipstick before heading back to the door.

'Lou, seriously, what are you up to?'

'I can't tell you... not just yet, you have to leave it with me.'

Nervously, she stood in the foyer, looked up at the clock and then she glanced outside to where Hattie paced up and down, presumably waiting for Adam and Luke. And, of course, then there would be Frieda, Finn and Noah, who would arrive together, in the funeral car that followed the hearse.

It had been almost four weeks since Sophie had died from her injuries and, with the police digging into everything, it had taken them a long time before the body had been released. A blessing that had come as a disguise. Finn's injuries had been so severe they'd thought they'd lose him too. He'd endured a long stay in hospital. One he hadn't liked and the first moment he could, he'd self-discharged, just in time for the funeral.

Back in the entrance to the crematorium, Louisa slowly breathed in. She had to come up with a plan and to do that, she had to work smart and, as Hattie walked in, she held out her arms and pulled her cousin into what she hoped would feel like a genuine loving embrace.

'Hattie... where are the boys?'

'They're coming.' Hattie waved her mobile phone around in the air. 'Luke just messaged, they're stuck in traffic. They should be here any minute.'

Steering Hattie to sit on a pew, Louisa took a long, admiring look at the way her cousin had dressed. She'd respectfully worn a longer length black dress and had a small pillbox hat sat neatly on the top of her head, with a veil that came down to cover her face. It was an outfit that had obviously been chosen with care. An outfit that looked fashionable and sophisticated, without vying for attention.

'I don't know why I wore all of this; I barely knew her...' Hattie murmured under her breath as she angrily pulled at the hat and dropped it down on the seat beside her. 'I'd only met her a couple of times and now, now look what's happened.' Lifting a hand to her face, Hattie swiped at the tears. 'I'm staying at a bed and breakfast while they scour every inch of my house and garden, Lou. I can't sleep, I can't eat and I just can't believe that all this is happening again...'

'Hey...' Louisa said as she placed a hand on her cousin's shoulder, picked up the hat and, with a spare tissue, lovingly dabbed at Hattie's tears before placing the hat back where it should be. 'I know this is hard, but you can't blame yourself. You didn't do this. Not any of this, now did you?' With a melancholy smile, she pinned the hat back into position. Pressed her lips tightly together and watched for the nod that Hattie gave her.

'I know you're right but it's all got too much. I haven't seen Finn, not since it happened and...' Hattie pulled in a deep breath. 'And all I can think is that I shouldn't have come back to the village, and I certainly shouldn't have dug around, looking for the truth, because now I know what it was, I really wish I didn't.' Slumping back against the bench, Hattie's red, bloodshot eyes once again filled with tears. 'If I hadn't come back, none of this would have happened. A whole new chain of events would have happened instead, and Sophie would still be alive and poor Noah...' She paused, gasped. 'Poor little Noah would still have a mummy.'

'Darling. None of this is your fault,' Louisa assured her. 'And the chain of events you're talking about all began before you were born, before I was born and...' She pressed a hand against Hattie's cheek and held her gaze for a moment too long. 'If it's anyone's fault, its mine.' She paused, gave Hattie a gentle, loving smile. 'It was me that took Mary to the sepulchre, we saw the massacre that had obviously happened there and Mary went on a rampage. She went crazy right in front of me and I wasn't strong enough to stop her. I was so torn up in my own grief that I didn't try and...' Staring down at the floor, Louisa felt her whole body sag with emotion, her shoulders drooped, and she leaned forward to hold her face in her hands in an act worthy of an Oscar.

'But...'

'No buts...' She shook her head. 'I can't do buts...' Sitting up in her seat, Louisa stared at the catafalque where Grant prepared the area in readiness for when the hearse arrived. 'All I can do is move forward, Hattie, and...' Once again, she took Hattie's hands in her own. 'I've made a decision, and I need to ask you a really big favour...' It was a question she knew she'd asked of Hattie at least a hundred times before, but this time she wasn't about to take her out on the game or ask her to become an escort to the rich or the famous and, for a moment, she stared at the floor before speaking. 'Your mum, one of the last times I spoke to her, I told her that I'd like to train as a counsellor and she'd said that I could raid her office for books. She said I could have examples of her case notes, which I know...' She paused, sighed. 'I know the police have taken a lot of things, but she told me of a few places where she'd hid some. Places in the house where I might still find them...' As she spoke, her words became lost as she saw Adam and Luke arrive and, just like Hattie, Luke was also dressed in black. His long, dark overcoat had been left open to show smart black trousers and a new white shirt, with a black tie that had been tied in a big bulbous knot. Adam looked as though he was struggling to walk. He leaned heavily against the wall, with his arm sporting a brilliant white sling that looked completely out of place against a smart black suit. It was, however, the way they naturally gravitated towards each other, and with an exasperated sigh, Louisa watched the way Hattie leaned in against Luke. The way his arm immediately slipped around her shoulders, in a loving and comforting way, and for a moment Louisa felt a surge of jealousy. It was the type of relationship she should have had, the sibling love and rivalry that was bestowed in equal measures and, for a moment, she took a step back, just as Finn's wheelchair was pushed into the entrance. He looked lost, deflated and broken, with eyes that even from a distance looked red and swollen and, with Noah sleeping peacefully on his knee, he was totally oblivious to the occasion he was about to attend, and protectively, Finn held him tightly against him.

For a moment, Louisa stood back. She looked from one cousin to the other and then back to Finn and Noah. The exchanges that went between them all were of a deep, understanding friendship. They'd all lost the ones they loved. Apart from Finn and Hattie, who still shared a love that had been relinquished a long time before. But one that would most probably be brought back to life, the moment it was respectful to do so. Which meant that once again, Louisa would be the one on the outside looking in. She'd be the outsider. Just as she'd always been. The only real family she had was Grant and the children and with an anger building up inside, she felt a desperate need to keep what was hers, no matter what she had to do to keep it. With a determined stride, she walked back to the office, to where she knew that Grant would be, finalising the arrangements before Sophie's funeral could begin.

Looking up from his ever-growing mountain of paperwork, Grant tipped his head to one side. Gave her an inquisitive look. 'Are you okay?' he asked as he continued to lift one file up after the other. 'I overheard you asking Hattie about Imogen's books and things and... are you going to do what I'm suspecting?' The words were a question and a statement all at once and seductively, she picked up his tie, and while using it like a leash, she pulled him behind her until they were stood outside the cremation chamber.

'I'm going to train to be a counsellor,' she announced. 'I'm going to set up a business.' Sensually, she leaned in and kissed him with passion before breaking off, and with a giggle, she playfully peeped around the corner to where distantly, she could see the line of mourners taking their seats. 'I mean, it's such a shame that the family business had to close down, isn't it...? There was a lot of money to be made and... just think about the excitement we'd have finding the right girls, the adrenaline of the birth and the satisfaction of...' She ran a finger across her neck. Pulled it sadistically from one side to the other. 'The kill.'

'Lou, you can't be serious... can you?' He searched her eyes with his and Louisa looked up to see the deep, burning desire within and again, she teased her mouth with his.

'Of course I'm serious. Look around you. We have the perfect tools.' She tapped on the door of the cremation chamber with her knuckles and smiled incredulously. 'With all of this at our fingertips, we certainly wouldn't be leaving any bones buried in the ground, waiting for others to dig them up... now would we?'

ACKNOWLEDGEMENTS

This story has probably been the most difficult of all of my stories to write. However, it was a story I really wanted to tell because I've always been a big believer that everyone has a secret that they wouldn't want anyone else to know. Every family has a darkness hidden within it, and most people can't honestly say that they know everything about every one of their family members, no matter how much they wish they could.

While writing this story, I've still been working full time as a Sales Director. My husband also retired, and I went out and did what all good wives do... I bought him a puppy, my Barney, who this book is dedicated to.

I'd also like to thank my ever-supportive editor Emily Ruston who has given me all the time I needed to make sure this story was told in the best way possible, and to my publisher Boldwood Books who I feel so privileged to have found. As always everyone in the team at Boldwood are a great support and after a lot of hard work and sleepless nights, we have a book to be proud of. Thank you.

And finally, to you... my reader.

Thank you for buying this book, *The Family Home*. I've really enjoyed writing it for you and I really hope you enjoyed following Hattie's story, along with that of Adam, Luke, Finn and of course, Louisa.

Like all authors, I've been on quite a writing journey, and I still find it totally surreal that my novels are bought and paid for by you, the reader. With that in mind, I'd love to know your thoughts and I'd be absolutely delighted if you'd take a moment to leave me a review on whichever platform you bought the book from.

Please feel free to contact me at any time. I'm on Twitter/X as @Lyndastacey, on my author page on Facebook as 'Lynda Stacey Author', and finally on my website, www.Lyndastacey.co.uk

Once again, thank you for reading this, my ninth novel. It was a pleasure to write it for you.

Much love.

Lynda x

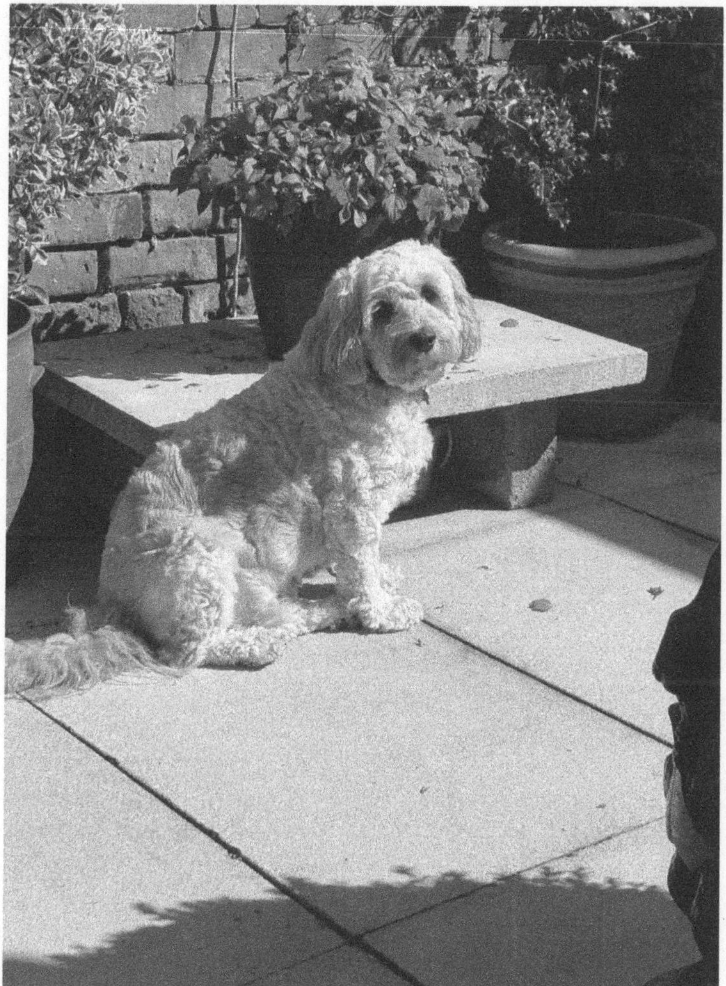

ABOUT THE AUTHOR

L. H. Stacey is the bestselling psychological suspense author of over seven novels. Alongside her writing she is a full-time sales director for an office furniture company and has been a nurse, an emergency first response instructor and a PADI Staff Instructor. She lives near Doncaster with her husband.

Sign up to L. H. Stacey's mailing list for news, competitions and updates on future books.

Visit Lynda's website: www.lyndastacey.co.uk

Follow Lynda on social media:

- facebook.com/LHStaceyauthor
- x.com/Lyndastacey
- instagram.com/lynda.stacey
- bookbub.com/authors/lynda-stacey

ALSO BY L. H. STACEY

The Sisters Next Door

The Serial Killer's Girl

The Weekend

The Fake Date

The House Guest

The Safe House

The Accident

Buried Secrets

The Family Home

THE
Murder
LIST

THE MURDER LIST IS A NEWSLETTER DEDICATED TO SPINE-CHILLING FICTION AND GRIPPING PAGE-TURNERS!

SIGN UP TO MAKE SURE YOU'RE ON OUR HIT LIST FOR EXCLUSIVE DEALS, AUTHOR CONTENT, AND COMPETITIONS.

SIGN UP TO OUR
NEWSLETTER

BIT.LY/THEMURDERLISTNEWS

Boldwood

Boldwood Books is an award-winning fiction publishing company seeking out the best stories from around the world.

Find out more at www.boldwoodbooks.com

Join our reader community for brilliant books, competitions and offers!

Follow us
@BoldwoodBooks
@TheBoldBookClub

Sign up to our weekly deals newsletter

https://bit.ly/BoldwoodBNewsletter

Milton Keynes UK
Ingram Content Group UK Ltd.
UKHW040143181124
2888UKWH00007B/46

9 781801 626088